Three Fiddles

Megan K. Bickel
Elizabeth A. Dow
Ellen P. Cooke

This book is dedicated to our parents, Mike and Peggy Crawford, for always encouraging us to express ourselves. And to our husbands, Luke, Jonathan and Richard, for immediately understanding the importance of our sisterly bond.

Crawford Content

Contents

Prologue

Kate

My sisters call me the Angel of Death. They've also compared me to that cat that lives in a hospice and inexplicably knows to go and sit with a person a few hours before they shuffle off this mortal coil. I'd love to be able to say that my sisters are overly dramatic and ridiculous, but the fact of the matter is that I have an odd relationship with death. For one thing, I can see it coming.

So, it didn't come as much of a surprise when I answered the phone to hear my mother's voice filled with tears.

"Hey honey, my dad died this morning," she said without preamble.

Just two days ago I packed up myself, my husband, and our four boys and left my grandfather after a fall break visit to Boston. I knew the moment I watched him say goodbye to my sons that he wouldn't last the week. He had been declining for months, years really. But as I watched him rest a hand on each boy's head and saw the look in his eyes when he turned to say goodbye to me, I knew I'd never see him again.

As we drove to the airport, I debated what to say to my mother and aunts and uncles. Should I tell them their father was going to die? How do you warn someone of something like that without sounding like an insane person or a worry-wart? There was no medical evidence to suggest a reason for pessimism, so I chose to send a delicate email telling them he "seemed worse." I decided to keep the "imminent death" thing to myself.

And I sure as heck didn't tell my sisters. Knowing my death-predicting history and the depth and breadth of my "creepy" afterlife experiences, they would have freaked out. Despite the way we often joked about this strong connection I seemed to have to death, I wouldn't want this prediction on my track record if I turned out to be correct.

"I just wasn't expecting this," my mom said. "He was sitting up with Mom and the home health aide in the living room, then he slumped over and was gone."

My shoulders drooped with the news. "I'm sorry, Mom," I said. "I'm so sorry. I loved him so much."

"I know, sweetheart. Me too." She paused and blew her nose. "I have to get to Boston right away to help. I don't know any-thing yet, but you'll need to start looking at flights. Can you call your sisters, please?"

"Yeah, sure," I said, not surprised by her request. I could hear that she wanted to get off the phone. It cost her a lot just to get the words out once. "Just let me know when you get details. I love you, Mom."

I hung up the phone and turned around in my kitchen to see four sets of eyes turned in my direction. My boys. It was one of the rare days when everyone was home after school. They were converging on the snack drawer in a blatant effort to ruin their dinners. They all froze when they heard my voice become thick with barely-controlled sorrow.

"Mom?" Christopher ventured. He looked at me and then glanced at his younger brothers to see if they had picked up on the situation.

I did a brief social-appropriateness evaluation about the proper order to notify people of a death. Should I call my sisters before I told my boys? Should I call Steven at the office and wait until he got home so we could tell our sons together? Hell. My boys were watching me and the tears were threatening.

"Boys. Can you all put the snacks down for a moment? I have to tell you something," I said, my voice already cracking.

"What's wrong?" Alexander asked in his sweet ten-year-old voice. This would hit him hardest. He was my most sensitive child. He loved everyone and everything in a way that both astounded and frightened me. The world is no place for a male with a huge heart.

"That was your grandma on the phone." I paused and took a deep breath. "She was calling to tell me that Great-Grandpa passed away this morning."

"What!?" four voices exclaimed in unison. I watched as the four little faces I work so hard to protect crumpled in disbelief and sorrow, breaking my tenuous grasp on control. All four kids rushed forward into a group hug as we let the tears fall.

I could hear my voice murmuring all the comforting mom things that don't seem to have any foundation in conscious thought. They just tumbled out of my mouth unbidden. I hugged and kissed and wiped tears from cheeks. I assured them Great-Grandpa loved them all and he could still feel our love. Then I told them I had to make some phone calls and I gently guided them out of the kitchen with instructions to put on a movie and relax.

I sat at the table and took thirty seconds for myself. I replayed the brief conversation with my mom in my head. Look at flights. She told me to look at flights, didn't she? Oh, God. We still had half-un-packed suitcases littering the living room. The laundry pile was up to my waist and a good four feet in diameter. I'd have to ask for more time off work. So would Steven. The kids would have to miss school right after a break. I'd need someone to watch the cats. I'd have to cancel the mail. I'd have to cancel Phillip's dental appointment. Christopher would have to miss basketball practice. I'd have to tell the PTA that I wouldn't be able to help with the Scholastic book sale. And a hundred other things.

Focus. I needed to focus. I had to call my sisters. Time to be the Angel of Death.

Alice

"Hello?"

"Alice, it's Kate."

"Hey, what's up?" I said, surprised to be getting an actual phone call from Kate. We communicate regularly via group text with our younger sister Emma, but rarely do we talk on the phone. I turned up the volume on my Hyundai's hands-free system to overcome the loud hum of the highway beneath my tires.

There was a pause and I started to reach for the volume again when Kate finally spoke. "I have some bad news..." The tone of Kate's voice told me there was a death in the family. I know her so well. She continued, "Grandpa passed away this morning."

I drew in a quick breath. Hearing that a family member has died, whether expected or not, is always jarring. I tried to concentrate on the congested I-25 evening rush hour traffic, but my mind started to feel overloaded. It wasn't until the Audi behind me honked that I realized I was being ridiculously generous to my fellow travelers as I let car after car in front of me.

"Alice?" Kate said. "Are you okay?"

"Sorry!" I exclaimed. "I'm driving home from work. So, what happened? How's Gramma? How's Mom?" Kate described how my grandfather passed peacefully at home and how when she was with him last week, she knew it was coming. I remarked on her creepy ability to predict death and asked about funeral plans. To my great annoyance, plans were "unavailable at this time" so I was to "sit tight" until I heard back from Kate.

After we hung up, the audio book I had been listening to snapped back on and the latest weight loss guru explained the negative effects sugar has on the body. I turned it off and reached for the holiday Reese's Peanut Butter Cup I was saving for later. The pumpkin-shaped treat quickly worked its magic by letting me forget for a moment what Kate had just told me and enjoy one of my biggest pleasures: sugar. But after I licked the last bit of chocolate off my fingers, the sadness came rushing back. By this time, I had made it to Lincoln Ave.—normally five minutes away from my apartment but it took 20 minutes in rush hour. For a moment, my mind cursed all the people who had been recently flocking to Denver, crowding our streets, but then I remembered that I was one of them. I had only been living in Denver for about a year.

Kate's call slowly came back to me and I could feel the tears coming. Trying to remain focused on my driving, I refused to blink at first but quickly realized that just made my eyes fill to the brim like some cartoon character. I blinked and the tears came tumbling out. I reached into the back seat of my car for a tissue, but of course, Jake had moved them the last time he used the car. I used my sleeve to wipe at my eyes only to realize I was wearing my new white cardigan that was now marked by espresso Covergirl eyeliner. "Fuck!" I yelled out to no one. I wondered if I was already to the anger stage of grief but then realized I didn't know any other stages. I wasn't angry at my grandfather for dying, just at my own stupidity.

I decided to call my mom to see how she was doing until I remembered Kate said she was already on her way to the airport. I guessed her flight from Indy to Boston would get her there late and perhaps I should wait until the morning to check up on her. Besides, as soon as Emma heard the news, she would want full access to Mom, so better to not tie up the phone line.

I finally made it home and was greeted by Mr. Glenn Holland, my orange domestic shorthair cat. He immediately began alternating meows with licking his lips to indicate it was time for his daily kitty treats, as if I could forget. "Here you go, Glenn," I said as I threw a bunch on the ground. I wondered if I should be giving him fewer as his sizable belly gracefully moved into place so he could properly attack the treats. "Where's Jake?" I asked Glenn, not expecting a response. "Oh right, at work. How foreign." It was 6 p.m. and Jake wouldn't be home for another four hours. These days, I hardly ever saw him. Our work schedules just didn't jive. I changed out of my work clothes, ordered Chinese food from the GrubHub app on my phone, and plopped onto the couch.

While I waited for my food to arrive, I debated calling Jake to tell him the news but decided it could wait until he got home. So I reflected on the man my grandfather was and silently congratulated myself on my compulsion to have a box of tissues in every room in our tiny apartment—a trait I undoubtedly got from my mother. I felt alone. Glenn sensed my sadness and joined me on the couch for a minute but was quickly distracted by noises in the radiator, probably mice. I felt a twang of jealousy toward Kate who would have her husband and four sons to comfort her tonight. I made a mental note to call Emma later as she might be feeling the same loneliness in California as I was in Denver. Once the Chinese food arrived, I located my worn out *When Harry Met Sally* DVD and settled in for the night. The movie washed over me like a warm blanket, allowing me the ability to push my grief down until later. Eventually I reached for the Reese's pumpkin I had bought for Jake, ate it, and slowly closed my eyes. There was a lot to figure out and a lot of people to talk to, but it could all wait. I was depressed. Another stage of grief?

Emma

"This is going to be our most exciting issue yet! Stan's piece on the latest advancements in wisdom tooth removal is really eye-opening..."

I wasn't sure if Kenneth's enthusiasm for mouth surgery was sincere, but the man sure could talk about dental work. I suppose the editor-in-chief of *Tooth Magazine* has to stay upbeat during editorial meetings to keep the entire staff from resigning. I had been an employee for four days and already wondered what I had gotten myself into. Ignoring my doubts, I turned my attention to the recipe I had pulled up on my phone—butternut squash lasagna—and took a mental tour of my kitchen, searching for all the ingredients I would need that night. I was considering a stop at Ralph's Supermarket on the way home when I realized everyone around the large mahogany table was looking at me.

"Emma?" Kenneth asked.

"Yes?" I looked around. Was I already in trouble?

"Did you want to tell us a little about yourself? I don't believe you've met everyone."

"Oh. Right." I hated speaking in front of people, even a small staff of 12. I took a sip of water, a nervous habit. "Um, well...I recently moved to Long Beach from Indianapolis with my boyfriend, Charlie. I, um, like to watch movies, and, um, I have a gray tabby cat named Hoosier." The blank stares around the room told me none of these Californians knew what a Hoosier was. "People from Indiana are called Hoosiers," I offered, embarrassed. Still nothing. I took another sip of water.

"A cat! How great," Kenneth said, looking around the table for someone else to jump in. A petite woman with frizzy red hair accepted the challenge.

"Hi Emma! I'm Casey from accounting," she seemed to share Kenneth's extreme enthusiasm. Was that a requirement of the job? "Do you have any kids?"

"Oh God, no!" I said too quickly. She looked hurt. "I mean...no, I don't have any children," I corrected, looking down at the table.

Thankfully, Kenneth took this as a hint and concluded the meeting. My new co-workers began to file out of the conference room. I couldn't tell if they were avoiding eye contact with me or if I was being paranoid, but I wasn't sure I cared. Something told me these weren't my people.

I had just finished gathering the supplies I purchased for the new job—a fresh May Designs notebook and a pack of Staedtler pens—and was heading for the door when my phone lit up. It was Kate.

My stomach flipped. No one ever called me. Not for anything good, anyway.

I shuffled out of the room and down the hall, not really knowing where I was going in the unfamiliar office. I ducked into a restroom and answered the phone.

"Hey, what are you doing?" Kate asked, clearly trying to sound calmer than she was.

"I'm at work. What's wrong?" I bent down to check for feet under the stall doors. Thankfully, I was alone.

"Oh, right. You're three hours behind me. I was hoping to catch you after you left."

"What's wrong, Kate?" I asked, urging her on.

"Grandpa died this morning."

I froze. I had a million questions, but I couldn't put them into words.

"Emma?" she asked.

"I...yeah...I'm here. What...? How...? What happened?" As Kate filled me in on everything she knew, I stared at my reflection in the mirror. It was strange, watching myself as tears started to cloud my vision.

"How's Mom?" I asked. "Have you talked to Alice yet?"

"Mom is okay. She's sad. She's on her way to Boston. You could probably give her a call in a few hours. I called Alice first." Of course. The youngest is always the last to know.

"It's weird, isn't it?" I paused. Kate waited for me to go on. "I've always thought of Grandpa as the strongest man in the world. Larger than life. How can someone like that just be gone?" She didn't say anything. "You knew last week when you saw him, didn't you?"

"Yes. I could tell," she said, a little embarrassed.

"That's creepy, Kate."

"I know."

I smiled, then remembered that Kate's propensity to predict death wasn't funny this time.

We hung up and I let myself really cry for a minute. I continued to stare at myself in the mirror. It was almost comforting seeing my face crumble and turn red as my brown eyes flooded again and again. I was watching a movie; the pain wasn't mine. It belonged to the character on the other side of the mirror.

As I wiped away smudged eyeliner and pulled my curly brown hair into a messy bun, I realized I had been in the restroom for almost 15 minutes. I needed to return to my desk. I had to get through the next 13 minutes, then I could go home, snuggle with Hoosier and Charlie under a cozy blanket and put on *You've Got Mail*. Meg Ryan and Tom Hanks always made me feel better.

Weaving between cubicles, I kept my head down and walked as quickly as possible without causing a scene. Back at my computer, I began drafting an email to Kenneth to explain that I didn't have any details yet, but I would need some time off to attend the funeral. Four days in and I was already asking for time off. As I typed, tears continued to stream down my face. I closed my eyes and rested my forehead in my palm. I could feel a headache coming on.

"Um, Emma?"

I jumped and spun around in my chair. The woman with the frizzy hair stood at the entrance of my cubicle, looking concerned. I couldn't remember her name.

"Yeah?" I said, wiping at my eyes and runny nose. I cursed myself for forgetting to bring a box of Kleenex into the office.

"Are you okay?"

"Yeah, I just..." The tears kept coming. I couldn't stop them. "My grandpa died."

"Oh, you poor thing!" She leapt forward and flung herself at me, arms outstretched. "That's just terrible! Was he sick? Was it sudden? Were you close? Is there anything I can do?" She continued to embrace me, or hold me down, really, since I was still sitting. Stunned, I pulled my arm from beneath her and patted her back awkwardly.

"Thanks..." Kathy? Cindy? "...you." I gently stood up, forcing her to do the same, murmured something about needing to get home, and slid past her, leaving her in my empty cubicle.

Part 1

October

Chapter 1

Kate

All of my kids grew up in our van. We spent a large portion of our lives driving and waiting in it. As such, my van was an on-the-go miracle of modern life. Snacks? In the bin between the seats. Entertainment? DVDs in the pouch behind the driver's seat. Feeling sick? Plastic bags to catch puke, paper towels to mop it up, and Febreeze (to save the rest of us from joining in) are in the "Yak Kit" under the back seat. I also had sunblock, bug spray, hand sanitizer, umbrellas, a deck of cards, water bottles, Band-Aids, blankets, hats (both winter and ball cap), folding chairs, books, binder clips, nail clippers, a lighter, various utensils, and straws (Capri Sun and McDonald's) stashed here and there.

So, when I had to stand at a rental car counter for thirty minutes with four exhausted children who couldn't keep their hands to themselves and figure out if I wanted to prepay for gas or buy the what-if-a-meteor-hits-your-car insurance, just to get in a van that had nothing but seats and wheels, I got cranky.

"If you can't be still, go sit against that wall!" I barked at my children. Steven, my husband, went with them.

"I didn't mean you," I called after him.

"I don't want to be still either," he replied as he hopped up and down and shook like a dog from head to toe. My boys dissolved into giggles and followed their father to the wall. My over-wrought brain immediately both appreciated Steven for keeping things light for our boys and cursed him for winding them up even further.

I felt my phone buzz and pulled it from my pocket.

Alice: Are you here yet?

Kate: In Logan Limbo. May have to vault over car rental counter to pummel people.

Emma: I think they frown on that.

Kate: "They" can suck it.

Alice: You're in a great mood. I can tell.

Emma: We'll save you some chocolate.

Kate: You are heroes.

Alice: But we aren't suicidal, so if Franny finds the stash, you're shit outta luck.

I snorted to myself. We had long ago identified our great aunt Franny as "patient zero" in our collective chocolate addiction. The woman was not messing around.

"Long trip?" the rental car agent smiled at me.

"Very," I said, mentally commanding him to hurry.

"I hope you enjoy your stay here in Boston," he said.

"I'm here for a funeral," I replied.

"Oh, I'm sorry to hear that. My condolences," he mumbled as he turned back to the computer screen.

I shouldn't have said that. Why make this dude feel awkward? Because he made me wait for thirty minutes and believe that my own insurance was terrible and that there were no gas stations within thirty miles of Boston's Logan Airport. That's why.

With keys finally in hand, I walked over to the squirming pile that was my family. Thomas was holding a tissue to his nose, attempting to stem the flow of blood. My eyes flicked to Steven, who had the good sense to look a little guilty.

"It was an accident, Mom," Christopher piped up. "Phillip's foot hit Thomas's face when Dad picked him up and turned him upside down."

"As one does in a crowded airport. Of course." I gave Steven a "what'cha gonna do" shrug. "Let's go," I sighed.

My youngest, Phillip, bounced to my side. "Mom! We've been in our van, the shuttle bus, the escalator, two moving sidewalks, the airplane, three more moving sidewalks, two more escalators, a blue line bus, and now another van just in one day! Plus, lots of walking on our feet."

"Yes, Little Bit, I know," I said as I mentally counted carry-ons for the seventeenth time that afternoon.

Once we were all loaded into the van (where were the week-old french fries or quickly-forgotten-and-crumpled sports participation ribbons?), we headed for my uncle's house. The family was gathering for a cookout because all big Irish Catholic families know that funerals are just an excuse for food, drinks, and catching up with people you only see once a year—if the death toll stays in check.

As I drove and Steven provided directions to supplement the "British Male" voice on my phone's GPS, my children had an extensive discussion about how using their first initials in order–Christopher, Alexander, Thomas, Phillip–spelled "Cat Pee." Phillip especially found this hysterical, as he was the "Pee" part.

When we pulled up to the house, I parked the van, but didn't move for a moment. Everyone was already there. Even though I live among five other people every day, I'm actually a huge introvert. It took a physical toll on me to be social. To rally, I reminded myself that my sisters were in there too.

I took ten more seconds for vanity. In my normal life, I devoted very little brain power to my appearance. I usually knotted my thick light brown hair into a messy bun and swiped brown mascara over my eyelashes because I once read that brown mascara was best for blue eyes. After four kids, I had plenty to hide under my baggy travel clothes, but I still prided myself being in good enough shape to keep up with those same four kids. I mentally shrugged at my yoga pants and then pinched my cheeks to look a little more awake and counted that as "vanity."

Steven and I herded our children into my uncle's house with

whispered pleas for good behavior and warnings about not mentioning the cat pee thing. I then spent 10 minutes reintroducing my kids to people they only had very vague recollections of from weddings and funerals past.

"This is Christopher, he's 12 now...yes, middle school...you remember Alexander, 10 years old already...Thomas, no, not Tom, he's eight...and Phillip, a big six-year-old!"

I smiled through countless comments of how big all my sons had gotten and cheerfully assured everyone that our trip was "easy."

Finally, mercifully, I found my sisters. My boys visibly relaxed when they ran to the familiar embraces of their aunts. I carefully gauged how long to hug my sisters. We have a habit of dissolving into tears if the hug is too long, but the occasion warranted more than a quick squeeze.

Steven shook Charlie's hand and pulled him aside to give him a quick "in-law" debriefing. Steven recognized how intimidating our family could be to outsiders. Even though Charlie and Emma had been together for a while, Steven liked to guide the younger significant others of my siblings and cousins through the first few family gatherings.

"How was the flight?" Alice asked to deflect the emotion that always threatened to crash in on us when we were all together.

"The pilot said there is a crack in the engine, but not to worry, he'll take off anyway," I said with a smile.

"What?" great-aunt Franny said in alarm with a mouthful of chocolate Bundt cake.

"*French Kiss*," my sisters said in unison.

"It's just a quote from a movie, Franny. The flight was perfectly fine...and safe," I assured my ancient relative.

"How was it, really?" Emma asked.

"The kids were great, but it was still a 15-hour ordeal with parking and delays and rental cars. We could have driven in that time and not had to deal with airplane-appropriate packing, airport prices for snacks, and the horror of being jostled around with the general populace."

"Yes, God forbid you are without your own van, Kate," Alice said, rolling her eyes.

"That van is my kids' third parent," I argued.

Our Aunt Mary broke through the crowd and came to my side. She put a hand around my upper arm, as if ready to forcefully drag me away from my sisters. As the oldest of our mom's siblings, Mary had a no-nonsense business-like way of conducting herself at all times. As kids, we thought she was terrifying. Actually, we still thought that.

"O'Riley girls, nice to see you. I need to talk with Kate," she explained. With that, she led me away. I was not, technically, an "O'Riley girl" anymore. First of all, I had been married for 15 years and my last name was Bryant. Second of all, I was a good 20 years past "girl."

My sisters smiled at my misfortune and waved at me like lunatics. I attempted to catch Steven's eye for some help, but he was still talking to Charlie and helping Thomas through the extensive buffet that had been laid out in the kitchen. I could see the plate had one roll and five potato chips on it. It crossed my mind that my children had eaten nothing but carbs and junk for an entire day.

When we got to a quiet room, Mary got down to business. "You are staying at the Sheraton Needham, yes?"

"Yes," I said, hoping I answered correctly, like a kid surprised by a pop quiz at school.

"Good. Tomorrow you are on your own for breakfast, lunch will be leftovers here, and the wake begins at two. I'll need you to transport food for the family break room at the funeral home..." and on and on she went. Being the oldest grandchild in this family, I was used to this rundown. Leadership of the eldest of each generation was never questioned in this family.

"You'll be giving the second eulogy during the funeral. Five minutes. Get me a draft tomorrow at lunch," she concluded.

"Oh. Right. No problem." No problem?! Sometimes the ease of my own lies shocked me.

"Good. How are things going for you? Steven? The kids?" she asked. Now that business was taken care of, she switched into aunt-mode.

"Fine. All good," I said.

"What are you doing these days?"

"Well, Christopher is playing basketball, Alexander is finishing up the cross-country season, and Thomas..."

"I see all that stuff on Facebook. What are *you* doing?" she clarified.

"Uh...working?" I ventured.

"Still at the insurance company? You enjoy your work?" she

asked as she looked me over with a suspicious eye.

"No, but they let me work from home, so I can be there to drop the kids at school and pick them up and volunteer at the schools and stuff."

"And?" she prompted.

"And?" I was not enjoying this conversation.

"Your boys are growing up quickly." Oh, good, back to talking about the boys.

"I know. It's..." I began.

"They'll be gone before you know it," she interrupted. "And trust me, that's the worst time to find out that you are nothing more than a mother." She patted me on the arm and walked away.

I stood there, dumbfounded. Nothing more than a mother? What the frick? I stopped and noted quickly that I was editing my own internal monologue for curse words and rolled my eyes at myself.

Back to my outrage: Being a mother was the most important thing in the world! I was lucky to have a job that let me be there for my kids. My kids were happy and healthy and polite and smart. Everyone complimented me and Steven on how well-rounded and funny and kind my kids were. Strangers would stop us at restaurants to compliment the behavior of my children. The attentive and purposeful rearing of four boys in today's world required Steven and I to exert a great deal of effort every single day!

Alexander poked his head around a corner and caught me

in his sights. I saw the look in his eyes. With expert speed, I scooped up a trash can from the corner of the room as Alexander coughed once. I knew that single cough like I knew my own name. I was across the room in two steps and tipped my son's head forward as he began to puke into the waiting trash can.

"It's okay, honey. Don't worry," I soothed.

Steven walked in and froze. All our kids threw up a lot—when they were too hot or too nervous or had been in a car too long or unexpectedly bit into something crunchy when it should have been a "smooth" food or when they ate nothing but carbs all day. Despite this proclivity, Steven had never developed the iron stomach that I had.

"Can you go ask someone where the outside garbage is kept? Garage? Side of the house?" I asked, mercifully giving Steven a non-puke related task. He bolted from the room.

Alexander finished and looked up at me with a smile. "Sorry, Mom."

I rubbed his back reassuringly. "Feel better?"

"Yes. I'm fine," he nodded.

"Go wash up in the bathroom and don't tell anyone you threw up. They'll think you're sick and you aren't."

He skipped from the room as Alice and Emma walked in.

"What did Mary want?" Alice asked as she eyed the trash can suspiciously.

"To tell me the schedule, assign me homework, and judge my whole life," I ticked off on my fingers.

"Is that puke?" Emma asked.

"Of course," I said.

"I'm judging your whole life too," Emma said, crinkling her nose up in disgust and we dissolved into giggles.

Steven reappeared. He waited a beat for us to notice him and pull ourselves together. "Garbage barrel on the side of the house and there's a hose out there," he advised.

"Girls, can you collect my children and have them say good-bye to everyone? Steven, can you get a plate of food for us that we can take to the hotel? I'm going to go clean this out and then we're out of here."

"Already?" Alice asked as Steven gave me the thumbs-up and escaped, once again spared from a puke job.

"I told you I have homework. I have to write a eulogy."

"That's what you get for being the oldest," Alice said, moving out of my way with an exaggerated gesture as I slid past her with the offending trash can.

It took three calls down to the front desk for more pillows and blankets and an argument that resulted in Steven designing a spreadsheet to show who was sleeping on the floor on which night, but we finally got everyone to sleep.

I sat on the bed staring at the soft glow of an open Word document. How do you even begin summing up someone's life? What they meant to you and your life? My eyes began to fill up with tears. Steven reached a hand out to me.

"You can do this," he said. "Start by just making a list. You get to tell everyone what was amazing about him. Celebrate him. Don't focus on him being gone."

I nodded and started typing. I listed his professional accomplishments, his volunteer recognitions, his civic leadership roles, his hobbies, his passions, his faith, his friends in high and low places. Then, I started listing out the incredible experiences he provided for me when I was a child: tickets to the theater, VIP treatment during catered parties in hotel ballrooms, shopping trips for entirely new wardrobes, and lobster dinners.

Don't get me wrong, my childhood was not perfect. I had my fair share of dealing with bullies and the typical teenage self-doubt. I suffered from tragic hairstyles, awkward boyfriend experiences, and full-blown anxiety about grades and my future. But the dominant theme of my childhood was love. Love and support and encouragement to chase my dreams.

In fact, as I thought about it, that was the common thread running throughout my grandfather's family. Every single one of us—my mom, my aunts and uncles, my sisters and cousins —all of us had lives marked by love, safety, and support. Each member of the family had reacted to those gifts in different ways. Some rebelled against perceived injustices, some thrived in the freedom from hardship, some dedicated their lives to helping those less fortunate, some didn't bother acknowledging that they had anything special and were obliviously nasty.

But as I looked around the room at my children, I knew Steven and I were giving them the same thing that my grandfather gave my mother and her siblings and that they gave to me, my sisters, and my cousins in return. We literally had a multigenerational legacy of love and support. The gift of being able to be ourselves, whoever that may be.

Chapter 2

Alice

I've always felt like a bit of an outsider when I'm with my cousins. They are all so beautiful and cool. My sisters and I are like the geeky kids in class when we are all together. Who am I kidding though, we are the geeky kids in every situation we are in... except when my sisters and I are alone. In those occasions, Kate is the geekiest, I'm fairly neutral, and Emma is the cool one. But it never matters. We can always be ourselves when we are together. With our cousins, though, we kind of stick out.

As I wandered around the funeral home looking for a sister to cling to, I could see various cousins spotted throughout the crowd of people. They all looked terrible. One would think that perhaps they looked terrible because they were in such grief over the loss of our grandfather, which they were, of course, but I also knew they were hungover. Very hungover. I knew because I was with them the night before.

My parents, Kate, and Emma had ducked out of the cookout early and headed to the hotel. But I opted to hang out longer with my cousins. I hadn't seen them in a while and I always enjoyed being around them. I had planned to drink the night away with them talking about Grandpa and then eventually passing out on a couch. Unfortunately, someone over-ordered on the fruit and pumpkin flavored beers and the Sam Adams dried out way too early. Doubly unfortunate, I developed a bit of a tolerance for alcohol living a mile above sea level in Denver, and it seemed being at sea level made it harder for me to feel a buzz.

As the night wore on, I nursed a disgusting beer that tasted like a jack-o-lantern and sat back to watch my beautiful cousins get more and more intoxicated. I hugged a pillow to my body as if I was trying to hide my sizable middle. Like a little kid who hides his eyes and thinks he is invisible to everyone, I figured that if I hid my belly with a pillow, no one would see that I was overweight.

As the night progressed, we shared stories. We laughed. We cried. We dedicated far too many toasts to the beloved deceased head of our family. It was when one cousin pointed to the ceiling, said, "This one's for you, Gramps," and 'poured one out for his homey' on the carpet that I was ready to find my way back to the hotel. But alas, my cousins had a different idea.

I was making my way around the room saying goodbye to everyone when I heard one very young cousin tell another that his pot dealer had his stuff and he was just going to pop over to pick it up. "Wait, what?" I asked.

It was explained to me that the "party" ran out of pot and he just needed to run to his dealer's house to get some more. After further questioning, I learned that this dealer's house was five miles away and that I should not worry because my cousin would be there and back in no time and "oh man, wouldn't it be so much better if we all lived in Colorado where weed flowed like water?" I chose not to mention that he was still too young for that scenario to make sense.

I surveyed the room looking for a responsible adult to take control of the situation and it came as quite a shock when I realized *I* was the most responsible adult in the room. Uh, when did that happen? Since when could I not hang with my cool cousins? Go drink for drink with them? Oh, right...it was the moment some genius decided to fill the fridge with disgusting seasonal beer.

"Okay," I said to my cousin, "let's go." He looked at me confused, so I clarified. "You are in no condition to drive anywhere. I am not about to let you get behind a wheel to pick up drugs that are still illegal in this state. And don't get me started on the fact that you are underage for all of that alcohol you've been drinking."

He gave me a goofy grin and wrapped his long, lanky arms around me and said, "Thank you! You're the best!" He turned to the room, "Alice is driving me to my pot dealer's house, everyone!" The group cheered and we were off.

I really dislike driving around the suburbs of Boston at night. The streets are dark and narrow and curvy and always seem to be wet for some reason. I was nervous on the drive. I had two drunk cousins trying to give me directions, my contacts had dried out long ago which made it harder to see, and I was convinced I was going to be pulled over, most likely after we had acquired the illegal drugs. Thankfully, we somehow made it to the drop location, picked up the goods and made it back to my uncle's house without incident. Without getting out of the car, I advised my cousins I would see them in the morning. They protested and tried to convince me to join them for a smoke. I politely declined.

Before I drove off, one cousin yelled, "You're the coolest, Alice!" I smiled a weak smile and waved goodbye. In the past, I would have cherished that comment because it would have meant I was one of them. One of the beautiful and cool. But this time I knew it wasn't said to me as an equal. It was said to me the way a jock says it to the nerd who just wrote his term paper for him. I was ready to be back with my sisters.

"Oh good, there you are," I said to Kate as I took a seat next to her at the funeral home.

"How are you holding up?" she asked. I gave a small shrug and scooted over on the loveseat to make room for Emma.

Emma held out a plate of small cheeses to us. "No thanks," I said. "I'm lactose intolerant now."

Kate gave me a skeptical look. "Since when?"

"Since I realized that dairy products make me sick to my stomach. I won't go into details," I said, acting as if I was doing them a favor.

Kate rolled her eyes as she was used to my seemingly random diet schemes. She decided to change the subject. "Man, Great Aunt Franny does not look good."

Emma and I craned our necks to catch a glimpse of our aging aunt. She was being helped into a chair next to our grandmother. Like a line forming at a newly opened buffet, people hurried over to offer their sympathies to grandpa's widow and younger sister. I turned my head to Kate and said, "You know, you look like a normal person when really you are the Angel of Death."

"*When Harry Met Sally*," Kate and Emma said in unison, catching my quote from one of our favorite movies.

Kate continued, "I didn't say I thought she was going to die. I'm just commenting on how frail she looks."

"We all know what those types of comments mean coming from you," Emma said. "How soon after you said something about my fish did it die?"

"It was a fish!" Kate protested.

"You told me once that I looked ashen," I said. "So, I went home and prayed the rosary in hopes that I wouldn't keel over in the middle of the night." Kate rolled her eyes at us, used to our mocking.

Our mother came over to us seemingly to ask how we were holding up but really to encourage us to mingle because "many of your relatives haven't seen you in a very long time." Emma protested saying we hadn't seen *each other* in a long time, but Mom's side-eye eventually got us off the loveseat. We gave each other knowing looks because we knew we would find our way back to each other in about 15 minutes.

One of my mom's sisters, Darla, zigzagged through the crowd toward me as my sisters were each quickly pulled into different conversations. "Alice!" Darla said stretching her arms out to me. She pulled me into a big hug. Her strong grasp and familiar perfume made me feel like a child again. "Where's Jake?" she asked, looking around me as if he was hiding behind me.

"Oh, uh," I stammered. "He couldn't make it." Darla gave me one of those faux-pouts that encouraged me to explain. "He just got a new job, you see. We didn't think it was a good idea for him to ask for time off for *my* grandfather." I realized I had overstressed the word "my" and tried to recover. "I just mean...not his...well, I mean, Jake really loved Grandpa and he is devastated he couldn't be here. He's only had the job for three weeks and seeing as he hasn't been able to keep any job for too long..." I trailed off, internally kicking myself for reminding my aunt that Jake had never been the one to bring home the bacon, so to speak.

"That sounds reasonable to me," Darla said, saving me from my own babbling. "What is he up to now? How's Denver? How long have you been there?"

"Jake is working security in an office building downtown. One of those massive skyscrapers. He really loves the job. Plus, he works a lot of nights, so he can focus on his music during the days." I could tell I was speaking a little too enthusiastically to be believable, but I didn't know how to stop. "Denver is great, too. We've been there almost a year, I think."

Darla shifted her weight from one foot to the other methodically as we talked. I wondered if her heels were hurting her and was thankful I brought flats. "Do you think Denver is the final destination?"

"Oh, I think so," I said. "Jake just couldn't get into the saturated music scene in Austin and Seattle was so expensive. Denver just seems to have more potential, you know?" Darla nodded. "Plus," I continued, "I've found a pretty good job. Never seems to be too difficult to find a job in the insurance industry!" I said with entirely too much enthusiasm. I smiled weakly.

"Are you still creating art?"

"Yes," I said without much muster. "The job keeps me pretty busy, but I work on things in my free time." I tried to remember the last time I had picked up a paintbrush and then realized I had never actually unpacked my art supplies after the last move. I changed the subject. "How are you? The kids? South Dakota?"

Darla gave a quick recap of her family and then pushed the conversation back on me. "So how long have you and Jake been together? Should I carve out some time next year for a wedding, possibly?" She winked and I realized she had been talking to my mom who was undoubtedly trying to convince her siblings that two-thirds of her daughters weren't really "living in sin" because "Alice is on the brink of marriage." I relayed that Jake and I were coming up on seven years and that we had been talking a lot about the future and starting a family and hoped to have a date set real soon for a wedding. Darla pulled me in close and whispered, "You know, your mother gave me such a hard time when I lived with Phil before marriage. She must give you and Emma hell."

"No, no," I shook my head. "I was 29 when Jake and I moved to Austin. She didn't give me a hard time at all. She likes Jake and just wants us to be happy. Besides, we all know that is where Jake and I are headed." I smiled.

Darla pulled back, smiled a sickly smile and said, "Well, that's good. I wouldn't want her to be as judgmental with you as she was with me." She put a hand on my arm, tapped it a couple times and was off with her arms outstretched toward another relative. I grimaced at the cheerfulness of all the re-unions and wondered how many people thought this was just another family get-together and not a funeral for the man we all loved so much.

I made my way toward the coffin for a chance to kneel before my grandfather only to be stopped by a line that weaved through two rooms. I looked for a sister to make a snarky comment about the line being longer than the wait for a new iPhone, but couldn't find one. I decided to take my place in line to avoid further small talk for a while. Unfortunately, my Uncle Reed sauntered up behind me. I watched him take a swig from an unmarked flask before he registered that I, his god-daughter, was standing in front of him.

"Oh, hey there, Alice," he said while he put an arm around my shoulder. "Good to see you. How are you?" He pulled me in for a side hug and I wondered how I was supposed to hug back in this position. I awkwardly just patted him on his chest.

"Oh, you know," I said. "As good as can be expected, I guess."

I indicated toward the coffin with my chin and Reed nodded in agreement. He pulled out his flask again, this time offering me a drink. I waved it away and he took another sip himself.

"Where's good ol' Jake?" he asked. "He's always up for a drink." He surveyed the room, shaking the flask, hoping to see my absent boyfriend.

"He stayed in Denver," I explained. "He's really sorry he couldn't be here, but he just started a new job."

"Ah, that's too bad," Reed said. "I like that guy." He continued to look around the room as the line we were standing in very slowly inched forward. His eyes settled back on me and he seemed to be trying to think of something, anything to say. He finally settled on the topic I really didn't feel like discussing. "Your mom said something about a wedding next year?"

I half-smiled and said, "Oh, well, we've been talking about it. I think we are both anxious to have kids so..." I turned back toward the line and willed it to move faster, but Reed had more to say, so I repositioned to face him again.

"Good, good." He stepped closer to me and thinking the line had moved, I also took a step only to accidently bump into the person in front of me.

"Sorry," I murmured.

Reed took my arm and leaned in closer and whispered, "I hope you are going to do something about your weight before the wedding." I gave him a slightly shocked, slightly confused look. He continued, "We have all watched you struggle over the years." He made a sweeping motion with his arm to indicate the entire family. "Up and down with your weight and we just all know how your current weight obviously reflects your deep unhappiness." My eyes shot down to the ground in embarrassment. "We know how beautiful you can be and it will just break our hearts if you walk down that aisle at this weight. You deserve to treat yourself better. Plus, you'll need to lose weight if you plan to have a baby. Can't get pregnant like that!" He patted my arm, pleased with his effort to "save me," and indicated that the line was moving forward.

I turned away from him and my eyes filled with tears. I was mortified by his comments. I grabbed a tissue from a box sitting on a shelf next to me and prayed Reed would turn his attention to someone else. I subconsciously ran my hands down the front of my dress and willed my protruding stomach to shrink immediately. I recalled a few hours prior to when Emma and I were getting ready at the hotel. I had foolishly looked at myself in the mirror with pride, enjoying my reflection in my new black dress. My long blond hair was behaving nicely and Emma helped me with some waterproof eye makeup that brought out the different shades of brown in my eyes. We even took a selfie together and jokingly called it our "funeral selfie." I had happily shared it on social media. What a naïve idiot I was. How could I have seen a nice-looking person in the mirror, when obviously everyone else in the world saw an unhappy, fat person? Tears streamed down my face. Reed continued to talk to me, but I couldn't face him again. I continued facing forward. I didn't want him to see me crying. He asked me some questions and I nodded or answered curtly over my shoulder. Finally, thankfully, the line in front of me disappeared and it was time for me to visit with my grandfather.

I knelt next to the coffin. The body that laid before me was unfamiliar. It was obviously my grandpa, but it also wasn't. He looked plastic and fake. I longed to smell Old Spice cologne and not that clinically dead person smell. My cheeks flooded with tears as I tried to prevent the ugly cry from bubbling up, but a massive inhale of breath escaped me. I put my hand to my mouth and felt my shoulders shake. I mourned for the man who was always a big, comforting presence in my life and I cried in self-pity, angry at my uncle's comments. I blew my nose loudly in a tissue and felt alone in the crowded room. When I stood up from the coffin and turned to face the room, I saw Kate and Emma waiting to embrace me.

Chapter 3

Emma

As Charlie and I walked through the packed funeral home, strangers touched me on the arm and offered their condolences. This was the way it had always been at my grandparents' lobster bakes, birthday parties, and anniversary celebrations: hordes of old people talking to me like they had known me my entire life. I suppose they had. From the little girl stealing maraschino cherries from the bar and performing skits with her cousins to the woman in the corner trying to avoid everyone but her sisters, they had watched me grow up, one event at a time. Many of them looked vaguely familiar to me, but I had no idea who these people were.

"Your grandpa knew a lot of people," Charlie said, obviously impressed.

"Yeah. He was quite a man."

"Emma!" Before I had completely turned around, Judy, a longtime family friend who came out of the woodwork once every few years, had her arms around me.

"Hi, Judy. It's good to see you. This is my boyfriend, Charlie."

"Oh, I have heard all about Charlie," she said as she shook his hand and sized him up. "You're the one who stole my girl away from me and dragged her across the country!" Charlie's shoulders dropped and his smile faded. He was already worried the family was mad at him because we had moved for his job, but now this woman he hadn't even met before was giving him a hard time.

"That's not exactly what happened, Judy. We made the decision to move to California together." Why did she even care? She lived 900 miles away from Indianapolis. In no way had I left *her*.

"We thought it would be a good opportunity for both of us," Charlie offered, looking to me for help.

"Absolutely!" I said, exuding far too much excitement for a funeral home. "We love living in Long Beach and being near LA. We live super close to the water and the weather is always great." Charlie stood a little taller. "Plus, I have a great job at a magazine. It's a dream come true." Charlie sank back down a bit. He knew I was lying about that last part.

"Oh yeah?" Judy asked, looking skeptical. "What magazine? Anything I've read?"

"Oh, probably not; it's a business-to-business publication for the dental industry." I gave her my toothiest smile, no pun intended. She smiled curtly. "It's not exactly the subject matter I would like to be in, but it's definitely a stepping stone." Another lie. I knew *Tooth Magazine* would never help me break into the travel sector. Sure, I would get more experience there, but I would never meet contacts who could help me transition into consumer mags. The reality was *Tooth* was helping pay the bills in our now more-expensive home; that's it. I'd be out of there as soon as possible.

"Well, that's so nice to hear," Judy said.

"You should visit sometime," Charlie said. "You could even stay with us." He was always so gracious when it came to traveling. Like me, he had studied abroad in London and traveled extensively around Europe. It had had such an impact on him, he was always looking to pay it forward, to make it as easy as possible for others to travel. If that meant offering up our couch to people we barely knew or helping a friend cover the cost of a plane ticket, he would do it.

"That would be nice, dear," Judy said, clearly distracted, as she patted him on the shoulder and walked toward another mourner with outstretched arms.

"She was pleasant," Charlie said, once Judy was out of earshot. "I told you your family is mad at me."

"No, they aren't. And Judy isn't family; she doesn't know what she's talking about. She probably can't even name all of Kate's kids, let alone have a pulse on what's important to my family."

"What's important to our family?" Alice asked as she and Kate approached with a Diet Coke for me.

"Bless you" I said, accepting the caffeine boost. "Charlie

thinks the family is mad at him."

"For what?" Kate asked.

"For moving Emma across the country," he said.

"Please. People in this family have done much worse. Trust me," Alice said.

I sent Charlie to go hide in the family break room with Steven and the boys while my sisters and I continued to mingle, telling the same stories—what the kids were up to and where Jake was and how my new job was going—over and over again.

"We should have sent out a pre-funeral newsletter," I said when we finally made it back to the corner by ourselves. "It would have saved a lot of time."

"This just in: Kate spends all her time in her van, Alice is still not married, and Emma is using all her expensive degrees to write about tooth decay. See you all next death," Alice said sarcastically. We all laughed and were immediately hushed by our grandma who was walking back to her station near the coffin after a restroom break.

"Keep it down, ladies."

"Sorry Grandma," we said in unison, like little kids who had been slapped on the wrists.

As soon as she was gone, I smirked at my sisters. "A hotdog is singing. You need quiet while a hotdog is singing?"

"*You've Got Mail!*" they both exclaimed, loud enough that we received another glance from our grandmother. Immediately we split into three different directions and I was on my own once again.

I spent the majority of the next hour proactively seeking out people I knew I could talk to with ease, which was a surprisingly small number for a family gathering. A moment left standing alone was an opportunity for any fourth cousin twice removed to swoop in, which was always a gamble.

Everyone I spoke to wanted to hear about life in the big city (we actually lived south of LA) and how many movie stars I had seen (zero) and the infamous California drought (it had no obvious impact on our lives). I didn't mind talking about California, but the conversation always shifted to my job, and it was exhausting trying to pretend it was interesting or that it was going to propel me into a life of travel and adventure. Those who knew nothing about the industry believed *Tooth* was going to get me a job at *AFAR*, which depressed me more. Just one week into the job, I already knew I was in a dead end.

Luckily, I found my cousin Jen and we fell into an easy conversation about her latest trip to Mexico. Jen and her siblings had always been my favorite cousins, and I especially looked up to her. She was four years older than me, so I spent our childhood visits trying to do everything like her. I loved the way she dressed, her taste in music, her laidback attitude. She always came up with the best games when we were little, and I had followed her around as much as possible whenever the family got together. I guess I still did.

"You have to check out Puerto Vallarta," she said. "It's so much better than Cabo. My friends and I partied all night and sat by the pool all day, and the waiters brought drinks by every time we got low. It was paradise."

"That sounds awesome," I replied. "Charlie and I have been talking about taking a trip down there now that we're so close." I scanned the room for Charlie and saw him backed up against a wall with my Uncle Reed hovering over him. Compared to Reed's 6'3" frame, Charlie, at 5'5", looked small and trapped. I waved him over and he pointed in my direction, using me as an excuse to escape Reed.

Charlie weaved through the room and put his arm around my waist just as my Aunt Rachel joined our circle.

"I can't talk to any more of Dad's friends," she said. Rachel was the youngest of my mom's siblings, but she was actually closer in age to Kate than to my Aunt Mary, so she gravitated to the cousins more often than not. "What are you guys talking about?"

"Jen and I were just talking about traveling," I said. "I was starting to tell her about some of the trips Charlie and I want to go on."

"Oh yeah!" Charlie lit up like he always did when he was talking about any of his favorite topics: traveling, photography and pizza. "We're talking about going to Thailand next year," he said to Jen. Then he looked to me, "Maybe you told her already."

"No, not yet," I smiled. We were great at telling stories together. We fed off one another's energy and it never felt like one person was hogging the spotlight. Our best story was the one about how we met:

"I was a groomsman and she was a bridesmaid."

"He asked his friend about 'the one with the hair.'"

"She came over and asked me to dance."

"He said he didn't dance."

"But she pulled me on the dance floor anyway."

But travel was our second favorite thing to talk about. We loved dreaming about all the places we were going to go together and sharing our stories about the places we'd been and the things we'd seen.

"We want to go on at least one big trip every year," I told them. "So, Thailand will be the first of many."

"That's awesome," Jen said. Rachel looked from Jen to us and back to Jen, looking like she wasn't sure how to say what she wanted to say.

"But…" she started. "How are you going to go on a major trip every year once you have kids?"

"Oh," I said. Charlie looked at me expectantly. "We haven't worked out all the details yet. I'm sure we'll figure something out." Rachel didn't seem satisfied with that answer, but I wanted to talk about kids less than I wanted to talk about my job, especially with Rachel. "Anyway, in Thailand we're going to go to an elephant conservatory where you can bathe and feed rescued elephants! And there are tons of Buddhist temples we want to check out."

I continued to ramble on until I felt like it would be weird for Rachel to bring up kids again, seeing as how the conversation had shifted back to Thailand. Mercifully, she was called away moments later to greet an old man who had apparently worked with Grandpa. Charlie and I retreated to the family break room for another Diet Coke and chocolate chip cookies.

"Why didn't you tell your aunt we're not going to have kids?" he asked me.

"I didn't want to tell her," I said, shrugging.

"Why?"

"Because she wanted kids and wasn't able to have any. I can't just tell her that I am probably able to have kids and I'm choosing not to."

"But it's our choice," he said, defensively.

"It's not that simple, Charlie."

"Last night at the cookout, you didn't say anything to your cousins either when they asked about us getting married or having kids. Are they also all unable to have kids?"

"You don't understand what it means for a woman," I said, exhausted. We had had this discussion before.

"Lots of people don't have kids," he said. "It doesn't make sense for us. We want to travel and have the freedom to live the life we want, not the one we're stuck with because we have to spend all our time and money on children."

"I know that," I said. "But every little girl is told she's going to get married and have kids. It's ingrained in us. It feels like an obligation. I'm still trying to convince myself that it's okay to break out of that mold. I'm not ready to tell other people yet."

"So, you're not sure that you don't want to have kids?"

"No, I am sure, it's just..." I rubbed my eyes and tried to come up with a different approach. "The number one thing women without children are asked, regardless of how successful they are or what amazing things they've accomplished, is why they don't have kids. Famous actresses get asked all the time — Jennifer Aniston, Renée Zellweger — no one cares how awesome their show was or if they've won an Oscar, they want to know where the babies are. Ellen DeGeneres even named one of her dogs 'Kid' so people would get off her back!"

"Ok, fine," he said, seeing that I was getting worked up. Charlie hated a scene. "I just don't think it's that big of a deal."

"I know you don't, but you're not a woman." We just stared at each other. He couldn't argue with that, but it wasn't good enough for him.

"I don't know if you really don't want kids or if you're only saying that because I don't," he finally said.

"I really don't want to have kids."

"Then why won't you tell anyone?"

Before I could say, yet again, that he didn't understand the pressure on women, my dad poked his head into the room.

"Hey, Little Fiddle," he said, using the name he had reserved for me and my sisters. "The service is about to begin. I know Kate would appreciate having you front-and-center when she gives her eulogy."

"Ok, Daddio, we'll be right there." I turned back to Charlie. "Can we finish this later?"

"Of course," he said, softening. He pulled me into a hug and kissed me on the forehead. "Let's go say goodbye to your grandfather."

November

Chapter 4

Kate

Speedway, Indiana, is an incorporated town of about 12,000 residents that is completely surrounded on all sides by the city of Indianapolis. We have our own police force, fire department, library, town council, and school system. It is a fascinating mix of families that have lived in Speedway for generations and immigrants just settling into American life. There are apartment complexes on the very low end of the income spectrum and beautiful homes with stately front porches and stained-glass accent windows.

Our tiny school system of four elementary schools, one junior high, and one high school educates our 1,200 students. The town doesn't even have buses. Kids walk, bike, and carpool to school. Within that small population, nineteen native languages are spoken, yet we routinely beat state averages on testing and we graduate nearly everyone. The high school has a race car on display in the lobby and the school mascot is a Sparkplug, which, I believe, is the most awesome mascot in all of America.

This intimate mishmash of a community is true small town living with the convenience of big city amenities. We can be at the famous St. Elmo's Steakhouse in downtown Indy within fifteen minutes. Yet we can also go into any restaurant in Speedway and it's a guarantee that we'll see someone we know. We can enjoy the Haunted House at the world's largest Children's Museum in Indianapolis and attend the local Lion's Club Halloween party where they still give out a silver dollar as a prize, like they have for 50 years. There is no shortage of personality in Speedway. I think that's why I fell in love with it so completely.

Our morning breakfast table was the perfect place to see the wealth of personality in my own family. Showered and fully dressed, Christopher had headphones in, a book in one hand, and a spoon in the other as he ignored the rest of us and ate his customary four bowls of cereal. Alexander had serious bed head and ignored his food as he made Phillip laugh with crazy stories about his dreams. Thomas munched away on eggs that Steven made him. He had a blanket wrapped around him like a cocoon to disguise the fact that he was wearing nothing but his underwear. And Phillip hopped from one foot to another, standing next to Alexander's chair in mismatched socks and stuffing microwaved mini-pancakes into his mouth.

In twenty minutes Steven would take Christopher to the junior high and I'd be dropping the other three at the elementary school. It always amazed me we could go from that chaos to everyone-out-the-door in such a short span of time. But it always worked. Not to say we didn't have hiccups. There was always a shoe that couldn't be found, a forgotten book, a paper that had to be signed as we walked to the car, or a forgotten trash barrel for one of us to frantically wheel to the curb. Regardless, I was on my way to work by 7:50 every morning. Miracles do happen.

I always slipped, unseen, into my cubicle at the office and promptly put in my ear buds. In general, it was my goal to get as much done in as little time as possible. That allowed me the freedom to get out the door by 2:30 to pick kids up and begin the after-school-activity dance that was never the same from one day to the next. It took a great deal of coordination, patience, and gas to get it right.

This particular Wednesday had the added fun of a commitment for me after dinner. When I agreed to be a Confirmation sponsor for my niece, Mae, I had no idea it was going to take up one night per week for a couple months. When I went through Confirmation in high school, my sponsor was my aunt Rachel. She lived halfway across the country and she came in on the actual weekend of the service. No additional commitment required.

So, when my sister-in-law, Molly, called and asked if I would be Mae's sponsor, I didn't hesitate. I think I even said something about being honored. Like a sucker. Spending Wednesday evenings in "faith formation" classes with a bunch of uninterested high schoolers was not what I had in mind.

But, there I was. Mae and I found seats in the back of the room and settled in for two hours of fun.

"I have so much homework I should be doing right now. This sucks monkey toes," Mae said.

"Nice language in church, kid," I teased her.

"This isn't church," she said with a classic teenage eye-roll.

"It's the church's basement," I clarified.

"Fine. It sucks holy monkey toes," she smirked.

When I was growing up, my aunts played a big part in my life. I loved them all (even the scary ones) and looked up to them. Since my sisters didn't seem to be anywhere near having kids, getting to be an aunt when I married into Steven's family was a total bonus. I taught all my nieces and nephews that it was pronounced 'auuunt' and not 'ant.' Since my aunts were all East Coasters, there were no 'ants' in my family.

After enduring the most painfully awkward video ever produced, we were told to break into small groups. Sponsors were asked to share their own experiences of Confirmation and what it meant to them. As often happened in small groups, everyone turned and looked at me expectantly. Sometimes I think I have "take-charge oldest sister" tattooed on my forehead. "My most enduring memory of Confirmation is what the bishop said at the end of the service," I began.

"That's unusual," said another 30-something female sponsor in our group.

"Well, it's not for a good reason," I said.

"Uh, oh," she said.

There is a certain understanding among most Catholic women. She could see where this was going. "He said, 'I want you all to know that I'm keeping all of you in my prayers. I pray that some of the young men in this group will be called to and accept the calling of the priesthood. And don't think I've forgotten you ladies. I pray that you'll grow up, have sons, and they will be called to be priests."

"Ugh!" Mae exclaimed.

"Yeah. It made me really angry," I said. "In fact, I think it was the main thing that contributed to my decision to major in Religious Studies in college."

"You majored in Religious Studies?" a high school boy asked with a look of utter horror.

"Yeah, I found a real passion for theology," I said, remembering my college days. "There is so much fascinating work going on in the field. Innovative thinkers bringing amazing insight and new ways of looking at sacred texts and church tradition. Way more interesting than that video, anyway," I smiled.

"What do you do with a Religious Studies degree?" a man asked.

"Well, I loved it, but there aren't tons of options," I blushed. "So, nothing at the moment. But I also majored in Theater," I supplied.

"Cool. Are you like an actress or something?" a boy with bright purple hair asked me.

"Uh, no. I work in Regulatory Compliance for an insurance company." I was treated to blank stares. "Yeah, it's about as exciting as it sounds. But I have a really flexible work schedule and even work from home a lot. I can be home with my…sons."

It hit me like a ton of bricks. I saw it in the eyes of everyone in that small group. That bishop had valued me only as a boy-rearing machine. And that's what I had made myself into. I cleared my throat and looked down at my hands. Thankfully the other 30-something sponsor launched into a detailed story about the smelly holy oil dripping into her eyes. Mae put her hand on my shoulder and I wanted to cry.

As soon as my feet hit the parking lot, I texted my sisters:

Kate: I think I've become my own worst nightmare.

Alice: You became the voice of Vincent Price in the Thriller video?

Emma: I thought her worst nightmare was that giant snake that Jafar became at the end of Aladdin.

Alice: That was me.

Kate: Hey! Focus! I'm having an existential crisis here!

Alice: Hold, please. I need to get out my dictionary.

Kate: My life is not my own. I gave it all to my kids.

Emma: You love your life.

Alice: You are an amazing mom.

Kate: But is that all I am?!

Emma: Of course not.

Alice: Is this about what Mary said to you at the funeral?

Kate: Partly. And other stuff. I think I need to find myself again.

Alice: Look in the movie theater.

Kate: What?!

Alice: Before you had kids, you were always at the movie theater. Maybe you left yourself there.

Emma: Or maybe a Star Trek convention?

I walked in the front door to find Steven on the couch. He smiled at me as I dropped my phone on the table.

"How'd things go?" I asked.

"Pretty good..." he began. A mini stampede of feet came thundering down the stairs.

"Mom!"

"I was just about to say I got them all to bed," Steven offered. My children used me as an excuse to stay awake just a little bit longer and I used them to reassure myself that my life choices were legit.

"Okay, monkeys, get to bed," I ordered after I gave them all hugs.

"Mom! I forgot to write my summary for my reading homework!" Thomas skipped toward the kitchen.

"Freeze, Mister. You can do it at breakfast. Bed!"

"Mom! My stuffed kittycat has a hole in his tail!" Phillip said as he snuggled the poor animal that was more patch than original animal at this point.

"Leave it here and I'll fix it tomorrow. Bed!"

"Mom! My blanket smells funny," Alexander said.

"Alexander. Go. To. Bed."

Christopher saw his opportunity. "Mom, I need..."

"Bed!!" Steven and I yelled together.

Four little faces dissolved into giggles. They all fled upstairs, tripping over one another and yelling "Mom!" as they went. Steven and I couldn't help but laugh too.

"I never have to miss these moments now."

I froze mid-laugh and tears sprang to my eyes.

Steven looked at me, concerned. "Are you okay?" he asked.

"I just heard my grandfather," I gasped.

"What?" Steven came to my side. "I didn't hear anything."

"It was kind of in my head...but with my ears...or not. I don't know," I fumbled around for an explanation. Angel of Death. This sort of thing made me feel like a crazy person. I had considered that I just have an overactive imagination. But why would my imagination leap into a light moment like this with my grandfather's distinct voice saying something that both broke and melted my heart?

"Maybe you should sit down. It's been a long day," Steven said as he led me gently by the arm. I sank down next to Steven on the couch and leaned in to ground myself to him. He wrapped an arm around my shoulder and, mercifully, didn't ask me to go into it any further. I sent a "thank you" prayer up to God. Because when it came down to it, these little episodes were gifts. Over the years, I had had encounters with deceased loved ones about seven times. And those experiences had, ultimately, let me know they are okay and I will see them again someday. It's just that in the short term, they gave me goosebumps and freaked me out. I wondered how long it would be before I could tell my sisters about it without my voice breaking. I liked to share these things with them, but I didn't like to scare them.

Steven and I fell into our nightly debriefing. It was a habit we had established long ago. Every night we would share tidbits our children let slip about their lives like "Christopher blushed big time when he was telling me about partnering with Ali in Math class" and "Alexander keeps saying he doesn't like music class anymore, which is weird."

As I lay in bed that night, I blinked at the dark ceiling trying to get my brain to slow down. I was so tired and overwhelmed that I couldn't even narrow down what I should be worried about. The fact that I'm hearing my dead grandfather? How to tell my sisters about it? If my husband thought I was a losing my mind? My unfulfilling job? Judgmental looks from teenagers? Alexander's sudden aversion to a class he loved previously? Did I have any clean pants for tomorrow? If it rains on Saturday, how will we get the leaves raked? And it spiraled on and on until I finally surrendered to sleep.

Sunday night, after supervising bath/shower time had left me with damp clothes and a feeling that my children would never master the difference between the hot and cold knobs, my cell phone went off.

It was too late in the evening for me to be getting calls. When I looked down and saw "Alice," I sprang up from the couch and jogged back to the bedroom as I answered the phone.

"Alice?" I could hear Alice inhale a shaky breath and my

stomach clenched. She hadn't even said anything yet and I thought I was going to be sick. "What's wrong, Alice?"

"I think Jake and I are breaking up," she managed to say before sobbing.

"Oh, Alice, Alice, its okay. I'm so sorry," my voice trailed off as she cried into the phone. I wanted to tell her that this was for the best, but I knew that would not be appreciated at the moment. To be perfectly honest, I didn't trust Jake and I'd be happy to see him go. In fact, one of the only big fights I ever had with Alice was about Jake. I tried to tell her that he wasn't the one. That she could do better. But, like an idiot, I tried to tell her when I had had a few beers and it came out all wrong.

As I listened to her sniffle and try to calm down enough to explain what happened, I shook myself. The only thing that was important right now was that my little sister was hurting. She was hurting and all the way in Colorado. I couldn't hug her. I couldn't comfort her. I couldn't find Jake and punch him in the stomach, like I had done to a kid who made fun of Alice at the bus stop when we were kids.

"We had this huge fight that wasn't really a fight and he left and what am I going to do? All I did was ask why he was avoiding setting a date for the wedding and everything just crumbled." I let her continue to spill the story. All I could think was that this was so typical of Jake and I could feel my muscles twitching with anger, the strength of which was shocking to me.

Steven opened the door and peeked in. "Everything okay?" he mouthed.

I shook my head and formed the word "Jake" silently. Steven's face hardened and he nodded. No love lost there. He turned and walked away.

"What am I going to tell Mom and Dad? Mom's going to tell me to come home, but my life is here. I think I need to find a new apartment and get my..." she trailed off into tears again.

I could feel my own anger sharpen into a point and find a purpose. If I couldn't be there to take care of Alice, I had to make her take care of herself. "Listen to me, Alice. This is your chance. You have to take care of you. Stand up for yourself. It doesn't matter what Mom wants or what Jake wants or anyone else right now. Please."

Chapter 5

Alice

It might as well have been a divorce. That's what everyone was telling me. We had been together for seven years; living together for four. I must have known somewhere deep down that this was the only possible outcome for us. But for some reason, it still came as a shock to me. Even the exact moment I was saying the words, "I'm leaving you. I can't be in this relationship anymore," seemed unreal. As though I was outside looking back at myself. If you had asked me only 72 hours before I uttered those words, I would have told you that I would never leave Jake. He was my soulmate; my best friend. We were going to get married and have cute, artistic babies and live together for the rest of our lives.

The worst thing about time is being able to look back on yourself and see just how delusional you really were. Did everyone else see it? Was I the only blind one? Was everyone else talking behind my back? Probably. How could they not? I always considered myself an intelligent person, but when I looked back on my time with Jake, I could clearly see how good I was at only hearing what I wanted to hear. I would say, "I can't wait to get married and have kids with you," and he would say, "...yeah," but I'd hear, "Yeah! Me too!" I would say, "I think 33 is a good age to get married and start trying to have a baby," and he would say, "That would be a good time," (emphasis on "would") but I would hear, "I agree!" Ugh, it made me sick just thinking about it. How I trained myself to ask questions in such a way that he couldn't disagree because he knew that if he did, I would get upset and cry and we would argue and he would do anything to avoid one of those nights.

In the end though, I could no longer deny the facts. I was with a man for seven years and he had no intention of ever marrying or starting a family with me. It took him actually looking me in the eye and saying, "I've said this many times before, but you aren't hearing me. I don't want to get married." Those words hit me like a bullet. I finally heard them loud and clear. All sound went away for me at that moment. Time stood still. Everything went white. All I saw were his eyes. They were so familiar to me, yet not. I could tell it hurt him to say those words as much as it hurt me to hear them. The next words out of my mouth were to ask him to give me 24 hours alone in our apartment. He obliged and went to stay with a friend.

The next 24 hours comprised of hysterical phone calls to my sisters. To Kate first, then Emma, then Kate again. I had no desire to talk to anyone else. I didn't even consider talking to my parents because I needed to process what was happening. At first, I wasn't even sure if I was going to leave him, but when I got on the phone with Kate, the first words out of my mouth were, "I think Jake and I are breaking up." And then *Bam!* Just like that I knew it was true. It was really the worst 24 hours of my life, alone in that apartment. A constant stream of tears. I had to take a sleeping pill just to make them stop long enough so I could rest. When Jake returned, I'm sure he knew what was going to happen the second he walked into the door. My poufy red eyes and irritated red nose gave me away.

For the second time in just as many days, one of us was saying words that were hurting both of us. He stared ahead while I told him I was leaving. That I loved him, that he was my best friend, but I wanted a family. I couldn't be with someone who didn't want the same future as me. I watched the tears form in his eyes and spill over onto his cheeks. My own tear wells had yet to dry up and did the same. Seeing someone you love in pain, a pain you caused, is a terrible feeling. We had spent the last seven years comforting each other, but this was new territory.

He didn't say anything while I spoke. He just nodded his head and silently cried. Finally, he said, "I knew this was a possibility, but I really didn't think this was going to happen." He then asked to be excused and went for a walk to process our new reality.

The breakup happened on a Sunday night. I was a zombie at work the entire week. I didn't tell any of my co-workers. I didn't think I was strong enough to formally verbalize my new reality to anyone. My supervisor could tell something was wrong and thankfully gave me some space. She knew I would tell her eventually. Without even telling me, she quietly took me off new claims for a couple of days so I could just work on my existing heavy workload. About half way through the week, I asked her if it was a slow week for new claims and she shrugged and said, "I thought you might need some time to catch up." She smiled at me knowingly. I thanked her and went back to my desk where I put on my headphones to drown out the office.

It was Tuesday before I called my parents. I hoped I would have a better handle on my emotions at that point, but as soon as I heard my mom's voice, I broke down. I asked her to put Dad on the other line.

"Are you okay, Fiddle?" he said as he got on the extension. I quickly got into why I was calling, and I could sense my mom getting angry on the other end of the line. That's the thing about my family: They are quick to defend, protect, and comfort. *Someone hurt you? That bastard. How can we fix this?*

In the course of the conversation, I found myself trying to defend and protect Jake. I understood my whole family was going to be angry at him, but I needed them to see that he and I brought the relationship to this point together. The more they berated him for failing to commit, the more I needed them to see that I was blind and let myself go along with something I knew deep down was never going to end how I wanted it to. "Mom," I said finally, "I know you are angry with Jake, but I don't think I can hear about that right now. It's too fresh. You need to remember that he did love me, just perhaps not in the same way I loved him."

"I understand, honey," she said reluctantly. "I'll only talk bad about him to your father."

I smiled. "Thanks, Mom."

And then as if a silver lining occurred to my mom like a flash, her voice brightened. "Does this mean you are going to move back to Indianapolis?"

I smiled again, thankful for the predictability of my parents. "I've been thinking a lot about that actually." I took a deep breath. "I think I am going to stay in Denver." I explained how when I first decided I needed to leave Jake, I did think I was going to move back to Indy. But as time went on, I realized I was mourning my lost relationship and I had started to mourn moving away from Denver. It then occurred to me that I didn't have to break up with the city. I could stay. "I know I haven't been here long and I don't really have any friends, but something is telling me to stay. Moving back to Indy somehow feels like a step back. You know, been there, done that? Whereas Denver feels like...I don't know...possibility."

My mom let out a little, "yeah, I guess," while my dad made a practical comment about me already having a job in Denver. I told them about my plan to go look for a new apartment that weekend and they told me they would send me some money to help with the moving costs. As they were saying goodbye, my mom told me she was so proud of me for standing up for what I want. "I know this is going to be a hard transition for you, Alice, but you are so strong and resourceful. Please call us if you need anything." Tears filled my eyes again and I gave a shaky acknowledgment and goodbye.

The week was excruciating. Thankfully, Jake was working most nights so I had the place to myself when I got home from work. When he wasn't working, he was out drinking with friends. That was how he handled the situation. He needed to be surrounded by distractions, whereas I just needed my large stock of rom-com DVDs and chocolate. He had asked if he should sleep on the couch, but I said that would be stupid. We could share a bed a little longer. On Thursday night, he came in after the bars had closed, slid into bed and wrapped his arms around me. As he held me tight, we both cried, not saying a word. Neither of us knew it would be our last night in the same bed.

Friday night after work, as I was deep into *While You Were Sleeping* and a batch of from-scratch chocolate chip cookies I somehow had the energy to make, there was a knock on the door. It scared Glenn, who had been snuggling on my lap, and he dug his claws into my legs. My heart pounded, unsure of who could be at my door at 9 p.m. I pushed Glenn off, brushed the cookie crumbs from my top, and tried to smooth down my crazy hair. When I opened the door and saw my visitor, my face crumpled into a mess of tears. Kate dropped her bags and pulled me into a long embrace.

"Thank you," I said between sobs. "I really need you here."

"I know," she said. "I know."

After what seemed like the world's longest hug, Kate told me to pack a bag for the weekend, my collection of DVDs and the fresh baked cookies. She summoned an Uber and before I knew it, we were stepping into an enormous suite on the 10th floor of the Sheraton Denver Downtown Hotel.

Once we had settled in, I looked at her and asked, "How?" She knew that word carried the multitude of questions I had about how she could leave her crazy life for a whole weekend and how she could afford the flight and hotel and most importantly, how did she know I really, really needed her there with me.

"Mom, Dad, Emma and I had a conference call about you late Tuesday night," she explained.

"Obviously," I said and smiled.

"We all agreed you needed some support and I volunteered," she continued. "Emma and Charlie pooled their frequent flier miles to pay for most of the flight and Mom somehow got Uncle Reed to give us a voucher for the room." She pointed to a huge fruit basket and noted that it was likely from Reed who was some kind of VP for Sheraton Corporate.

"What about your kids?" I asked.

"Believe it or not, they can survive a weekend without me," Kate said. "Besides, I have a great husband who has been well trained. And let's not forget, that *you* are my first kid." I smiled remembering the stories of how she thought I was her baby doll when my parents brought me home from the hospital. "Come on," she said gesturing toward the large sofa, "let's put on our comfy clothes and watch something ridiculous like *Clue* or *Oscar*."

The next morning, Kate was up before the sun. She blamed it on the time change, but I suspected she hadn't slept more than six hours a night since Christopher was born. She had showered, called her family, made four appointments at apartment buildings we had looked at online the night before and gone out to get us bagels all before I woke up. By 2 p.m., I had the keys to a new apartment in my hand and we were heading to Target to stock it up.

"I think you are being too generous," Kate said. "You bought everything in that apartment."

"I know," I said, sheepishly. "I just want to start fresh. When we go through the apartment tomorrow I will take what I need, but I don't want to leave him with nothing. I'm not heartless."

"Of course you're not," Kate said. She scanned the aisle of dishes and pointed to a pretty set.

"Those are nice, but maybe I should go the economy route." I picked up a box of red and white plates and put them in the cart. "Besides, when I meet 'the one' within the year, I will get to register for my dream items..." It was the kind of joke I had been trying out all weekend. I wasn't buying them yet, but Kate laughed in agreement. My smile faded quickly and my mind went back to the dark place. I looked at my sister and, like a little child, asked, "What if I never meet 'the one'? What if I've just broken up with the only person who will ever date me and I am single for the rest of my life and I don't ever have the chance to start a family?" The tears started to come again.

Kate placed her hand on my arm and said, "I truly believe that won't happen. You made a brave move to change your life for the better. It may not seem like that now, but it will one day. And whoever said you needed to be with 'the one' to start a family?"

"The Pope?"

Kate laughed then said, "You run your own life. Give yourself a timeline. If you aren't anywhere near a relationship at that point, then just have a baby. Start your own family."

I gave her a small nod and smile and wiped the tears from my eyes. She pulled her hand away from where it was resting on my arm and I said, "Geez, your hands are so hot!"

"I know. I can't help it!"

Kate left Denver after dinner on Sunday. I felt cleansed as she hugged me goodbye. With her help, we had packed up my things and moved them to the new apartment. Glenn had already found a cozy spot to call his own. She encouraged me to take a few days off work and I had a hand-written schedule on my new fridge advising me when Macy's, the moving company, and Comcast were scheduled to be there within the following 48 hours. Before she left, I thanked her profusely for her help. She shrugged it off and said, "Anytime, Al-gal. I love you so much. Call me if you need anything."

Chapter 6

Emma

I was pulling books out of a box and organizing them on our bookshelf from tallest to shortest when my phone buzzed. I looked up and saw it across the room on the couch. Too lazy to retrieve it, I went back to the task at hand and switched Amy Poehler's Yes Please, which I stole from Alice, with Neil Patrick Harris' Choose Your Own Autobiography, which was slightly taller. I hadn't read either of them or any of the other books that moved to California with me.

I was notorious for collecting books that I never read. My parents were big readers. When I was little, even before both of my sisters had moved away for college, evenings were pretty quiet in our house. We'd turn on The Carpenters or John Denver and my parents would read while the three of us did homework. On those evenings, I rarely saw my mom or dad without a book. Stacks took up every nook and cranny of our home, which was probably why I enjoyed having them in my own apartment. They were comforting, even if I never read them.

My phone buzzed a few more times and I knew my sisters were texting. I climbed over the two boxes in front of me and slid through the little path Charlie created from the hallway to the couch. I sat down beside Hoosier, who was sleeping through the buzzing, pet him on the head, and opened my phone to a conversation about the cable man in Alice's apartment.

Alice: He's just standing here, watching my TV.

Kate: Is he done hooking it up?

Alice: I think so. It seems to be working.

Emma: What's he watching?

Alice: The Help. We just saw the part with the pie and he cracked up and literally slapped his leg.

Emma: Well, that's a good movie.

Alice: One of his favorites, apparently.

I laughed just as Charlie came in from the kitchen, catching me in my little break. "I thought you were unpacking," he said as he broke down another box.

"I am, but my sisters are texting."

"Uh huh," he muttered as he rolled his eyes and went back into the kitchen. He had been working late every night and occasionally on weekends, so this was the only time he had to unpack boxes. He wasn't going to let me slow his progress.

Alice: Once he leaves, I think my apartment will be all set up.

Emma: What?! You've been there like a week. Charlie and I are still climbing over boxes and putting furniture together.

Kate: You've been there for three months.

Emma: It's only been two and a half. And we've been busy! Charlie practically lives at his office.

Alice: I had to get everything in order. I couldn't live in limbo anymore.

Emma: Want to come help us now?

Alice: No. The cable guy just started petting Glenn. I think he lives here now.

After another glance from Charlie, I got up and went back to unpacking, but it wasn't long before another distraction knocked on the door. Charlie and I froze at the sound, looked at each other and immediately put our fingers to our noses. *Not it!* He pointed to me to signal I had lost that round, and I went to answer the door.

"Hi, I'm Cynthia!" A short blond said, smiling at me expectantly.

"Hi," I said cautiously. What was she selling?

"I recently moved in across the way," she said, pointing to the building on the other side of the courtyard.

"Oh hi!" I said with a much friendlier tone. I was always on the hunt for new friends. Other than Charlie and my weird coworkers, I didn't know anyone in Southern California, and I was starting to go a little stir crazy. "I'm Emma and this...Charlie! Come here." Charlie poked his head around the corner and I waved him over. He pushed a box out of his way and came to the door to shake our neighbor's hand. "This is Charlie."

"Nice to meet you guys," Cynthia said. "Did you just move in, too?" she asked, glancing over our shoulders at the mountain behind us.

"We've been here a couple months," Charlie said. I could see the judgement on her face.

"We've been busy," I said defensively.

"Oh, of course," she said. "I know moving can be so hectic. My husband and I really had to scramble to get things in order for our housewarming party. And of course, keeping the kids out of everything was a total disaster."

"You have kids?" I asked, wondering how anyone could fit more than two people into these apartments. *The corner unit must be a two-bedroom*, I thought, looking in the direction of her apartment and wishing we had a spare room for all the stuff we had yet to unpack.

"We have two girls. Harper is 3 and Evie is 14 months."

"Cool," I said, not knowing what else to say. I didn't know how to talk to people about kids who weren't related to me. She glanced from me to Charlie and back to me, clearly waiting for us to say something else.

"Do you two have kids?" she finally asked.

"No, it's just us," Charlie said happily, putting his arm around my shoulder. "And our cat Hoosier." He pointed to the couch where Hoosier was stretching and repositioning to continue his nap.

She glanced over at the couch, unimpressed. "Oh, well, maybe you'll have a child before too long and he or she can play with the girls!"

"Oh, um, we're probably not going to have kids," I shrugged and smiled.

"Really? Why not?"

"We just don't think kids are for us," Charlie said matter-of-factly.

"Oh, you'll change your minds," she said, giving us a dismissive wave.

"Probably not," Charlie countered, holding his ground.

"But kids are so fun," she persisted. "Sure, they're a handful, but they're so fulfilling. You'll see when you have your own." She gave a toothy grin.

"Yeah," I said, cutting Charlie off from saying anything else. I raised my eyebrows at him and turned back to Cynthia. "Maybe we will," I smiled.

"Harper and Evie would be so excited to have a baby in the neighborhood!" she exclaimed, happy that I gave into her demands that we have children.

"Sure they will," Charlie said, defeated.

"Anyway, like I said we're throwing a housewarming party and we can't seem to find our wine opener. We must have lost it in the move. Any chance we could borrow yours?"

"Sure," I said, the friendliness in my voice all but gone. I started to turn into the apartment but Charlie stopped me.

"I'll get it," he said, clearly avoiding being left alone with our new neighbor. I could hear him rifling through the kitchen drawer as I just stared at Cynthia in the doorway, her fake smile still plastered on her face. I was fairly certain this was not the new friend I had been looking for. After Charlie returned with the wine opener and handed it to her with a little too much force, Cynthia thanked us and retreated to her side of the courtyard. I shrugged at Charlie and we returned to our boxes.

After a few minutes, however, he was back in the living room. "You don't actually think I'll change my mind, do you? Because I won't."

"No, Charlie," I sighed. "Do you think I'm going to change my mind? You forget I knew I didn't want kids long before I met you. Sure, I thought maybe I would want them once I met the right guy, but here you are and I still don't want them, so you have no reason to be concerned. I could just tell she wasn't going to back down."

"So, you just gave in and said we're going to have kids?" he asked.

"It wasn't a binding contract! I just didn't want to justify myself to a complete stranger," I said exasperated.

"So, you didn't mean it?"

"Of course not."

"Ok," he said, pulling me in for a hug. "I just don't want you to wake up in a few years and realize that we weren't on the same page. I don't want to waste your time." He was talking

74

about Jake.

Charlie hadn't been around for the bulk of Jake and Alice's relationship, but he caught on quickly. He knew their split hadn't just hurt Alice; in a way it had hurt me, too. Sure, I had mixed feelings about Jake over the years; I had spent more time with him than anyone else in the family. We had some great times together, but there were also times when I couldn't stand to be around him. When he was angry, he would recount whatever injustice had happened to him repeatedly to anyone who would listen. When he was drunk, he became the life of the party, always trying to make someone laugh. He passed judgments on my life that made me so mad, but ultimately, I knew he wouldn't have said them if he didn't think of me like a sister. As much as I knew Alice could do better, I never thought they would break up. When they did, I was shaken, and Charlie could see it. He knew my confidence in men, in relationships in general, took a hit, and he didn't want to disappoint me the same way Jake had disappointed Alice.

"You're not Jake, Charlie. You've been honest with me from the beginning, right?"

"Yeah," he said, not letting go of me.

"Then we're on the same page."

The next day, Charlie and I went to Target to get some things for the apartment. I was choosing between chevron and polka dot shelf liners when I noticed he was getting antsy.

"Do we really need all this stuff?" he asked, glancing at the growing pile in our cart.

"Yes," I said. "You want our place to look nice, right?"

"Yeah…" he said cautiously.

"Well, 'nice' costs money." I smiled and continued down the aisle toward the decorative dish towels. This apartment was our first together, and I wanted to make it perfect. He told me he wanted me to make it "homey," a complete change from the bachelor pad he lived in before we moved in together, but we had different expectations of how I would make that happen.

"Do we really need more towels?" he asked. He was definitely the practical one in our relationship.

"How else will we mark the seasons in this California climate if our dish towels don't have little snowmen on them?" I smiled, throwing them into the cart.

"You're a crazy person," he teased, poking me in the side as I jumped away from him and giggled. "Are we about done?"

"Yes, we just need to get the stuff for our earthquake kit."

"Our what?" I could tell he was losing patience.

"Our earthquake kit. They were talking about it on the news. There's an increased chance that an earthquake will hit soon. And it's going to be a big one."

"How much of an increased chance?" he asked skeptically.

"It's only like .5 percent, but!" He rolled his eyes. "But, the anchorman said this is more of a reminder to have your kit ready!"

"Fine," he sighed. He knew I worried about everything and that he wouldn't win this one. "What goes into an earthquake kit?"

"We need to have enough nonperishable food and water for each person for three days."

"How much is that?"

"I'm not really sure how to know if we have enough food, but I know we need one gallon of water per person per day."

"So, you want to buy six gallons of water?"

"At least," I said, making my way to the grocery side of the store. "And a full gallon for Hoosier."

When we tracked down the water, I could tell I wasn't the only one working on her kit this weekend. "See!" I said, pointing to the shelf that was nearly empty.

"Let's just get four for now," he said. "I don't want to carry seven gallons of water."

"Fine, but if the earthquake hits this week, I get some of your water."

"Deal."

February

Chapter 7

Kate

Growing up, hobbies were a hobby in my family. Our mother had fairly steady hobbies: puzzle books, reading, and baking. Our father had an ever-changing cavalcade of hobbies: Civil War reenactment, biking, hiking, sailing (in Indiana!), and gardening. My sisters and I were a combination of our parents. We had primary hobbies, with random bouts of other obsessions.

My freshman year of high school, I decided to make theater "my thing." I thought this was a great extension of my love of movies and TV shows. Part of being an introvert, for me, is avoiding drama in real life. So, embracing drama in the world of theater made total sense to me. I only had one close friend, Vicky, and we never fought or gave into teenage ideas of rebellion for the sake of rebellion. Part of me needed to lash out though. Theater was my chance to do that without dealing with ramifications in my real life.

I continued with theater through college and even did a show with local company after I graduated. I have no clue if I was any good or could have continued down that path. The majority of my information came from my adoring husband and my supportive-to-a-fault family. Adorable, but unreliable.

But then I had kids. Christopher came when I was twenty-four and I spent the next six years of my life with a baby or pregnant or both. I was exhausted on a molecular level. I didn't have energy to devote to rehearsal schedules and performances. Plus, there is no need to go seeking the dramatic when your life includes physics-defying diaper blow outs while sitting in a traffic jam or toddler tantrums in Kohl's because his socks are "too red."

As I did the junior high carpool on a cold February morning because Steven had an early meeting, Christopher told me he was going to be auditioning for the school play, so he wouldn't need a ride until 4:30 that afternoon.

"Wait, what?" I stammered.

"Yeah, I signed up for an audition time," he shrugged.

"What play? Do you have a monologue to perform? Since when are you interested in acting?" I started in as I pulled the van up to the school.

"Mom. I have to go. I have a makeup test before first period."

"Oh, sure. Okay, see you at 4:30 then," I said, distracted.

As I drove away from the junior high school, I realized I was jealous of my son. But not for the reason I would have thought. Initially I figured I was jealous that he would be part of a theatrical production. I still loved the theater and the person I was when I was in a play. But it went deeper than that. I was jealous that he had the time and freedom to decide on a whim that he was going to try something out because it sorta-kinda interested him. There was no way being jealous of your 12-year-old could lead to good things, right? Something had to change.

When I snuck into my cubicle 20 minutes later, I didn't dive into my work. Instead, I texted my sisters.

Kate: Christopher is trying out for the school play.

Alice: Cool!

Emma: Are you going to become a theater mom now?

Kate: No, thank you. I want to do something I want to do.

Alice: That sentence is confusing.

Emma: Why can't you do what you want to do?

Kate: I don't have time.

Alice: For what?

Kate: What I want to do!

Alice: But what is it you want to do?

I put down my phone. What did I want to do? I had no idea. How could I have no idea? For the past 13 years, all I wanted was to have kids and be a mother. And I still wanted that.

So much of what you do when you're a mother is dictated by your children. Parents project the illusion that they are in charge, but really, they are just reacting to whatever situation their children put them in. I needed something in my life that I could direct. But it also had to let me be a mom. So, I was looking for something to give me freedom that also allowed for a total lack of freedom. Awesome.

Alice: The fact that you're not answering leads me to believe you're either (a) not at home, (b) home but don't want to talk to me, or (c) home, desperately want to talk to me, but trapped under something heavy.

Emma: When Harry Met Sally!

Kate: Sorry. I have no idea what I want to do.

Emma: How can you not know?

Alice: Start with your hobbies.

Kate: I don't have any hobbies anymore.

Alice: How is that even possible? That would make me crazy!

Kate: My kids are my hobby.

Neither of my sisters responded to that. I could imagine them both looking at their phones and shaking their heads. Was I really this pathetic? Anger flared in my mind as I got defensive again. Being a mom and being interested in my kids was not a character flaw. It didn't make me boring; it made me a good mom.

Shut up, I told myself. This isn't about being a good mom. It's about being a good Kate. There can be more to me and it doesn't have to diminish the mom part. Right?

I opened a Word document and at the top of the page I typed "Interests." Then, I wrote "my family" and promptly deleted it. I already had my family. That wasn't changing and it wasn't up for debate, so why put it on this list?

After a full five minutes of staring at the page, I got up. I walked around the building, making stops at the cafeteria, the bathroom, and the coffee station. This was ridiculous. Okay, if I didn't have any interests anymore, I would start with what they used to be.

Months ago, Alice had told me to look in the movie theater. I had barely seen anything that wasn't animated or a heart-warming animal-based story in almost 13 years. There was a time in high school when I couldn't go see a movie because I had seen every single film playing at the local multiplex. I would anxiously await the Oscar nominations and be sure I had seen each nominee for Best Picture and as many of the others as I could fit in.

I pulled up the movie schedule for the local theater. The latest installment of the rebooted Star Trek was playing. I used to love Star Trek. I followed The Next Generation TV series, I went to opening nights of their movies, and I even read books based on the series. I hadn't seen the preceding reboots, but surely, I could catch on. I was well versed in the Star Trek universe.

I checked my watch. The first showing started in an hour and it would be done before I needed to pick up the kids. I looked around the wall of my cubicle. My boss wasn't in today. Could I really just leave? Play hooky? Well, maybe this was my big chance to be a rebellious teenager.

I shut down my computer, grabbed my coat, and used my

years of experience sneaking into the building to sneak out of it. My heart pounding, I made it to my car and started the ignition before I lost my nerve.

Kate: I'm going to a movie.

Alice: That's nice. Thanks for sharing.

Kate: I mean I'm leaving work and going to a movie.

Emma: Like when people think you are working?

Kate: Yes. I snuck out.

Alice: Who is this? Who has Kate's phone?

Emma: What are you going to see?

Kate: The new Star Trek.

Alice: Never mind. Obviously Kate still has Kate's phone.

I pulled into the movie theater and checked my phone. No work emails had come in yet. I bought my ticket and stood in the lobby. When we came to the movies with the kids, I would sneak Capri Suns and candy in my purse. By myself, I could afford something at the concession stand. It was only 10:15 in the morning, but I bought popcorn, Buncha Crunch, and a large Diet Coke.

When I got into the theater, there were a few other people already there. I sat in the row against the back wall with my stash of totally overpriced and time-of-day-inappropriate food. One more look at my phone and the lights went down.

The previews were for movies that were rated PG-13 or R— a world of movies I had long been absent from. And each preview was for a sci-fi or fantasy film. And I wanted to see all of them. My boys had been asking for years to see the Marvel movies and, as I watched a preview of one, I realized that I could see them, even if my kids couldn't yet. I had so much catching up to do.

In two hours and some-odd minutes, I felt something inside me wake up. I fell into the familiar world of science, adventure, exploration, and aliens. I watched Kirk and Spock work a problem from the emotional and logical angles respectively. I let everything melt away and gladly suspended my disbelief. When the familiar theme song played over the closing credits, I cried.

Driving home, I got a call from the elementary school principal.

"Mrs. Bryant?" came the familiar voice.

"Mr. Price? Is everything okay?" I asked, immediately thinking of broken bones or other tragedies.

"Well, we wanted to let you know there was an incident with Alexander today. If it had happened earlier in the day, we would have asked you to come pick him up. But as it is, I'll just keep him in my office until dismissal," he said, as if doing me some giant favor.

"What? What happened?" I asked. I could hear my voice ice over.

"He head-butted another student," Mr. Price explained.

"Excuse me?" I said. This had to be some kind of mistake. Alexander did not have one violent or angry bone in his body. He was my little love. Friends with everyone. I could feel my heartbeat increase and the blood rush to my head.

"In the hallway after specials, he head-butted the student in front of him in line. As you know, we do not tolerate physical violence of any sort in our school. I've had Alexander and the other child in my office and we've had a discussion together," he finished.

"So, Alexander is okay?" I asked, still feeling off-balance. None of this made sense to me.

"Yes," he said.

"And he can come back to school tomorrow?" I asked.

"Yes," he agreed. "As long as he understands that any further incident will result in a suspension."

"Right," I said and then I hung up without bidding the man goodbye. I was in a blind rage and I didn't even have the whole story yet.

My mood did not improve when I saw Alexander walking toward the car. His face was contorted in that horrible way that little boys have to prevent themselves from crying in front of friends. The instant the van door slid shut, he burst into tears.

I unbuckled my seatbelt and folded myself in half to clamber into the backseat. I scooped Alexander into my arms and held him tight without saying a word.

We stayed that way until I saw Phillip skipping toward the car. I pulled a tissue from a seat pocket, handed it to Alexander, and climbed back into my own seat. By the time the van door opened again, nothing looked out of place to Phillip.

When Steven got home, the three of us closed the door of

Alexander's bedroom and had a chat.

"Okay, buddy, tell us what's going on," Steven began.

"Zander, in my class, is so bad in music and Ms. Cooper never does anything," he said, tears springing to his eyes already.

"Bad, how?" I asked.

"He puts bad words in the songs and tells inappropriate jokes when she isn't listening and pokes me in my back or messes up Kendall's hair or steps on K'wan's toes," he said. It was like a faucet had been opened. He spent the next couple of minutes getting every observed or experienced offense off of his chest.

Eventually, we got to the bottom of the "headbutt," which was the result of months of frustration boiling over when Zander called my son a particularly nasty name and pinched him. Alexander showed us the bruise on his upper arm and my heart leapt into my throat.

After Steven and I calmly explained to Alexander that physical retaliation was never appropriate and would always be caught, we suggested he go find his brothers and play for a while and let us talk alone.

"What the hell is wrong with that school?" I unleashed as soon as the door shut. "How can all of this be happening and the one thing they see is our son pushing back? I know that kid, Steven. He's a piece of work. Thinks he's above every single other kid. Plus he's twice Alexander's size! How could they think Alexander is a threat to *Zander*?"

"Calm down, Kate. This seems to be isolated to one class where one teacher isn't paying attention to one kid. Maybe we just need to alert her to the issue so she can watch for it," Steven said, reasonably.

"Or maybe I can quit my job, follow Alexander around all day, and trip Zander in the hallways during passing periods," I suggested.

"I do think we need to tell Mr. Price about the bruise on A's arm. He didn't mention that part, did he?" Steven asked.

"No! Our kid was hurt too! But he had the nerve to talk to me like I was raising some kind of hooligan," I jumped on the unfairness of it all.

In the end, Steven and I sat down and wrote a couple of (too?) polite letters. One to the music teacher to let her know that things seemed to be happening in the classroom and we'd appreciate it if she could keep an eye out and, perhaps, separate Zander and Alexander. The other to Mr. Price expressing our regret that things had turned physical, our assurances that we had spoken to Alexander about it, and our dismay to find the rather large bruise on Alexander's arm.

Kate: Some little punk has been bullying my son!

Alice: What? Who?

Kate: Alexander. He got in trouble for fighting back today.

Emma: Alexander fought with someone? Like physically?

Alice: Must have been bad.

Kate: Yes! It was! Next time I'm in that school, I am staring that kid down.

Alice: Uhhhh…

Kate: I'll just dress all in black, maybe do a nice smoky eye and leer at him.

Emma: We don't have bail money. Redirect, woman.

Easy for them to say! I felt like someone had kicked me in the stomach. While I was sitting at a movie, my sweet boy had reached a breaking point. For the second time that day, I cried.

After putting the kids to bed that night, with extra kisses and attention for Alexander, I flopped onto the couch next to Steven. I put my head on his shoulder and sighed.

"You okay?" he inquired.

"I cried at the Star Trek movie today," I admitted.

"I'd cry if I had to watch a Star Trek movie too," he joked.

"Because I loved it and missed it," I said as I punched him lightly in the arm.

"You missed Star Trek?" he asked me with a confused scowl.

"I missed how it made me feel. Not just Star Trek, but movies. Science fiction, fantasy, the journey of the characters, the magic of it all," I explained with a knot in my throat.

"Why did you stop going to movies?" he asked.

"I shouldn't have gone today," I said, heartbreak making my voice crack.

"Why on earth not?" Steven asked.

I couldn't bear to voice the guilt that was eating at me.

"When Alice broke up with Jake you were able to take off for a whole weekend and we all survived. I think we could manage a couple hours here and there."

"I know..." I hesitated.

"I want...we all want you to be happy, honey," he encouraged.

"But that's the thing. I am happy! It's not like I feel like I have this terrible life. I have the life I've always wanted. And today, I should have..." I trailed off.

"What? Should have what?" Steven challenged. "Been sitting out in the hallway? Been in music class with him?"

"I don't know. But it almost feels like I'm being..."

"If you say 'selfish' to finish that sentence, I will make you sit in the time-out chair," he scowled at me.

"Well it does feel like that!" I argued, lamely.

"Do you think I'm being selfish when I go play tennis with my brother?" he challenged.

"No! Of course not!"

"Then why would it be selfish for you to get away every once in a while? Don't make me be the feminist in this family, Kate. You do not have to be chained to this house to be an amazing mother."

"If I let myself get back into all this stuff, I may become a big old nerd again," I warned.

"Hey, I fell in love with that nerd."

I hugged him tight.

"Besides," he continued, "you never stopped being a nerd."

Chapter 8

Alice

The amazing thing about having a birthday two days after Valentine's Day is that I could trick myself into thinking beyond the dreaded Love Day. "Oh, is there a holiday today? I didn't realize. I'm busy planning my awesome birthday, which is in two days." I was not looking forward to my first Valentine's Day in seven years without Jake, not that Jake ever paid much attention to the day. The first few years of dating we did the obligatory eating out at a fancy restaurant. Some years I received flowers, some years I did not. Usually, Jake didn't have much money, so my birthday was lumped with Valentine's Day, and we would eat out on my birthday so not to be bombarded with all the "commercial love crap." It was fine. It didn't bother me.

Okay, okay. It did bother me. Every other girl gets dinner and flowers and gifts on BOTH days. Why should I be denied a Love Day simply because my birthday is two days after and Jake was cheap? Not that I could ever actually complain about this out loud though. One little "I want to celebrate both my birthday and Valentine's Day" comment and the Christmas babies would jump down my throat. "You want to talk about gift injustice?? Don't get me started on combined gifts!" Yeah, yeah, yeah...

Anyway, there I was on Valentine's Day. It had been almost exactly three months since the breakup. The previous three months had not been great. A major breakup days before Thanksgiving leads to a lot of holiday gatherings with friends and family and the obvious void that was Jake. I did a pretty good job at keeping my composure until I was a couple of glasses of wine into the night. It never failed that the second glass seemed to cue someone to look at me with that slight head tilt and say, "So, how are you?" Ugh. Instant tears. Thanks, friend whom I love dearly, way to ruin the party.

Three months into the breakup, I had learned how to hold back my tears in public. I saved them for the shower most days. There was something comforting about not being able to tell the difference between shower water and tears. I just hoped my salty tears could wash away the day as well as the shower water.

I had planned ahead for the weekend of Valentine's Day and my birthday though. My best friend, Helen, flew to Denver from Washington, D.C. to be with me. She had recently gone through a breakup as well and was seriously considering moving to Denver to get away from her ex. I was desperate to have her with me and the weekend was going to be the good will tour that convinced her to make the move.

"Okay, Helen. Operation: Ignore the Obvious Heartache Weekend has begun!" I said to her as she hopped into my car at the airport.

It was Friday night and the holiday was in full swing. "First, we are going to enjoy the night life, which you will be happy to know is full of men, hence the name Men-ver."

"I like the sound of that!" Helen said.

"Then tomorrow we are going to Red Rocks for a hike up the stairs. Then to Morrison for some lunch and then maybe to the Coors Brewery?"

"Nice."

"Other things we could do while you're here is go to the DAM aka the Denver Art Museum or to Boulder to visit Pearl Street or the Celestial Seasonings factory. Or maybe we drive further into the mountains and check out Idaho Springs or Georgetown..."

"There is so much to do here!" Helen said.

"Oh you have no idea. Hopefully by the end of your trip you will see why I had to stay here. Denver is bustling and the mountains are gorgeous and there is just this great sense of being in the right place at the right time."

Once out of the airport traffic, I drove us directly to The Shoe, my favorite neighborhood bar. The Shoe was fantastically dressed up as that emo kid you knew in high school. You know, the one who hated anything and everything commercial? Driving by other bars we could see the red paper hearts spilling out of the entrance ways. But not at the Shoe. The only red in sight was the blood red carpet that I'm sure used to be a wonderful bright red, but years of traffic and alcohol spills have left it dark and sticky.

"Coors Light?" Frank, the cute bartender, asked me as soon as I walked through the front door.

"Make that two!" I shouted over the crowd as I pointed out Helen. We stood behind two occupied stools for about a minute before they freed up and we grabbed a seat. "Frank, this is my friend Helen who is thinking about moving to Denver!"

Frank nodded hello to Helen and popped open our cans of beer. "Welcome to Denver! You'll love it here. These are on me," he said with a wink.

"I could get used to this!" Helen said.

Helen then proceeded to ask me the only line of questions I seemed to get those days: How are you doing? Have you seen Jake? Are you dating again? I went beyond my standard answers of "fine, yes, and no" with her though. I told her about how every day seemed to be a little better, but the heartache was still quite fresh. I told her that Jake and I met for coffee the other day to "catch up" and it went well. I explained how a "weening-off" program seemed to work well for us because, "I just don't know how people go from being best friends to being acquaintances so quickly. I know it has something to do with a non-contentious breakup, but I just can't hate him or remove him from my life so easily." And I told her about how my dreams were helping me to think about dating again.

When Jake and I first broke up, the thought of dating anyone, or really the thought of just dating in general, made me completely nauseous. Literally sick to my stomach. For so long, I only had eyes for Jake. I never found myself (or let myself?) think about another man. I always believed that people who cheated in their relationships were obviously in the wrong relationships. It seemed so clear. Not happy equals cheating. I was happy. I could not ever fathom cheating on Jake and I assumed that meant that he was my "one." So, when I realized he was not my one, it left me with this horrible pit in my stomach. Like when a dog cautiously takes the piece of bacon from its owner's hand after years of being taught not to beg at the table. I was conditioned to see Jake and Jake only. Because of this, I assumed it would take many months, maybe a year before I even looked at another man. But my subconscious knew better. It must have had an agreement with my biological clock or something, because before I had even vacated our shared apartment, the dreams started. They came without warning. One by one, night by night, the dreams came to me. They were tame at first and then they started to grow in intensity. One could argue that they weren't really dreams, but memories trying to break free from my psyche.

The first dream was so innocent and distant. I was four or five and at a daycare center. My little friend, Greg, was giving me a hug. He put his arm around me and his other arm around his friend, Adam. "You are my best friend," he said to Adam. "And you are my girlfriend," he said to me.

I woke up from that dream feeling nostalgic for my first "boyfriend." Mostly though, I felt nostalgic for my first feeling of "like" toward a boy.

A few nights later, I was visited by Mikey, the blond boy who declared his love for me in the fifth grade. I was too busy scoping out the swing set situation to fully hear him pour his heart out to me. It wasn't until I was securely on a swing that I looked back at him, yards away, and I realized what was happening. He looked defeated as I swung higher and higher.

More and more dreams came. All leaving very distinct feelings as I slowly woke from them. Every boy who impacted my life in some way appeared to me as I slept. Ian from middle school, James from high school, Nick from freshman year of college—all my crushes and boyfriends came to me as I recovered from the breakup that jolted me the most.

By the time the boys of my 20s started appearing to me, I was waking up to feelings of lust and desire. On and on they came to me until one night, I got the final visitor. He was a measly blip in my story, a race car driver I had a quick and passionate affair with mere weeks before I met Jake. I had long ago forgotten his name, but there he was in my dreams, just like the rest. I woke up from that dream feeling both flushed and calm. That morning, I knew deep down that something had changed in me. It took probably two and a half months, not the year I had predicted. Finally, I was ready, conditioned even, to start thinking about other guys as possibilities again. Another chapter in my life could finally begin.

"Good," Helen said. "You're ready to start dating again. How do you plan to meet new people?"

"I...I don't know," I stuttered. "Shouldn't I be focusing on getting into shape or something?"

"Getting into shape" to meet potential suitors terrified me. I was a typical American woman who had never been happy with my weight. I had yo-yo dieted my way through eight different sizes of jeans and I was currently at the top of the jean-size swing. I had met Jake at my lowest jean size, and I really believed it wreaked havoc on my mental happiness with him. I had been struggling with my weight my entire life and so when I met Jake at my lowest weight, I was so worried that I would gain all the weight back and he would leave me. So, I subconsciously sabotaged myself into gaining all the weight back to test my theory. In the end, he never did leave me because of my weight. I know it started to concern him, but he said he loved me and my weight would never change that. And now that I was on the precipice of dating again, I feared I would repeat the horrible experiment if I lost the weight before I met someone. I had convinced myself that I would be better off meeting someone at my highest weight and then losing it so I didn't feel like I needed to test their love. It was a ridiculous theory. My mother always made it very clear to me that the people who really loved me would always love me no matter my appearance. I knew she was right. I knew I needed to be healthy for myself and myself only, but I couldn't help but think that life would be easier if I met my future husband at my highest weight and lost it once I was with him.

"I don't even know where to begin," I said to Helen. "How do I meet people? It's been so long since I've dated. Is it all about online dating these days? Jake and I didn't even have Facebook accounts when we met!"

"Well, there is always the standard methods of meeting people at bars, work, through friends, etc."

"Right...I work in insurance with a bunch of old dudes, don't have too many friends in Denver yet, and you see the kind of bar I like to hang out at," I said as I swept my hand around The Shoe. A regular at the end of the bar downed a shot and let out a primordial yelp as if to prove my point.

"You can try online dating like Match.com or eHarmony."

"Don't you think those sites are for the more serious daters? People looking for their life partners? I'm not ready for that. I'm just looking to get my feet wet, not dive in head first." I looked around the bar and started to look at the various guys as possibilities and felt fairly disheartened as a group of guys downed Irish Car Bombs and hive-fived each other as one seemed to throw up a little back into his glass.

"Oh!" Helen said. "I've got it. What about Tinder?" She picked up her phone, flipped through the screens and selected an app and held it up with confidence. I gave her my "you have three heads" look and she began explaining. "It's a dating app that uses your location to find people you might be interested in within your vicinity." She showed me her own Tinder account on her phone and continued. "Based on the criteria you give it, age range and distance from you, it populates various possibilities and allows you to flip through and select people you like."

I scrunched my face and began to protest, "I don't know. Sounds..."

"The great thing is," she continued, "when you say you 'like' someone, they have to 'like' you back for a chat room to open for the two of you to communicate. So, you aren't getting unwanted messages from creepy guys. You can only talk to someone if they say they like you and you say you like them. Plus, it's like a game!" She began swiping left and right on the faces on her screen. "If you like someone, you swipe right and it logs that you like them, and if you don't like someone, you swipe left and they just disappear." As she said this, she swiped right on a guy's face and just like that, it said they were matched and a chat room could be accessed.

"Hm," I said as I took the phone from her. "So, you can only talk to someone who has already expressed interest?" Helen nodded. "And it doesn't give away any personal information?" She nodded again. "So, if I talk to someone and don't like them anymore..."

"Then you block them and they disappear from your phone forever."

"Hm," I said again. Frank picked up my beer can, shook it, popped open another, and placed it in front of me. I nodded my appreciation and looked back at Helen. "Why don't I just date Frank? He's so considerate."

Helen laughed, "Considerate?"

"He anticipates my every need!" I said as I held up my fresh Coors Light.

"Well, I guess it's a start," Helen said. "But I don't think you would be happy with a guy who simply supplies you with beer that in the end determines how much tip he will be getting."

I smiled, "Are you saying my current relationship with

Frank is purely capitalistic in nature? I won't believe it!" I winked at Frank and he winked back as he blew a kiss across the bar to another one of his adoring customers.

Chapter 9

Emma

E mma, how are your 2,000 words on plaque buildup coming?" My boss, Kenneth, smiled at me from the entrance of my cubicle.

"Well," I muttered, looking down at my notes that were mostly doodles, "I'm still working on finding my angle. So... not great, honestly."

Kenneth's smile faded. He could tell I did not share his enthusiasm for dental journalism, and I was pretty sure he was losing patience with me.

"I think things will pick up after I interview Dr. Harris," I offered, trying to avoid a lecture on how important this piece was for our readers. "I have a call with him on Tuesday."

Kenneth perked back up. "Excellent! I can't wait to read the finished story." He placed a piece of sugar-free gum on my desk, his signature "keep-up-the-good-work" incentive for the staff, before bouncing along to the next cubicle. As soon as I heard him chatting happily with one of the copy editors, I dropped my head onto my desk. How did I get here?

Over the years, I had fallen into my fair share of weird and unsatisfying jobs. In college, I was a certified Bear Builder at Build-A-Bear Workshop for about four months. I was the one sitting at the fluffer machine, helping kids (and adults) bring their furry friends to life. I actually didn't mind leading the "heart ceremony," because I was able to inject a little creativity into the process. Every bear's heart needed to be warmed up, kissed, and wished upon, but I often added extra steps to give the bears some personality: "Squeeze the heart in your hand and jump up and down so your bear will be energetic. Rub the heart on your forehead so your bear will be smart, just like you. Tap the heart on your funny bone so your bear will have a sense of humor. Put the heart on your foot so your bear will be a fast runner." The kids loved it, but my favorite customers by far were the reluctant teenage boys who were clearly trying to impress their girlfriends. I always gave them extra goofy tasks to see if they would play along. Many of them didn't.

Even on the best days at Build-A-Bear, when I thought I was really killing it with the heart ceremony and the bear-themed songs on repeat weren't driving me crazy, my manager constantly told me I wasn't enthusiastic enough. I considered myself a fairly upbeat person, but my manager didn't seem to think so. Short of skipping through the store, I wasn't sure what else I could do. I greeted customers with a smile and stayed chipper even when I got fluffed (the industry term for when the fluffer machine arm came out of the bear's back while it was activated and the fluff went everywhere, including in my mouth and eyes). No matter what I did, it wasn't enough to please my manager. I guess I wasn't cut out for working with kids. This shouldn't have been surprising, considering I didn't really like kids and had no desire to have children of my own.

Next, I went to the other side of the spectrum and worked at a nursing home for veterans. I was in the recreation department, which sounded more exciting than it was considering all my residents were in wheelchairs or used walkers. Every morning, I gathered the residents in the common room, served coffee and donuts, and read the newspaper aloud. Based on the vacant stares around the room, I knew no one listened to me as I read the day's stories, but I was more informed at that time than I had ever been before.

The residents only cared about two things: the horoscopes and the obituaries. Beyond that, they only stayed because they weren't allowed or able to go back to their rooms without assistance. One morning, I was reading about the latest environmental disaster when I noticed that everyone in the room was asleep. I turned to my supervisor who was organizing the snacks in the corner.

"What do I do now?" I asked.

"Keep reading. The schedule is approved by the state, so you have to keep doing what it says you'll be doing. You have 25 more minutes with the paper," she said. I never liked her.

As I continued reading out loud to no one, I knew working with the elderly wasn't my cup of tea either. That job lasted about three months.

Even before I took those jobs, I knew I wouldn't last long; I just needed the money. To be honest, kids and old people freaked me out, unless we were related. Besides, I had known what I wanted to do since middle school. When I was little, I always wanted to be an actress, probably because my sisters and I loved movies so much and Kate was into theater, but I very sensibly realized that lifestyle wasn't for me. Instead, I turned my sights to journalism. If I couldn't be a star, I would write about them. As I grew older, my interests expanded to include all forms of entertainment, food, city life and, most of all, travel. Dental work was not on the list.

Getting my master's degree in publishing only solidified my love of magazines, and I had been trying to break into the industry ever since. I spent two years after grad school as a copywriter for an office supplies catalogue. There were only so many ways to describe desk chairs and ballpoint pens, so that gig got old fast. After about six months, I wanted to quit, but I had rent to pay and magazine jobs weren't exactly booming in Indianapolis. Despite the fact that I was bored and knew I could be doing so much more, I stayed because I hated job searching more than I hated writing about tape dispensers. Charlie's promotion and relocation to California was the saving grace that gave me the excuse I needed to quit.

When we moved, Charlie and I had been dating long-distance for a year and a half. We had spent months trying to figure out how we were going to end up in the same city. It made the most sense for him to move to Indianapolis, but his company treated him well and didn't have any offices nearby, and he wasn't ready to leave them. We toyed with the idea of me moving to Cincinnati, since I wasn't committed to my job anyway, but there weren't many opportunities for me there either. In the end, our solution was to move more than 2,000 miles away from everything we had known. Our families weren't thrilled, but we were excited about starting a new adventure and exploring the unknown together.

After staring at my computer for another couple hours and still not having more than a few disjointed sentences, I was finally able to go home. Charlie was working late again—an unfortunate side effect of his promotion—so Hoosier and I watched *You've Got Mail* for the zillionth time over a dinner of cold leftover macaroni and cheese.

When Charlie finally got home around 9 p.m., he immediately fell onto the couch, exhausted and starving. I brought him a personal-sized pepperoni pizza, a couple breadsticks, and a glass of milk. He was one of the only people I knew over the age of 10 who still regularly drank milk with anything other than pancakes or fresh-baked cookies.

"Thanks, babe," he said without looking up from his phone.

"Whatcha doing?" I asked, sitting down next to him.

"Just catching up on Facebook. I didn't have ten minutes all day to even look at my phone."

"Yeah. I texted you a few times."

"I know," he said, not looking up from his phone. "I'm sorry

I didn't have time to respond."

"I just missed you," I said in a whiney voice I hated but couldn't stop myself from using with Charlie.

"I missed you, too," he said. Finally, he lifted his head to address me. "Tell me about your day."

"It wasn't great," I said. "This story on plaque is going to be the death of me. It makes me want to gag every time I do research. And Kenneth is breathing down my neck about it. It's not my fault it's such a boring topic! No one could make this story interesting; trust me. And he acts like there's something wrong with me because I'm not all about it."

"That sucks," he said, clearly still distracted by the phone in his hands.

"I just don't know how long I can do this job," I went on. "I don't care about anything I'm working on and what good is it doing for me? Working there will never get me in at a top magazine."

"Yeah," he said as he watched a video of a dancing dog.

"Are you listening to me?" I asked, more aggressively than I intended.

"Yeah, I'm listening," he shot back. "I just don't know what to say right now. I'm exhausted, babe."

I had run into this problem my entire life. I was an extrovert, but everyone in my family was an introvert. At the end of the day, I always wanted to talk and interact with people to get my energy back, but my family craved quiet to decompress. When I was little, my mom used to say, "Okay, Emma.

Talk." And I would go on and on. After a little while, she would say, "Okay, now it's time to be quiet." And I would have to find something else to do while my family recharged. Being raised that way, I adopted some of their introverted qualities, but I still talked a lot, and it still got me in trouble.

"I just need to relax a bit," Charlie said, clearly deflated. "I've been talking all day."

"Yeah," I said. "But you asked me about my day." I could hear myself getting defensive, but I was annoyed that he wasn't addressing my complaints about my job. "I just want you to acknowledge what I'm saying, especially because you ignored me all day."

"I didn't ignore you." Now he was getting frustrated. "I was working."

"I know you were working," I said. "I didn't mean you ignored me intentionally, just that you weren't able to talk." I was backtracking, but I knew it was too late. I had come off meaner than I had intended. Charlie prided himself in being attentive, and he often texted me just to let me know he was thinking of me. Accusing him of ignoring me was like blatantly calling him a bad boyfriend. Even if I had only been talking about one instance, he took it like a blanket statement that he was failing. Since he hadn't done anything wrong, he got mad.

"I had an incredibly busy day," he said. "Even when I left the office, I had four messages on my voicemail and countless emails that I will have to deal with tomorrow. I know you don't like your job, but honestly, we can't afford for you to quit unless you find something else first. I physically can't work anymore than I already am."

"I'm not asking you to work more," I snapped. "I just want you to listen to me when I'm talking to you."

"So, I never listen to you? Is that what you're saying?"

"I didn't say 'never.' You're always so dramatic."

"Ok, well you're being rude and I don't really want to talk to you right now," he said, getting up from the couch and making his way to the bedroom.

"Can we just talk about this?" I yelled after him. "You're misunderstanding what I'm saying!"

"Not right now," he said before he closed the bedroom door and I broke down in tears.

This was pretty much how all our disagreements went. One of us said something that the other took the wrong way, we both got defensive and spoke in hyperbole which just made the other mad, then he would storm off and I would try to latch onto him to close the gap he had physically created. He wanted time to process and cool down, and I just wanted to fix whatever the problem was the moment it happened. And I always cried.

We knew early on that we had different styles of arguing, but we hadn't quite figured out how to meet in the middle. We also had different ideas of how long was long enough to cool down, so when I thought I had given him the space he wanted, he thought I was ignoring his request to be left alone.

After crying by myself for a few minutes, I knocked on the

bedroom door lightly. When he didn't answer, I opened it anyway. "Can I come in?" I asked meekly. He said yes and I went around to my side of the bed and sat down. "I don't want to fight anymore."

"It didn't seem like it," he said.

"I'm sorry I was mean. I know you were busy today."

"I'm sorry you felt like I was ignoring you," he responded. "I would have texted you if I could have. This job is just much more demanding than I thought it would be."

"It's okay." We didn't talk for a few minutes. I picked at a hangnail because I didn't know what else to do. As always, I was the one to break the silence. "I don't know how to fight."

"I know you don't," he smiled.

Honestly, my parents didn't properly prepare me for arguments; they never fought. I had no idea how to have a disagreement without getting defensive, feeling the need to explain my side in great detail and saying something that I later regretted. I remember one time in my entire childhood that my parents fought, and it wasn't even a verbal altercation. In fact, I had been there at the start of the argument and I didn't even know it was happening.

It started with a flat tire on the side of a dark highway. My mom wanted to call AAA, but my dad insisted on fixing it himself. I'm not really sure what was said outside of the car as I was curled up in a blanket in the backseat, but somehow the disagreement led to a week of the two of them barely talking to each other. I believe it was resolved via letters, which is how their relationship started in the days before email and cell phones. There was never a blowout. No one yelled or said anything mean to the other. It happened right in front of me and I had no idea until it was brought up years later.

The only fighting I had ever really witnessed was between Alice and Jake, and that didn't work out so well. I knew it was normal for couples (other than my parents) to argue, but it still scared me every time.

Charlie pulled me into him. "You have to give me space to cool down when things get heated," he said. "I walk away because I don't want to say something mean to you, but you need to not freak out when I do. I'm not going to leave you."

"Ever?"

"Never." I continued to cry with my head on his stomach until my nose was so stuffed that I had to get up to blow it.

"Do you think we can still be friends?" he asked. That was his thing. He said it at the end of every disagreement. It was his way of saying that we were going to be okay.

"Always," I replied.

May

Chapter 10

Kate

May in Speedway, Indiana, isn't a month. It's a historic and cultural milestone. People around the world, people who don't speak English, people who have never watched a car race in their lives, people who couldn't find Indiana on a map, know the Indianapolis 500. And the truly wild fact of the matter is, the Indy 500 is not run in Indianapolis. The Indianapolis Motor Speedway is entirely within the town borders of Speedway.

Indianapolis gets in on the action, of course. They host the largest (or second largest, depending on the year) mini-marathon in the country as part of the festivities. The 500 Festival Parade goes through downtown Indianapolis the day before the race. Speedway certainly couldn't provide the necessary security and traffic support without the resources of Indianapolis. But on race day, the population of Speedway explodes from 12,000 to roughly 350,000.

The town welcomes visitors from around the world. We smile as the local grocery and liquor stores get stocked with beer to the point that you can't get your cart down any aisle. We marvel at the people who show up on Thursday to camp out in the Coke Lot until after the race on Sunday. We patiently avoid all the major streets in town when the Carb Day concert lets out.

And we park cars. We park cars for days, everywhere in town. We park cars to raise money for the high school band, for the junior high and high school exchange trips, for the church youth groups, for the robotics team, for the Lions Club, for the Optimists Club, for the Legion. We park on town property. We park on local business' property. We park on Indianapolis Motor Speedway property. We park on private property. We park in every church and shopping center parking lot in town. The primary experience for Speedway residents is parking.

For me, May also meant driving my car constantly. As the school year winds down, the number of events and commitments ramp up. One major reason being that it was the end of the rec soccer season. This particular year, because I must have deeply offended the gods, all my boys decided to be in soccer. Steven and I always encouraged our boys to be involved in something. We didn't care what, just something to break up the hours of staring at the Kindle Fire/Nintendo DS/iPhone. Usually we had a mishmash of activities, but somehow everyone had decided soccer was the way to go this spring.

At 2:30 p.m. on Friday, I left the office and drove to the spot in the neighborhood where I picked the kids up when the elementary school let out. I propped my phone up on the steering wheel and opened the calendar. Then I dug in my purse for two note cards and a Staedtler pen that Emma had given me for Christmas. On the top of one I wrote "Steven" and on the other I wrote "Me." Then, looking at the calendar, I tried to map out how we were going to tackle the end-of-the-season tournaments that loomed that weekend. When the van door was thrown (THROWN) open ten minutes later, I was on my fourth attempt.

"Mom! Pete asked if I can come over tomorrow," Alexander said as he climbed over the middle seats and flopped into the very back of the van. I burst out laughing.

"No way, kiddo. This weekend is all soccer all the time. All hands on deck," I explained as I scrutinized him in the rear-view mirror. "How was school?" I asked with the small lump in my throat that still crept up, even after months of nothing more concerning than the occasional comment about a small perceived injustice.

"Good. Boring," he replied.

"I'll take boring," I said. "Where are your brothers?"

"Remember? Thomas has that movie thing and Phillip has library duty."

Right. "Movie thing" meant that Thomas's class had finished reading some book and they were watching the movie version after school for a couple days in 45-minute bursts. Just long enough to make me have to come back to the school. And

Phillip had an after-school "job" in the school library restocking books. That lasted only 15 minutes.

I fired up the car and swung around the neighborhood so I could go park closer to where Phillip would be coming out of the building.

"Can I go home? I'm starving," Alexander whined.

I threw my blinker on at the last second and turned down our street instead of going straight around to the school. I found myself wondering again why I didn't just let my kids walk home. Then I remembered the Amber Alert that had been issued just a few days earlier. Right. I'd never forgive myself if something happened and I was just sitting at home because I was tired of driving.

I pulled into the driveway and Alexander hopped out. I rolled down the window.

"Freeze, mister. First, shut the van door. Second, go in through the garage. Lock everything behind you. I'll be home in a half hour, after I get Christopher, too. No answering the phone or the door."

"K, Mom!"

As I pulled out of the driveway, I watched to make sure he closed the garage door, then drove around to the side of the school.

I pulled into a spot and took out more notecards to try the schedule again. The infuriating thing was tourneys were ultimately question marks. If a team lost, they may be done. Or they may be in the "losers" bracket depending on the age group. I realized I'd have to make situational notecard schedules for us—"if Christopher's team wins game 2" and "if Alexander's team loses game 1" and so on. I was going to need to stop at CVS to grab more notecards.

Another 10 minutes and the van door was thrown (THROWN) open.

"I finished another book today in my series, Mom," Phillip said as he tossed his backpack into the van before treading on it to get into his seat. "Can we go to the library tomorrow to get the next one?"

"Sorry, munchkin. All soccer this weekend," I explained.

I pulled out of the parking spot and turned toward the junior high school.

"Can't I be dropped off at home? I'm starving!" came the same whine from a different kid.

"No time."

"We're passing the house!"

"Snacks in the snack bin. Christopher doesn't have anything after school today, so he's done at the normal time," I said as we crossed Crawfordsville Road.

Five minutes later, I wove through the maze of other cars waiting for their students and found a spot in the side lot. I was there a whole four minutes early. I used the time to answer a few work emails that had come in since I had left work an hour before.

Then, my phone buzzed.

Christopher: Mom, I have a meeting with the cross-country team about summer training.

I silently cursed the age of cell phones. It was like coaches didn't bother sticking to a schedule because they knew kids could text their parents and change plans at a moment's notice.

Kate: Fine. Text me when you're done.

I fired up the car and headed back across Speedway.

I pulled into the driveway and let Phillip out, rolling the window down again.

"Freeze, mister! First, close the van door. Second, go in through the garage. Tell your brother he's babysitting. I should be back with Thomas in 15 minutes."

"K, Mom!"

As I pulled out of the driveway again, I watched, again, for the garage door to shut.

I parked on the side of the elementary school again and looked at the clock. Thomas should be out in 10 minutes or so. The timing of all this was bonkers. Not enough time to go into the house and chill, too much time to just swing by and grab a kid and keep going. I contemplated quitting my job and just becoming a Speedway-only kid-Uber. I knew other families did this dance every day, too. Crisscrossing Speedway over and over and over. I bet people would pay me to do it for them. I'd pay someone to do it for me.

My phone buzzed.

Christopher: Done.

Seriously?! It had been all of 10 minutes since I left the junior high!

Kate: Hold tight. Have to wait for Thomas, then I'll be there to get you.

I spent the next five minutes willing Thomas to hurry up and come out to the car. I hated making my kids hang out at a school and wait for me. I could picture teachers, anxious to go home, looking at my kid and thinking, "Where is his mom? I know she doesn't work in the afternoon." Of course, I did work in the afternoon. I was supposed to be working from home. But no one seemed to understand that.

The van door was thrown (THROWN) open once again, five minutes late. "I told Mark he could come over tomorrow. Is that okay?" Thomas said as he repeatedly tried to extend the seat belt too quickly and it locked before he could get it long enough to fasten.

"No, that is not okay. Soccer. Be gentle with the seat belt!" Thomas exaggerated his show of being gentle with the seat belt and got it fastened. I pointed the van toward the junior high again.

"Oh, can't I be dropped off at home? I'm starving!" came the familiar whine.

"No! Snack box!"

I parked in front of the junior high this time and texted Christopher that I was waiting. Five minutes later, I was still waiting with no response from him. I started to get nervous about Alexander and Phillip at home alone. I texted Christopher again. And again. Where was that kid?

Finally, I got out of the car, dragging an unamused Thomas with me. I went to the front door, which was locked, of course.

I pressed the intercom.

"Can I help you?"

"Hey Debbie, It's Kate. I'm looking for Christopher."

"Oh hey, Kate. I know I've seen him around. I'll page him and tell him you're waiting out front."

"Thank you."

Thomas hopped on and off the cement benches. I had visions of him falling and smashing his face, or scraping his knee, or breaking an arm. I gave him a look. He caught my meaning and sat down with a sheepish smile. Some people thought I was nuts for reining in my boys on things like this. There seemed to be a general attitude of allowing boys to "blow off steam" or whatever. I ran a household full of boys. If I let them be wild animals, we'd be in the ER every week. As it stood, we'd only made one ER trip for injury in 12 years. That's not luck.

Finally, the front door was thrown (THROWN) open and Christopher came out. "I was watching for you on the side!"

"I texted you that I was at the front."

"My phone died."

"Of course it did," I said as I led them all back to the van.

When I finally pulled back into my driveway, it was 4:00—a full hour and a half from when I'd left work to pick up the kids. I'd spent 90 minutes in my car to pick up four kids who go to school within a three-mile radius of my house.

The boys congregated in the kitchen to raid the snacks. I could hear a bag of pretzels being opened and knew that it would be empty in 10 minutes. I milled around, absent-mindedly picking up wrappers and graded papers while I had a mental argument with myself about how I didn't need pretzels too.

"Can we go to the comic book store tomorrow?" Christopher asked through a mouthful of pretzel.

"NO!" I screamed.

"Why not?" Christopher asked, startled by my outburst.

"Soccer!" everyone said together.

"New rule. I'm not talking to any of you people until we're all together."

During halftime of soccer game #11 on Sunday afternoon (why did these kids all have to be on winning teams?!), I closed my eyes and let my mind wander. In 45 minutes, the soccer season would finally be over. The last day of school was just three days away. The Indy 500 was seven days away. And then, a break.

I took out my phone.

Kate: I'm one week away from being able to breathe.

Alice: I don't think holding your breath for a week is healthy.

Kate: Soccer, school, and the race will be done. Everything will slow down, finally.

Emma: What are your plans for the summer?

Kate: Usual stuff. Camps, road trips, swimming lessons, sports practices...

Alice: That's your idea of slowing down?

Kate: Well, now that you made me think about it…

I stuffed my phone back in my pocket as Christopher took the field. Even though I watched the rest of the match and made all the appropriate mom noises, I don't think I saw anything that happened. I was too busy going over the summer schedule in my head. I had been looking at the 500 as this big finish line when things would slow down and I might be able to take five minutes to figure out what to do about that nagging feeling in the back of my mind that I should be doing something for me.

But it wasn't a finish line. It was just a marker for the ending of one set of obligations and the beginning of another. I wasn't going to be less busy. I was going to be different busy. And after that, I'd be busy with school starting and fall sports. And after that I'd be busy with the holidays. And after that…

There was no magical "me time" coming. No retreat to allow me to do some serious self-reflection. No time to suddenly be able to pursue some fulfilling activity outside of the home. As I watched Christopher's face beaming when the coach called his name to get his medal and I got a text from Steven showing Thomas proudly displaying his ribbon, I knew I didn't resent any of this or want to change it. I just needed to work within it. I needed a creative outlet and I needed to make a concerted effort to make it fit in my life.

I just needed to figure out what on earth that could be. As I loaded my folding chair and oversized umbrella into the trunk of my van and Christopher took his shin guards off and tossed them on top of the chairs, I looked at him.

"What? I'll remember to get them out when we get home. I promise," he said.

"What do you like to do?" I asked.

"Huh?" he eyed me suspiciously, like I was baiting him.

"For fun. Not video games. What do you like to do?" I asked again.

"Soccer?" he ventured.

"And?" I prodded.

"Uh, drawing, reading, watching YouTubers, movies, and Netflix. Why?"

"Just trying to get some ideas."

"For what?" He was truly baffled by this line of inquiry.

"A creative outlet," I explained.

"Like a multicolored extension cord?" He broke into a goofy braces-laden smile.

"Ugh. Your father is turning you all into dad-pun machines." I hopped into the driver's seat and punched our home address into my phone. I had no idea where we were or how to get home. Soccer fields in Indiana are often in the middle of absolutely nowhere. Christopher popped his ear buds in, so I left the radio off and used the time to brainstorm. I ticked options over in my mind.

Forty minutes later and I concluded that I needed to go to a library. The Speedway library wasn't open on Sundays, but as long as I didn't check anything out, I could hit a Marion County library. I called Steven to explain my quest and dropped Christopher at the house. I parked in the underground garage at the Central branch and made my way up to the fourth floor. After taking a moment to appreciate the view of downtown Indy, I started wandering the stacks.

I didn't have much of a plan, but I started in the theater section. I wandered slowly down the aisle and back up the other side. Another person came into the aisle, so I moved along to another one. I looked down and saw a slim white book with a giant fishbowl on it. I pulled it out and read the title, "Something Startling Happens."

The back of the book promised to reveal what tons of movies have in common that makes them successful. The list of movies was a crazy mix of widely disparate genres and I was intrigued. I pulled out my phone and bought the book on Amazon and got back to browsing. I picked up books on writing children's books, poetry, and magazine fiction. I followed that with books on developing word puzzles, cross stitching, and making sock monkeys. In desperation, I flipped through books about birdwatching, geocaching, and pottery. Finally, the library was about to close and I had to get home.

After the kids were all in bed, Steven and I settled in for some Sunday Night Football. Since the Colts weren't playing, I decided only half of my attention was required. So, I opened my digital copy of "Something Startling Happens" and began to read. I quickly realized this book wasn't just an interesting examination of movie structure. It was aimed at screenwriters.

Chapter 11

Alice

May has always been one of my favorite months. The excitement that surrounded the Indy 500 growing up stuck with me long after I left my hometown. Spring is in full swing and summer starts to become a real possibility as the cold days become fewer and farther between. And thankfully, my thoughts of Jake had become fewer and farther between as well. I was officially "on the market." My first few encounters with the opposite sex had been awkward and not ideal.

My first physical encounter with a guy since my breakup (unsurprisingly) came after a night of drinking at The Shoe. It had become my habit to find my way over there on various "off" nights when the loneliness seemed to be strongest. Sundays and Tuesdays were my favorite nights because it wasn't crowded and I could meet new people easily.

One Sunday night, I walked in, was greeted by Frank and sat down at the corner of the bar. Frank introduced me to some of his friends who had gathered and the night spiraled into a warm glow of good conversation, beer, and mild flirting. To be honest, I don't remember his name. He was tall, had dark hair, and was young. Much younger than me—possibly by a good eight years. I made a mental note that he *seemed* to be the right age, probably because he was the age I was the last time I was single and out on the town. But unlike an astronaut who had been in space on a seven-year mission, I had aged. The guy didn't seem to notice our age difference though. He seemed to be on the prowl, hoping for some kind of connection with anyone. Honestly, I was as well. Any sign that I could still be an attractive option to someone, anyone. Even if that someone and myself were slightly tipsy and we both knew we would mean nothing to the other in the morning.

When Frank announced last call, I closed my tab (tipped well) and walked out the door. A few steps down the street and my flirting partner came after me. He reached for my hand and asked where I was going. I gave a nod toward my apartment building and told him I was heading home. He pulled me close, looked me in the eyes with the dreamy, far-off look that only a drunk person can give, and murmured something about walking me home to make sure I arrived safely. I nodded drunkenly and linked my arm with his.

By the time we reached the front door to my building, I was feeling a little nervous. It hit me during the short walk that I had not kissed another guy in years. I encouraged my drunk self to look past this fact and provide me with some sort of confidence. It worked until he asked me if he could come up. I gave him a sheepish grin and said no. Visibly disappointed, he tried to sway me with a kiss. The kiss was full of faux-passion and tight squeezes. It felt good to be held like that and to kiss back. We tried to desperately cling to each other and I wondered if he was getting over a breakup as well. There was an underlying need to connect, to feel, but no matter what I tried, it all felt fake. He put his hand to my face and looked at me with expectations but all I could offer were my "goodnights" and "goodbyes."

When I finally made it back into my apartment, I decided it would be a good idea to text Jake. We had plans for me to go over to his apartment after work the next day so I could get the last of my boxes that I had been putting off. When he didn't answer immediately, I texted again:

Alice (2:36 a.m.): If you don't want to see me, just let me know when you aren't going to be home and I'll just let myself in.

Alice (3:01 a.m.): I understand if you don't think we should hang out anymore. You just said that I could come get my things, so whatever.

Alice (3:23 a.m.): I just threw up EVERYWHERE. But I guess that isn't your problem anymore.

I was brutally awoken a few hours later by my phone making too much noise. I reached over and saw multiple texts from Jake.

Jake (6:04 a.m.): OMG. Are you okay? I was sleeping!

Jake (6:06 a.m.): Of course you can still come over tonight. I'd like to see you.

Jake (6:07 a.m.): Text me as soon as you get this so I know you are alright! I would have come over if I heard my phone. I'm sorry I didn't see your texts until right now!

I squinted at his words as the previous night began to come into focus again. I scrolled up to reveal the passive aggressive texts I had sent and I didn't know which felt worse, my headache or my guilt for making Jake feel so bad for something that really wasn't his problem anymore. I typed back telling him I was fine. I had too much to drink and I hadn't throw up "everywhere," but, in fact, I had thrown up neatly in the toilet.

When I finally had the courage to meet up with one of the guys I had been talking with on Tinder, it was also...not great. I had been chatting with Carl via the Tinder app for about a week. His photos portrayed him as a geeky kind of guy interested in karaoke, books, and puppies, apparently. Our conversations seemed rather smooth and we actually had a distant friend in common according to the "shared friends" link on the app.

When we finally agreed to meet in person, I suggested a bar close to my apartment so I could make a quick getaway if necessary, but I was certain this guy was going to be quite harmless. Thirty minutes before we were scheduled to meet, my palms started to sweat and my hair decided not to participate in "Operation: Look Halfway Decent." I had to eventually put it up in a ponytail. I told myself it was going to be fine; it was just meeting up for drinks. It was basically my first "date" since leaving Jake...so no pressure. To calm my nerves, I downed a Coors Light before heading out the door. On my way out, he texted that he'd be wearing a Hawaiian shirt and a "white leather sports coat," whatever the hell that meant. I hoped he was joking about his attire. I texted back that I was in a ridiculously pink zip-up hoodie (not a joke).

While walking to the bar, I saw him from a distance. He was easily recognizable by the white leather and the bottom edges of a Hawaiian shirt poking out. My image of us hitting it off and living happily ever after vanished while I prayed he would be taller than he looked from a distance. But closing the gap between us only made him grow smaller. In the end, he turned out to be a good six inches shorter than me—not something a girl with weight issues is hoping for. The last thing I wanted was to appear like the great bearded lady towering over her husband, the incredibly tiny man.

Determined not to judge a book (yadda yadda yadda), I greeted him warmly as we sat down at the bar and began an engaging conversation. We talked about movies and books and travel, and we seemed to have so much in common. While his loud shirt distracted me at first, his words overcame my prejudices and we had an enjoyable evening.

I was often judged right off the bat because of my size so the last thing I wanted to do was to write this guy off for his. I'm sure it is something he has battled his whole life as well. While his height did bother me a little, it was something I could look past until there was one piece I could not get over: his hands. They were small. Small hands. They were more distracting than his terrible choice of clothing. I wanted to be with a man who could make me feel safe and secure, and I could just see us being attacked by a stranger and me being the one to fight off the bad guy. Barf.

When the night ended, I was feeling a little better about Carl, but I wondered if I had just found a new Denver friend as opposed to a new boyfriend. Carl walked me to the street corner for us to part ways and we made plans to go to a movie in a week. He leaned in for a kiss and…nothing. I honestly felt nothing! I heard people talk about "no spark" dates, but I never experienced it before. If I had a brother, I imagined that is what it would have felt like to kiss him. It was weird. When it ended, I gave him a half smile and walked away.

I was sure he felt the lack of spark as well because our supposed "second date" day came and went with no communication. So, I was surprised to get a text from him a week later asking me to get together. I agreed, thinking it might be fun and I really shouldn't write someone off so easily. We decided to meet at a restaurant at a certain time, but apparently something happened to him on the way to the restaurant because he never showed. I checked my past messages and confirmed that I was at the right place at the right time and day, but after sitting alone for 45 minutes, I knew I had been stood up. I texted him to see what was up, but nothing. No response.

There really isn't a worse feeling than being stood up by a person you didn't have any feelings for in the first place. I was convinced he must have died, because who does that? Makes plans, then completely falls off the face of the earth? Did he hear me talking to Helen about the first date? Did he hear that I called him "Small Hands" to Emma and Kate and that I told them he had the most hideous taste in clothing? Was he exacting revenge against me by making me sit like a fool at a restaurant by myself? Sadly, I will never know the answers to these questions. I did check the obituaries for a couple days looking for his name or photo, but he could not be found. In the end, I decided he must have been hit by a city bus, was in a coma for weeks, and when he woke, his short-term memory had faded and he had no recollection of me. I could live with that.

The dates that followed these first two encounters weren't much better. There was another awkward Tinder meet-up with a guy who yelled the f-word at a poor valet who was just trying to help, there was the musician who turned out to be seeing multiple people at once and I apparently didn't make the cut, and then there was Maintenance Man...the actual maintenance man in my apartment building who hit on me after repairing my garbage disposal. By the time I needed help with a light bulb in the hallway, he was sending up a pinch hitter so he wouldn't have to run into me again.

It was the first week in May when I decided I needed to shift my focus on to something other than dating, because I was starting to get more and more depressed with each new bad encounter. Painting had always been a creative release for me, but it was something I hadn't devoted much time to in the past few years. I decided to join an art co-op to motivate me to get back to painting. I had enough inventory to display a few pieces at first and I hoped being within the creative community would inspire me to put paint on canvas once again. I was also hoping to meet a different type of guy than ones I was meeting through Tinder or at my local bars.

I was nervous for my first co-op meeting. I brought a few of my paintings to hang up, but I was worried the *serious* artists would see right through my prosaic landscapes. But the reality was that the co-op was...lived in. It wasn't a clean cut, top-of-the-line art gallery that sold Banksy's pieces for more than what I paid for rent in a year. It was a community of adults looking for a place to display their creative outlets like me. The walls were cluttered with everything from amazingly unique pieces to "seen it a million times before" pieces.

I settled into a fold-out chair a good 15 minutes before the meeting was supposed to start. About a minute later, a man sat next to me and nodded a silent "hello" in my direction. I pretended to play with my phone while I waited for the meeting to start. People and voices swirled around me, and I absorbed it all in trying to get a good feel for the place. It was a couple minutes before I realized that the guy next to me was making quiet commentary on the action. I couldn't tell if he was talking to me or if he was just a crazy person talking to himself. But when he finally said something that made me laugh out loud, I turned my head to smile at him. I then realized his commentary was indeed for my benefit. He smiled back at me and I was struck by his beautiful, dimpled smile and blue eyes. I took a moment to fully take him in. He was rather unassuming at first glance, but like his quiet, funny commentary, his attractiveness slowly seeped into my consciousness.

"I'm Alice," I said, offering my hand.

"Eddie," he replied. "First time here?"

"Yup," I said sheepishly, trying to hide the canvases at my feet.

"Well, welcome to the nut house." He gestured around the place. "You will find these meetings fairly unorganized and the curation that follows downright exhausting, but at the end of the day, we get a lot of foot traffic and exposure." I smiled and nodded not sure what to say back. So he continued, "May I see?" He pointed to my canvases.

I picked up the canvases and immediately started to make excuses. "These are rather old. I really joined for some inspiration..."

He held up his hand to stop my excuses. "I will be the judge," he said with a fake pompous accent. He pushed his glasses down to the edge of his nose, tilted his head back slightly, and peered down at the first canvas I handed him. "Hmmmm," he said dramatically. "Very nice...very nice."

I blushed as I took the canvas back. "What do you do?" He pointed across the gallery to a large metal piece that looked like a baby crib with a creepy metal mobile hanging from it. I craned my neck to see it better. "Hmmmm," I said, mocking him. "Very nice."

Then the meeting started. While people went over the various meeting topics, I remained highly conscious of Eddie. His chair was situated in such a way that I could spy on him out of the corner of my eye. Though sitting, I could tell he was tall and from the hand shake we shared earlier, I knew he had big, strong artist hands. Immediately my mind filled with him as a possibility. There was just something about him that made me instantly comfortable. It was probably that smile. I was a sucker for a good smile and I felt honored to have seen it in all its grandeur so soon. I got the impression he didn't let everyone see it so easily.

When the meeting wound down, I tried to think of an excuse to talk to him again, to make him smile again. He had pulled out his phone to check the time. "I didn't think they made those old flip phones anymore," I said, nodding toward his phone. "The hamster that powers that thing must be 70 years old by now."

Eddie looked down at his phone than back at me. I worried I had offended him until he let out a loud guffaw and said, "Hey, it's not *that* old!" He smiled brilliantly at me again and that was it...I was smitten.

Chapter 12

Emma

With nearly nine months of living in California under our belts, Charlie and I were finally starting to get the hang of our new surroundings. I could successfully get to the grocery store and the centers of nearby towns without GPS, and after four trips to the DMV, we finally had our California licenses.

That process was a bit of a disaster. Before our first visit, I had scoured the California DMV website to ensure we would have everything we needed. Although we each were only required to have two documents proving our residency, I had about fifteen utility bills and pieces of mail from our insurance companies with me. Because the DMV was only open from 8 a.m. to 5 p.m., Monday through Friday, we had to take a few hours off work to make our appointment. That was strike number one.

With Charlie dressed in his navy suit and me in my favorite striped pencil skirt, we confidently walked into the biggest DMV I have ever seen. In Indianapolis, you'll find about five old ladies behind a single line of desks and 20 to 30 folding chairs in the center of the room, but chances are only 10 of them will be filled. I've never waited more than 15 minutes at a DMV in Indy. This one, however, was massive. Forty cubicles took up the center of the room and nearly every chair in the building was occupied by people waiting to renew their vehicle registration or take the driving test. Thankfully, we bypassed the line that snaked out the door and made our way to the "Appointments" desk.

The first woman we encountered was immediately rude to us. Before we could really explain why we were there, she asked us for our passports, which we didn't have. "I checked the website for what we needed to bring with us," I said. "It didn't say anything about passports."

She slammed a pamphlet down on the desk. "It says it in here."

I picked it up and started skimming while Charlie asked why our out-of-state IDs didn't suffice.

"No," I said, rushing through the bulleted list of required documents. "This says a state-issued ID will work."

She plopped a second pamphlet in front of us. "This pamphlet explains which state-issued IDs count. What you have doesn't fit in those categories."

I stared at her. "But I looked online." She shrugged at me. "You're telling me I needed two pamphlets to figure out what I can use, but it's not on the website?" Strike number two.

"I don't make the website," she said.

"So, I can use my Indiana license to get on a plane, but it's not good enough here?" I asked.

"We don't know what other states require to issue their IDs, so we need a passport or birth certificate," she said. "You can register your vehicle today and come back for the IDs later."

"Fine," Charlie said. "Let's do that." We were then sent to another desk where the woman handling our registration asked for our drivers' licenses.

"Oh, so now our IDs will work?" Charlie asked sarcastically. The new woman shrugged her shoulders at us the same way the first woman had, like it was the state-mandated response to angry customers.

"You'll need to get a smog test," she said.

"No," I said again. "The website clearly said we don't need a smog test if the vehicle was purchased in the last four years. He bought it new last year." I pulled up the website on my phone to prove to her that I had read it correctly.

"That's only for vehicles purchased in California," she said.

"Are you kidding me?" Charlie was frustrated. "Do you think the car I purchased in Ohio was made differently than one purchased here?"

"I don't understand," she said.

"When the car is on the assembly line," I offered, "do you think they differentiate by cars coming to California versus Ohio? Do you think they make the Ohio cars worse on purpose?"

"Well, no," she said, getting as annoyed with us as we were with her. "But we don't know what other states require, so you have to get a smog test." This was our first experience with California elitism. It felt like we had moved to another country instead of just another state. Apparently, our IDs and cars just weren't good enough for California. Strike number three. In the end, Charlie paid $427 for a piece of paper that said we had to get a smog test.

Our second attempt was more spontaneous. I was working from home and Charlie was home sick, so we decided to give it another shot instead of taking more time off work. We got the smog test on the way and headed to a different branch, hoping we'd have more luck with different employees. Because we didn't have an appointment, we filed into a long line, passports in hand. While in line, we filled out the paperwork the first lady at the other branch had given us before she realized we didn't have proper identification. When we made it to the front of the line 45 minutes later, we had everything ready to finish our vehicle registration and get our new IDs.

"Hi!" I said, trying to sound upbeat and friendly. "We're here to turn in our smog test and get our driver's licenses."

The woman behind the counter shook her head and I could instantly tell she was going to ruin our day. "You can't take the written exam without an appointment," she said. "So, you can't get your licenses." What comes after strike number three?

"Are you kidding me?!" Charlie said, a little too loudly.

"Sir, lower your voice," she peered at him. "We can make an appointment for you, if you'd like, but nothing is available until the middle of next month." She handed us a number to meet with someone about finalizing our registration, but Charlie was too angry about standing in the first line for nothing, so we left.

For attempt number three, we had an appointment, we had our passports, we had added to the number of documents proving our residency, and we had studied for the written exam with online practice tests. None of it mattered, however, because every DMV in Southern California was experiencing a system outage that prevented them from issuing IDs or registering vehicles.

Needless to say, I held my breath through the entirety of attempt number four. I ended up at the window of the second woman from our first visit. "I helped you before, right?" she asked.

"Yeah, I think so," I said shyly, hoping she didn't remember that Charlie and I got mad at her.

"Yeah, you were registering a vehicle before," she said. "Why didn't you just get your ID then?" *Don't even get me started, lady!*

An hour later, Charlie and I walked out of the DMV as official residents of California and I finally exhaled. We celebrated that night with burgers and milkshakes from In-N-Out.

Paperwork aside, the hardest part of settling into our new community was making friends. When you're a kid, friends just appear. They are in your neighborhood, your class, and your Sunday School group. As adults in a new town, Charlie and I had no idea how to make connections with people. Luckily, Charlie's coworker Leo and his wife, Casey, invited us to a dinner party in early May, which gave us the chance to meet some people and check out their condo that overlooked the ocean.

While on the grand tour of the impeccably decorated three bedrooms and four bathrooms, we met one of Leo's high school friends who told us all about his son's baseball team. "What about you two?" he paused to ask. "Any kids?"

"No," Charlie said. "We're not planning on having kids."

"Oh, okay," he said, "That's cool. I didn't think I wanted kids either, but mine are great." He went back to bragging about the run his son had scored earlier that day.

At dinner, we sat next to one of Casey's coworkers and her fiancé. Halfway through dinner, we learned the two of them were in the process of buying a house in Irvine. "We love being near the ocean, but the schools are just so much better inland," the woman said. "How are the schools where you guys live?" she asked. Charlie and I looked at each other, mentally playing nose-goes and hoping the other would speak first.

"We have no idea," Charlie said bluntly.

"Oh," she said, looking concerned. "Well you really need to look into that. In so many places you should have all that figured out well before your kids are actually old enough to go to school. Spots fill up so quickly."

Charlie looked to me to respond this time. "Well, we're not

planning on having kids," I said.

"What? You have to," she blurted out.

"Excuse me?" I asked, nearly dropping my glass of wine.

"I just mean, you're smart and successful and you could give children a great life."

"But we don't want them," I said defensively.

"You have an obligation!" she said. I could tell she really believed that, too. To her, my feelings and opinion of what I wanted to do with my life and my body were irrelevant. "I didn't have a great support system growing up," she said, "so I'm going to do everything I can to love my children and give them everything they need."

"What does that have to do with me?" I asked, feeling my face flush.

"You have to make it better for future generations," she said with conviction.

"I can do that without having kids," I said, matching her tone. "Why can't I just be a kickass aunt or a great role model to other people's kids?"

"It's not the same," she said, shaking her head. "You have a duty to have kids of your own and raise them properly." I glanced at Charlie, who stared at the woman, mouth agape and unsure of how to respond to her hostility. He had never experienced this reaction and everything I had told him about the pressure women face was starting to click.

In the car after dinner, Charlie couldn't wait to talk about what we had encountered. "I couldn't believe that woman!" he said in the high-pitched voice he used when he was upset or caught off guard. "I mean, I've had people tell me that I might change my mind or that I would love my own kids if I ended up having them, but no one has ever told me I have an obligation to have them!"

"Honestly, I've never been berated like that before either," I said, still in shock. "And by a complete stranger!"

"Who does she think she is?" he continued.

"I don't know," I said, shaking my head in disbelief. "And she doesn't know our situation! What if we wanted kids but were unable to have them? If my Aunt Rachel had been there, she would have lost it!"

"It was completely insensitive," Charlie agreed. "I guess that's kind of what you meant when you said you didn't want to tell your aunt, huh?"

I nodded. "Having kids is such a sensitive subject for so many women, it's easier to just keep it to ourselves."

"I'm sorry I didn't get it," he said.

"It's okay," I said. "So, do you think those people will be our California friends?" He laughed and assured me we'd keep looking.

The following week, we learned that Charlie was being sent out of town to pitch an ad campaign he had been working on for months. It was an awesome opportunity for him, but I was bummed he was leaving. We had tickets to see Aziz Ansari's stand up show, and because I didn't have any friends to take his ticket, I texted Alice.

Emma: What are you doing?

Alice: Drinking at The Shoe. You?

Emma: Drinking at home. Anybody good tonight?

Alice: No. I'm not really looking though.

Emma: Why not?

Alice: Just not interested. I'm focusing on me and my art, remember?

Emma: Oh yeah. How's the co-op?

Alice: It's great! I love the vibe and the other artists are great. I'm going to a movie with one of them tomorrow.

Emma: Cool. A guy?

Alice: Yes.

Emma: Is it a date?

Alice: I don't think so.

Emma: Bummer. Anyway, do you want to come visit me and go see Aziz Ansari?

Alice: Yeah!

Emma: Yay! It's in two weeks.

Alice: Wait. Really?

Emma: Yeah. I'll split the plane ticket with you. Charlie will be out of town for work and I don't have anyone else to go with.

Alice: I'll be there.

Two weeks later, I picked Alice up from LAX. She looked like a different person from the one I saw at Christmas. As it turned out, her "not-a-date" had, in fact, been a date and she had been hanging out with Eddie ever since. He dropped her off at the airport that afternoon, and she was still beaming.

"He does these metal sculptures that have so much character," she said. "We're actually working on a mixed-media piece together."

"That's cool. Is he a full-time artist?" I asked, trying to subtly ask if he was unemployed like Jake had been for much of their relationship.

"No, he has a real job like a real adult," she said, playfully hitting my arm to let me know she had caught my jab at Jake. "He's never been married. He doesn't have kids, and he's kind and funny and wonderful."

"That's great, Alice. Really. I'm so happy for you."

Back at my place, we brought a bunch of blankets into the living room and snuggled up with some of our favorites: *Father of the Bride* and *My Best Friend's Wedding*. Around the time that Rupert Everett started singing "I Say a Little Prayer," Alice turned to me. "I'm going to marry him," she said. I smiled and placed a Kleenex on her head just like we had when we were kids playing wedding. We giggled and sang along with Rupert.

The next night, Alice and I grabbed tacos before heading to the theater and I told her about my encounter at the dinner party. "I couldn't believe how aggressive this woman was.

Why does she care if I have kids or not?"

"That's insane," Alice said. "What did Charlie think?"

"He couldn't believe it either. The good thing is that he gets it now. He understands why I was hesitant to tell people."

"Well that's good. So, has he stopped bugging you about telling Mom?"

"Oh, I did tell her."

"What?" Alice asked, putting down her drink. "When? How did she react?"

"On Mother's Day…" I said, sheepishly.

"Emma! You told her on Mother's Day? What is wrong with you?"

"It just happened!"

"So you broke mom's heart on Mother's Day?"

"Well, when I called her she was with Kate and the boys. She said they've all gotten so big. They're basically all self-sufficient now and she said she misses having babies around. Then she said that she doesn't know what she'll do when you and I have kids because we won't be close by for her to cuddle them. So I said, 'Well, I don't plan on having kids, but I'm sure you can stay with Alice as long as you want when she has kids.'" I smiled and shrugged my shoulders.

"So not only did you crush her, but you told her she can live with me when I have kids?" Alice asked.

"Basically, yes."

"You're the worst. What did she say?"

"She didn't seem that upset, actually. I mean she didn't seem happy about it, but she basically said it was my choice and she would support me either way."

"Wow," she said. "Maybe she doesn't think you're mother material."

"Hey!" I threw my straw wrapper at her.

"I'm kidding! But I guess this really puts the pressure on me, huh?"

"Oh yeah, she's expecting you to have kids like yesterday," I teased. "And get the guest room ready."

Part 2

October

Chapter 13

Kate

D o we have everything?" I prompted.

"If we ain't got it all, we sure got enough!" came the enthusiastic reply.

Since I was a child, this had been the traditional start to all trips that required luggage. As a mother, it was now my cue to throw the van into reverse and back out of the driveway. We were off to Denver!

This time last year I was hauling all my family to a funeral, so it only seemed a fitting "circle of life" sorta thing that we were heading to a wedding this October. The fact that it was Alice's wedding when we didn't even know Eddie existed last year was still a little dizzying.

As I pulled the van onto I-465 in the direction of I-70 and the DVD player was fired up in the back seat, I couldn't help but grin. I had been so worried that I'd be going to Alice's wedding this year, but my concern stemmed from the fact that I thought the groom would be Jake. When I met Eddie for the first time, it was like all my concerns about my sister evaporated. Like the world suddenly made sense again. And I was thrilled for Alice.

That is not to say that my protective older-sister-sense didn't kick in when she told me they were getting married so quickly after meeting. As much as I loved to think of myself as a very worldly and liberal young woman, I was almost middle aged and I'd led a traditional by-the-rules life. Sometimes I had to remind myself that just because I played into the social norms, I didn't have any particular allegiance to them. I'd known for a long time that my path was not the right path for my sisters.

"Mom, what are we doing again?" came Phillip's small voice in the far back, under a pillow pile.

"Alice is getting married," Christopher supplied.

"But I thought Mom said we were going to be gone for a long time," Phillip replied, confused.

"It takes a long time to drive there, buddy," Steven answered.

"How long?"

"We're going to take three days to drive," I jumped in.

"THREE DAYS!?" he exclaimed.

"But we won't drive all day long and we're going to stop and see fun things along the way and then we'll spend three days in Denver for the wedding and take three days to drive back," I said, hoping to get him excited for the road trip.

"But what's fun on the way there?" he whined doubtfully.

Steven elbowed me and pointed at a billboard. It boldly stated "World's largest golf tee. Next exit."

"We're going to see the world's largest golf tee!" I exclaimed loudly.

"What? Now?" Christopher laughed.

A quick look in the rearview mirror showed me four little faces suddenly looking out the windows instead of at the DVD screen. I pulled off and followed the little signs to a golf course and pulled into the parking lot. Everyone piled out of the van and Steven led the way down a path to, well, a giant golf tee.

The boys laughed, delighted at the absurdity of this small detour. After a few pictures and a bathroom break, we piled back into the car. It took all of 15 minutes. On the way back to the highway we saw the "world's largest token" in front of a bank. The boys decided it was "super dumb," but we thought the "world's largest wind chimes" were much better.

Back on the highway a short time later, Steven took to the internet to look for other roadside gems and amazing restaurants. We had already planned our route based on an essential meal at Sweetie Pie's in St. Louis, but beyond that, we were open to whatever the road offered. It was a bizarrely liberating experience. Our lives were so scheduled that the luxury of meandering across the country was almost too amazing to grasp.

When Steven took over driving a few hours later, I took out my phone. It was time to address something that I'd been putting off.

Kate: Uh, we're supposed to be giving a toast in a few days, ya know.

Emma: Yeah, you should get on that and get me my lines.

Kate: Nice try. Your job is based on writing! Get to writing!

Emma: My strength is editing. You write. I'll edit.

Kate: Bah! Woman!

Emma: Besides, you've started writing, too!

Kate: Unless you want to act out, film, edit and show a movie for this toast, I am not your gal. Plus, I haven't actually written anything yet.

Emma: Okay, let's come up with a concept. Then we'll each write our parts and weave them together and you can do most of the talking because I'll be crying.

Kate: At some point in our lives I'm going to have to stop being the speaker-by-default because you people can't keep it together.

Emma: Sure, sure. But this is not that point.

A few dozen texts more and we had a nice outline of what our speech would be and self-imposed deadlines. I pulled out my iPad and got to work. Well, almost.

"Mom! I can't hear the movie and Thomas looks like he's gonna puke."

I undid my seatbelt, stashed my iPad between the center console and my seat, and vaulted into the back of the van. In 10 seconds, I had a bag in front of Thomas's face and a can of Febreze air freshener in my hand. Steven eased the van slowly to the side of the road as Thomas let loose.

"It's okay, baby," I muttered as I willfully suppressed my gag reflex.

Steven pushed the button to open the sliding door, and I crawled/fell out of the van. I deposited a bag of puke on the side of the road and stuck my head back into the van.

"Are you leaving that there?" Steven asked, nodding to the bag.

"He ate hot dogs for lunch. Do you want me to bring it back in the car?" I asked, pointing to the sign a little ways up the road that indicated the next exit was fifteen miles away. Steven read the sign, considered the problem, and mimed buttoning up his mouth and throwing away the key.

"So, why the vomit, little comet?" I asked Thomas.

"I got too hot," he explained.

I maneuvered around Alexander to get to Thomas. I adjusted the vent on the ceiling (why are these things where kids can't reach them?) and put a blanket a few inches out of the window so I could close it and hold it in place as a sunshade. Then I wired the DVD sound through the speakers of the car with an auxiliary cord, sprayed some more air freshener, handed everyone a bottle of water and a snack, and got back into the front seat. All told, we only lost eight minutes. Bam.

That night in St. Louis, when the kids were snoring/grinding teeth/talking in their sleep, I fired up the newest app on my iPad. It was called Final Draft and it was for writing screenplays. It's the same software that most people in Hollywood use. The industry standard. The desktop version was way out of my price range, but the app was only $30.

I had spent the past several months immersing myself in screenwriting. I read articles about it. I read real scripts of movies I'd seen and movies I'd wanted to see. I began building a network of screenwriters, both professional and amateur, on Twitter. I bought and absorbed The Screenwriter's Bible. And all the while, I turned over a few concepts in my mind. I tried to start writing longhand. Then I tried using Microsoft Word. Finally, I came to the conclusion that I needed software to even start to take this whole thing seriously.

"You going to write or just stare at that program forever?" Steven whispered.

"I'm going to write," I said. "Eventually."

"Stop overthinking it. Write. Then sell it and be my sugar mama," he said, wiggling his eyebrows at me.

"I won't sell one," I said, matter-of-factly.

"Don't say that. You don't know."

"If I start now...if I write and learn and write and read and write and make connections and write, maybe in ten years I'll be good enough for someone to take a serious look at one of my screenplays. Not buy it, but look at it," I explained.

"Okay," Steven said, contemplating my timeline. "We'll be

empty nesters by then, which means you'll only have me to spoil. So, I'd like a classic Corvette."

"Deal." We shook hands.

I opened a new document in Final Draft, looked at the blank screen, and typed "Fade In."

The next morning, we took in the amazing (and free!) St. Louis Zoo. Basically, we were just killing time until Sweetie Pie's opened, but it was a really good way to kill time. When we had all stuffed ourselves silly with fried chicken and corn bread and the most incredible macaroni and cheese on the face of the earth, we got back on the road.

With each passing mile, landmark, roadside attraction, and state, I grew more excited for Alice's wedding. I always considered Alice my first baby. It was both a relief and a joy to know she'd be married to a man she so obviously adored and who adored her right back. She was happier in these last few months than I could remember her being in recent history.

But more than that, I was thrilled to be spending a few days celebrating Alice. As the middle child, she always got the short end of the attention stick. Not this week! I was ready to let her make all the decisions or none of the decisions, whatever her perfect little heart desired. I'd get to brag about her in the toast and cry over how beautiful she is and point out all the amazingly artistic touches she integrated into the celebration.

I gave my boys a briefing on what to expect out of a wedding and the corresponding expected behavior. Then Steven and I fielded roughly 20 questions that covered everything from whether the DJ would play "lame" music to why Alice was going to change her last name. When we finally pulled into the Denver city limits, we were locked and loaded for a wedding.

Chapter 14

Alice

I woke up at 6 a.m. the day of my wedding. I couldn't sleep. Not exactly unusual, I suspect. There is just so much happening on a wedding day. I tried to prepare by planning every bit of the weekend down to the exact time people needed to leave the hotel to get to the venue for the ceremony. At 6 a.m. on my wedding day, there wasn't anything left to do. It was done. The day arrived and it was out of my hands. I had to think about being the bride and about going with the flow and not trying to control everything. So, I sat on the couch in my apartment that I wouldn't live in anymore after today. Most of my things had already been moved to Eddie's house, so the apartment was bare, with the exception of the bigger pieces of furniture, my honeymoon bag, and Glenn.

"Hey there, buddy," I said to Glenn as he lazily crawled onto my lap. "Sorry, everything has been so crazy this week." He purred loudly in my arms as I petted him. "The pet sitter will check on you all week and then when I get back, we will move in with Eddie!" I scratched his ears. "You like Eddie, right?" Glenn meowed weakly, still tired. "I know it's been a bit of a whirlwind, but every bone in my body is telling me this is the right thing. He is the right one. I love him so much and he is everything I never knew I needed. Mom and Dad, Kate and Emma love him...he just fits so perfectly into our family! I can't believe I'm getting married. He has a house that will now be ours and he wants a family, just like me." I smiled while I spoke about my future husband and Glenn continued to purr loudly.

A knock at the door made Glenn dig his claws into my leg and leap off my lap. "Ah!" I screamed. "Who could that be?" I went over to the door and peaked out the peephole and saw Kate looking ready to go and Emma yawning behind her. "What are you guys doing here so early!" I exclaimed as I let them in.

"I knew you wouldn't be sleeping. No one sleeps in on their wedding day," Kate said handing me a coffee and a bag that would be holding a whole wheat bagel with peanut butter. "Besides, I'm on Indiana time. It's eight my time."

"It's NOT eight my time," Emma said with a scowl. "This crazy woman made me leave my fluffy hotel bed before the sun rose so we could be first in line at the bakery. Then she wouldn't even let me wait for the donuts that were cooling on the rack and smelling amazing!"

"I've stopped eating sugar," I said. "So, no donuts for me!"

I saw Kate roll her eyes at me and then say to Emma, "Oh,

you're worse than my kids." She bent down to let Glenn sniff her and deem her worthy of being in our apartment.

I hugged them both and thanked them for coming over so early. "I didn't know what I was going to do this morning. My TV is already at Eddie's and there is nothing left for me to do for the wedding!"

Emma pulled an index card out of her pocket and said, "Yeah, my schedule doesn't even start until 10." Then she looked at me and said, "When did you find time to make these index cards for everyone?"

I shrugged and said, "I just wanted to make sure nothing was forgotten. Planning a wedding in 30 days is nothing to be lackadaisical about!"

"Remind me again why such the rush?" Emma said, yawning again.

"Oh, who cares about the timeline," Kate said, setting the bagels out on paper towels. "She met a great guy who wants to start a family with her so there is no reason to delay."

"Yeah," I agreed. I took my bagel and sat cross-legged on the couch and my sisters followed suit.

Kate put her hand on my leg and said, "He really is great, Alice. I think you guys will be very happy."

I smiled and reached for my phone after it buzzed to life. It was a text message from Eddie that said, "Good morning, Sweetpea." My smile broadened and my sisters knew who it was.

"Doesn't anyone in Denver sleep?" Emma asked.

By 11 a.m., I was in a makeshift hair and makeup chair in my bathroom. My stylist had already masterfully given Kate and Emma beautiful updos and my time had come.

"How are you feeling?" the stylist asked.

"Pretty good," I said.

"I'm told by most brides that this is the moment it really sinks in."

I contemplated that comment for a second and said, "Yeah, I guess so. I'm getting married today!" Then shouting out to my sisters I repeated, "I'm getting married today!!"

"Woo!" they exclaimed from the living room.

I could feel my face start to sweat with the reality of the day. The stylist noticed and said, "Take a deep breath. Just relax and I'll get started on your hair."

I did as I was told and took a deep breath. I couldn't wait to see the final product…me as a bride. I had done a makeup and hair run-through a couple weeks prior and left it all on for Eddie to see. His reaction wasn't exactly what I expected.

He said, "Alice? Is that you?"

"Don't you like it?" I asked concerned.

He hesitated. "I do…" I gave him my best frown and he continued. "I just mean, you look amazing, I'm just not used to seeing you with so much makeup!"

"So, you don't like it?" I asked.

"No, no, I really do," he said. "I just think it is a lot of makeup. Do you need all of that? I love the way you look normally, with no makeup!"

I could tell he was trying to be careful with his words, but I wanted to cry. I understood that he preferred my natural look and I loved that, but this was for our wedding! "I know it's a lot of makeup," I said. "But this is the one day of my life when I really want to look amazing. The makeup is mostly for the pictures...so they turn out nice. I want to look like the bride! Not the weird, single, out-of-town aunt."

Eddie laughed at my strange comparison and pulled me close to him. "You look beautiful. I am going to be the proudest groom in the whole wide world. I am thankful you don't feel the need to wear this much makeup all the time, and I promise to react properly on the wedding day."

"Mmm-k," I said, not convinced. "When you see me on the wedding day, you will get to see the whole package. I won't be in these sweats."

Eddie laughed and kissed me on the forehead. "I cannot wait."

So as the stylist was doing her magic on the big day, part of me hoped Eddie really would be shocked and awed by his bride.

"Alice," Kate said, coming into the bathroom holding a phone out in front of her. "Mom wants to talk to you."

The stylist moved to a part of my head away from my ear so I could hold the phone up. "Hello?"

"Hi, honey," my mom said on the other end of the line. "How's it going? Feeling excited? Nervous?"

"I'm feeling pretty good," I said. "I can't believe it's almost time!"

Not missing a beat, my mom got down to business. "Just wanted to give you a quick update because I know how you worry. I just left the venue, it looks amazing. All of the vendors arrived on time. I just swung by Eddie's house and he is looking happy and relaxed."

I smiled. "He doesn't seem nervous at all?"

"Nope," she said. "He's just Eddie. Do you need anything? Your dad and I are getting dressed now."

"I'm good. Thanks, Mom. See you soon!"

Once at the venue, the photographer did some preliminary shots and was ready for the big reveal. She positioned Eddie outside the Bridal Room with his back to the door, then told me to come out. When she gave Eddie the go ahead to turn around and see me, I held my breath. I'll never forget the look he gave me. His eyes widened and brightened and his smile went from a small smirk to the huge, dimpled smile that made me fall in love with him so quickly. He closed the gap between us and held me and said, "You are the most beautiful bride I have ever seen. I love you."

By the time the ceremony started, my head was spinning. It was so strange to plan so much for one day that it didn't seem real when it came. After my father gave me away to Eddie in front of the minister, a million emotions and thoughts were going through my head. My face already hurt from smiling too much, causing my lips to quiver slightly, which Eddie noticed.

He gave me a small "You okay?" look and I managed a bigger smile to reassure him. The introvert in me wanted the day to speed up so I could just relax with Eddie one-on-one again. The perfectionist in me was cursing the DJ who screwed up my entrance song. The worrier in me was fixated on Eddie's face for any sign that he thought he might be making a mistake. (It wasn't there.) The caregiver in me was hoping everyone was having a good time and didn't sense my underlying stress about the day going as planned. The dieter in me scolded myself for not losing one pound of weight prior to being the center of attention for a whole day. The entertainer in me tried to engage the crowd with the occasional exaggerated expressions. The maternal instinct in me shot one of Eddie's nephews a side glare when he started to bounce around distractedly. And the optimist in me knew Eddie and I would live happily ever after.

Thankfully, even with all of that running through my mind, I managed to say the right words at the right time and ended up married. Once the reception began, I could relax a little.

Before the food was served, my dad said a prayer and ended it with, "And bless the marriage of Alice, my middle fiddle, and Eddie, a welcomed addition to our family."

As Eddie and I made our way to the buffet line, he asked, "Remind me again why your dad calls you three his fiddles?"

I smiled at the endearing nickname Dad gave me and my sisters. "When we were young, my dad would make pancakes on Saturday mornings. We would all hang around the kitchen and dining room getting the table set, listening to music and dancing along. It was usually folk music and often John Denver."

"Hence your John Denver father/daughter dance?" Eddie asked.

"Yes," I replied and continued. "In the song 'Thank God I'm a Country Boy', John Denver says, 'Well I got me a fine wife, I got me an ole fiddle. When the sun's comin' up, I got cakes on the griddle.' My dad thought it was funny that he had 'cakes on the griddle' but he didn't play a fiddle, so he changed the song to 'Well I got me a fine wife, I got me three fiddles.' And thus, we became his three fiddles."

"That is both nerdy and adorable," Eddie said as we made our way back to our table to eat.

"You've just summed up the O'Riley Clan perfectly," I said. Then holding up my iced tea, I said, "Welcome to the family!"

Chapter 15

Emma

I spent the majority of Alice's wedding day worrying about my part: the maid of honor's speech. I made Charlie take my water bottle away from me so I would stop gulping water nervously. Luckily, Alice had also picked Kate as her matron of honor, so we shared the responsibility of being funny and nostalgic and charming in front of 150 people. After we helped Alice into her dress and before we had to gather for pictures, I sat in the corner of our holding room going over my notes again and again.

"Stop worrying," Kate said. "We're going to do great and everyone is going to love it."

"Easy for you to say! You're a natural-born performer!"

"That's true," Kate joked, trying to get me out of my head. I laughed and flung one of my notecards at her before realizing I needed it and frantically picked it back up and made sure my notes were in the right order.

Thankfully, I was distracted from worry during the ceremony because I couldn't get over how happy Alice looked. Tears came to my eyes when I saw my big sister, the woman I had admired and looked up to my entire life, get everything she had ever wanted in a partner. Watching the way Eddie looked at her, and she him, I knew this marriage was right, even if it had happened at a speed that made Charlie use his high-pitched, squeaky voice when I first told him they were engaged. "It's not you, honey," I told him. "Calm down."

After the ceremony, I put off mingling to look over my notes once more. Charlie handed me a beer, but I put it straight on the table without taking a sip. I didn't want to risk slurring my words. I already had to compete with Kate's "theater voice."

When the time came, Kate and I stood in our matching black dresses and started our witty banter about our sister. I got through my part about Alice's inspiring creativity with relative ease and I could breathe a sigh of relief as Kate took over to finish our toast with a story about Alice when she was a little girl playing "house." As soon as I saw Alice wipe at her eye, all hope was lost for me. I was thankful I didn't have to say anything else as I sniffed back my own tears and crossed the stage to hug my sister and new brother-in-law.

With my speaking duty behind me, I could relax and enjoy the party for the rest of the evening. I knew Alice would be worried about whether or not people were dancing—she was the one who taught me that getting people to dance was a major responsibility of the bridal party—so Charlie and I spent much of the evening pulling my cousins and Alice's friends onto the dance floor with us. We sang our favorite songs to each other and Charlie spun me around and pulled me into him. Although Charlie wasn't normally a dancer, this came naturally to us. Our relationship started on a dance floor at a wedding; it was our place.

After a trip to the bar, Charlie and I stopped to talk to a group of Alice's friends from Indianapolis. "You two looked adorable out on the dance floor," one of them gushed.

"So happy," another agreed enthusiastically.

"I suppose it won't be long before you two are dancing at your own wedding, huh?" The women giggled like teenagers at a sleepover and made their way back to the dance floor.

I smiled at Charlie innocently and shrugged. "They said it, not me," I joked.

"We're not in a rush!" he said, all high-pitched again. I laughed and kissed him on the cheek.

"I know," I said, leading him to find a new group to catch up with.

On the side of the dance floor, we found Kate talking to our cousin Jen and Aunt Rachel. Charlie and I joined their circle as Kate was filling them in on the fast facts about Eddie, including what he did for work.

"He does something with steel," Kate said tentatively. "I'm actually not entirely sure what he does, but I know he doesn't work in the insurance industry, so he's not one of us just yet," Kate joked.

"What about Emma?" Jen asked, turning to me. "You're not part of the family club either."

"Actually, I am," I said.

"You're not at the magazine anymore?" Rachel asked.

"No, I had had enough of dental journalism," I explained. "I just couldn't get excited about tooth decay."

"Uh yeah," Rachel said, making a face. "That sounds disgusting."

"It was," I laughed, glancing at Charlie because he had heard all my complaints about working at *Tooth Magazine*.

"Are you a claims adjuster now, too?" Jen asked.

"No, I'm a copywriter for an insurance company," I said, trying to hide how much I already hated my new gig. "I guess I wanted to be like Kate and Alice." I smiled weakly.

"I didn't realize insurance companies had copywriters," Rachel said. "What kinds of things do you work on?"

"Mostly informational brochures and blog posts for the website," I said. "It's not really what I want to do either, but it will do for now."

"We're going to find her something in magazines again," Charlie jumped in, putting his arm around my waist. "This will just tide us over until then." He smiled at me. He knew better than anyone that I had been struggling to find work that I was interested in. I had hesitated about taking the copywriter job because I knew I would get bored quickly, but the money was good and the office was closer to home than the *Tooth* offices. In Southern California, a shorter commute was everything. Being able to avoid the 405 alone was worth the job change. "Just give it six months," he had said, and he assured me I would find a better opportunity in that time.

After a few more conversations with family members we only saw twice a year and a few more dances, the reception was coming to an end.

"Alright folks," the DJ said. "At the request of the bride, we're going to wrap things up with one last song." John Denver's "Country Roads" came over the loud speakers and without prompting, the remaining guests gathered in a circle on the dance floor, arms wrapped around each other. This was a tradition Alice and her friends had started in Indy. I was proud to have been in a number of "Country Roads" circles in various bars and living rooms over the years, but this was by far the coolest iteration, with our parents, cousins, and even nephews swaying and singing along at the top of their lungs.

March

Chapter 16

Kate

W hen we bought our little Cape-Cod-style house in Speedway, the thing that bothered me the most was the fact that two bedrooms were on the main floor and two were upstairs. There was no scenario in which I was on the same floor as all my kids.

We settled on an arrangement where Steven and I had a room on the first floor and Christopher had his own room next to ours. Upstairs, Alexander had his own room and the two little guys shared the other. I wasn't thrilled that it was the youngest ones who were furthest away from me, but the sizes of the rooms made most of the decision for us. To compensate for this feeling of unease, I used a baby monitor long after I had any "babies" in the house. I was terrified one of the kids would need me upstairs and I wouldn't hear him.

Of course, there was never any danger that I wasn't going

to hear them. I always heard them. In my family, that mainly meant I heard when kids started throwing up in the middle of the night. I'd hear the tell-tale cough and I'd be up those stairs before the kid was even fully awake or aware that he was about to throw up.

March 11 was different. I didn't hear anything, but I woke up quite completely and all at once. There was no gentle creeping awareness of consciousness. I was sound asleep and then I was wide awake, as if someone had shouted my name. But the house was silent. The gentle static from the baby monitor hummed in my ear and Steven's even breath didn't waver beside me. But I could feel someone.

I tipped my head up and looked around my room, half expecting one of the kids to be lurking in a corner, trying to work up the courage to approach and tell me about a nightmare. But there wasn't anyone there. I rested my head back into my pillow and tried to get a grip. I could already anticipate my sisters' reactions when I told them I was awakened in the night by the feeling that someone was in my room. I smiled and decided to humor myself.

"Grandpa?" I whispered into the dark.

At that moment, a small cough sounded over the baby monitor. It was a type of cough that I hadn't heard before. Immediately my heart began pounding in my throat. I knew something was wrong. Really wrong.

With no regard for how noisy I was being, I sprang from bed and threw open our bedroom door. By the time I heard Steven's sleepy voice call out to me, I was already half-way up the stairs.

When I got to the hallway, I stopped by the bathroom door. I looked in one bedroom and saw Alexander sleeping soundly. I looked in the other and saw Thomas' and Phillip's angelic faces. There didn't seem to be anything wrong. I was confused. I'd been so sure something was amiss.

Then my world toppled.

As I turned to head back downstairs and assure my husband that his nutty wife was just paranoid, the ceiling of the bathroom collapsed in a shower of fire and embers. Smoke poured down into the room and out into the hallway. The smoke detector began to blare as I screamed Steven's name.

In a panic, I slammed the bathroom door shut and turned into Thomas and Phillip's room. "BOYS! UP! BOYS!" I screamed at them.

"Kate! What is it?" Steven yelled as he took the stairs three at a time.

"Fire! Get them!"

Out of the corner of my eye I saw Steven dash into Alexander's room. I grabbed a very confused Thomas by the arm and scooped Phillip up. I got back to their door in time to see Steven and Alexander running down the stairs as Steven screamed Christopher's name.

"Mom! What's happening?" Thomas managed to say before he started coughing against the smoke that was quickly filling the upper floor of the house.

"Remember in school, baby? If there's a fire, you get low, get out, don't go back," I intoned as I pushed Thomas down to the floor where the smoke wasn't as thick.

"Yes," he squeaked.

"So, let's go," I commanded.

I got down on the floor and half-crawled as I still cradled Phillip against my body. We had to pass the bathroom to get to the staircase. I paused by the door and let Thomas crawl past me, thinking I would shield him a little from the heat radiating from the door. I angled my back toward the door, keeping Phillip shielded as well, but he started to whimper from the heat or my death grip, or both.

When Thomas got to the top of the stairs, Steven was back already and instructing our son to come down to him quickly. I took one last glance over my shoulder to see fire, wood, insulation, and drywall rain down in the room I had just pulled my sons out of. A guttural howl shook my entire body as I flew down the stairs.

"Kate? Are you hurt?" Steven asked, panicked by the sound I had just made. Thomas burst into tears as he gripped his father's leg.

"The boys?" I demanded.

"Across the street in Ruth's yard."

"Cats?"

"Christopher has them."

"Let's go!" I said as I grabbed Steven's arm.

"I should get --"

"NO! It's too much! We'll use Ruth's phone."

With that, the four of us joined Alexander and Christopher in my neighbor's yard across the street. Steven immediately began pounding on Ruth's door and I touched each of my boys on the head, the shoulder, the back to reassure myself that they were all there and all unharmed. I took the panicked and flailing cats out of Christopher's arms and tried to soothe them, too.

Ruth came to the door and I heard her gasp in alarm. Only then did I turn back to look at our house. The entire second story was engulfed in flames and portions of the roof had already collapsed in.

The next few hours were a blur of sirens, questions, and tears. I told the story of what had happened over and over again. I lost track of how many times I described fire falling from the ceiling, each time driving a bolt of remembered panic into my heart. I watched numbly as the firefighters battled our house, which did not seem to want to be extinguished.

Ruth provided blankets, pillows, and air mattresses, and we set up shop in her basement. Once the kids were sleeping, or at least resting, we knew we had to call my parents. I sobbed into the phone as Steven rubbed my back. It took several tries, but I managed to finally explain that we were safe but homeless.

"Come up here, honey," my mom said. "It will be okay. We'll figure everything out. Here, talk to your dad. He's worried."

There was a rustling as the phone was transferred over to my father before I could respond.

"Kate. Are you okay, Fiddle?" came my father's calming

voice.

"Dad. Yes, but we don't have cars. They were in the garage."

"Oh, of course. We'll come get you."

"You and Mom will both have to drive, right? If there are six of us, plus two cats, plus you two, can we all fit..." I trailed off, too drained to do basic math.

"Right. No problem. We'll be there in the morning. Try to get some rest," he advised.

"We don't have phones, so just come to Ruth's house. The one right across the street. Looks just like ours...did," I finished lamely.

"Yes, okay. Hang tight."

"Thank you, Daddy."

I hung up and burst into sobs that I knew I'd regret in the morning. The kind that wrack your whole body and don't allow for anything other than a throat-ripping inhalation of breath between each one. Steven hung on to me until they subsided. Then I hung on to him as silent tears fell from his cheeks. Together, we watched through Ruth's front window as the sun came up and illuminated the near-total destruction of our home.

A few hours later, my family experienced the full weight of the Speedway community. A steady stream of neighbors showed up on Ruth's doorstep with everything from bags of clothes to pre-paid phones. The elementary school PTO president came with an envelope full of gift cards and said more would be on the way. This was the first batch that had come in since 6 that morning. It was only 8:30 a.m. The neighbors down the street brought two grocery bags full of food to "get you through breakfast." Someone even brought a litter box and explained that they had heard even the cats made it out safely, thank God.

The mother of one of Phillip's friends came with four brand new large stuffed animals.

"Sometimes, after a trauma, kids just need something to hug," the mother said, a little sheepishly.

"That is just so sweet. Thank you," I said as I accepted the fluffy offering. I hugged them to myself and thought I may need one too. I realized belatedly that I didn't know this woman's name. She was just "Dakota's mom."

With stuffed animals under one arm (even Christopher), the kids burrowed through bags of clothes to put together enough to wear up to my parent's house in the tiny town of Mulberry, Indiana. Steven started making phone call after phone call and I made list upon list.

By mid-morning, when my parents showed up, we had enough things to fill both car trunks and we still left a small stash of things in Ruth's basement. I climbed into my mother's car with the two youngest boys, and Steven went in my father's car with the other two and the cats.

I spent the car ride talking to my sisters. Both had been anxiously awaiting phone calls from me since our mother woke them up at ungodly hours to relay the disaster. I found myself comforting both of them because they were rattled on my behalf. It made me feel like me again. Older sister. In charge. Of course, everything would be fine. We were alive. That's all that mattered right now.

Even though the car ride was only 45 minutes, both boys were sound asleep by the time we got there. As we pulled into the driveway I turned to my mom to make a confession.

"Grandpa woke me up, Mom," I blurted out.

"What?" my mother looked startled.

"If I hadn't woken up until the smoke detector went off, the ceiling would have fallen on Thomas and trapped Phillip. They'd be..." I trailed off.

"Don't think like that, Kate," she comforted me.

"But I..."

"No. No 'what if.' You have enough 'what next' to deal with. Just hug your babies and thank God," she said.

"Right," I agreed.

"And maybe send a 'thank you' to your grandfather," she smiled.

Chapter 17

Alice

"A re you going to drive straight through?" Emma asked on the other end of the phone.

"No, we are going to stop in Kansas overnight. We will leave after work and drive six hours the first night," I answered. "Plus, I'm ovulating and we, uh, don't want this month to go to waste, so to speak."

"Right...thanks for that TMI! Do you think it's okay that I'm flying and not bringing a carload of things for them like you are?"

"Yes, of course. You live much farther away and Eddie and I have a lot of duplicate items since we combined homes and received so many wedding gifts. We have plenty to spare."

"It's just so crazy that they lost everything..."

"I know," I said. "It's hard to wrap my head around it. Thank goodness they are all okay."

"They are living with Mom and Dad. I don't know if 'okay' is the right word," Emma joked.

"True," I agreed. "Okay, I've got to finish packing the car. I'll see you soon!"

"Okay. Drive safe!"

"We will."

Eddie and I decided to stop by Speedway before we headed up to Mulberry to join the family. I wanted to see the house for myself. Not that I thought Kate was lying to us about the catastrophe she and her family experienced. It was just human nature, I suppose, to want to see what happened with my own eyes. We drove down the street, exhausted from driving all day, and really couldn't prepare ourselves for the sight. From way down the street, we could see the yellow caution tape blowing in the breeze. By the time we stopped our car in front of it, my eyes were filled with tears. The house was unrecognizable. The cute white and red house was now black and practically just a pile of rubble. We got out of the car and stood at the caution tape boundary. Eddie put his arm around me and I turned to cry into his chest.

"Shhh, it's okay," he soothed. "Everyone got out alive. This is just a house and those were just things that got destroyed."

"I know," I sniffed. "But they lost everything. Those boys must have been so scared! And Kate...I don't know how she can possibly be holding up through this."

"Well, let's get up to Mulberry and see them," Eddie said. "I bet when you get to hug all of them you will feel much better.

You will see firsthand that they're okay."

Eddie was right, of course. After the final 45-minute leg of our long road trip, we could take all six of them in our arms and see that they were all unharmed. It was such a relief when they came out of my parents' house to greet us. Kate looked exhausted and Steven looked stressed. The boys had a mixture of tired and stress on each of their faces, which lessened as they went down in age. Christopher looked older and more mature than I had ever seen him, and Phillip, the youngest, only showed the worry in his eyes as the rest of his face beamed when Eddie picked him up and gave him a bear hug.

"You really didn't have to come," Kate said when I hugged her last and longest.

"Yes we did!" I said, my tears returning. "Family is the most important thing and you need a distraction." I pulled away from Kate and did a bad impression of a tap dancer, twirling around and clapping my hands until the boys and Kate were all laughing. Eddie joined in and one by one, the boys all started jumping around to the music in our heads.

Emma and Charlie came out of the house, followed by our parents and Emma exclaimed, "A dance party without me? I think not!" and joined in our crazy front yard dance.

"Well, if the neighbors didn't already think we were the crazy family on the block, they do now!" Mom said and we all laughed.

Dad hugged me and Eddie and said, "It's good to have my three fiddles back home again in Indiana."

Kate, Emma, and I all shot each other looks and at the same time burst out into song, "Back home again in Indiana!" My parents jumped in quickly, "And it seems that I can see." Steven and the boys joined in like we had all been practicing for this moment for years. "The gleaming candlelight still burning bright." Eddie and Charlie rolled their eyes at each other and joined in song like obedient honorary Hoosiers. "Through the sycamores for me." Together we all finished out the song loudly, "The new-mown hay sends out its fragrance from the fields I used to roam. When I dream about the moonlight on the Wabash, how I long for my Indiana home!"

"Come on, crazies," Mom said. "It's cold out here. Let's get inside. I have dinner ready."

"I hope dinner is gluten-free!" I said. "I'm intolerant to gluten now. Did I tell you all that?"

"Seriously?" Emma said as we stepped into the house. I shrugged back at her.

After dinner, Kate, Emma, Mom, and I settled into my parent's sunroom. Emma and I flanked Kate on the couch, while our mom put her feet up in her comfy chair. None of us grew up in the Mulberry house. Our parents moved away from Indianapolis once we had all left the nest, but this house still felt homey to me. Mulberry is a quiet town, which seemed to make my parent's house feel more like a retreat. There was a gas fireplace to sit by when it was cold outside, an inviting kitchen to bug our mom in while she cooked, and my favorite room, the sunroom. The sunroom was surrounded outside by many bird feeders and no matter the time of year, you could be an amateur bird watcher and sit all day watching the natural world outside. But it was dark outside, so we all focused on Kate. She looked around and, knowing that her boys were in the basement playing and our men were in the living room watching TV, she finally felt she could let her guard down.

"I'm still in shock," she said while looking down at her hands. Tears began forming in her eyes, then mine, then Emma's.

Emma sniffed and passed out tissues, "I have a strict rule that no one cries alone in my presence."

"*Steel Magnolias*," Kate and I said in unison.

"How do you replace a whole life? A whole household?" Kate asked.

"Well, thankfully you were well insured," Mom said.

"And once you have the insurance settlement, you can rebuild!" I said. "Imagine that. You'll finally get that upgraded kitchen you've always wanted!" Kate smiled a small smile. "And I brought what I could so you don't have to buy everything right away."

"Thank you."

"And until then," Emma said, "You get to live with Mom and Dad!" Kate and I snickered.

"Hey," Mom said defensively. "At least they have a place to stay."

"We are very grateful, Mom," Kate said. "It just all sounds so exhausting. So much to do." Kate put her head back on the couch and stared at the ceiling. "My brain can't handle thinking about it anymore. Alice, time for some of that distraction you promised."

I sat up on the couch ready to do my duty. "Anyone want to play Skip-Bo?" Everyone nodded and we rearranged ourselves around the coffee table. I don't know how it all started, but Skip-Bo became our family's go-to distraction card game many years ago. We all had a copy in our homes and almost any gathering had the game close at hand. My parent's copy was the most worn. "Did I tell you guys that Helen is pregnant?" I said as I dealt the cards.

"What?" Kate said, "No. How long has she even been in Denver?"

I explained that ever since my friend, Helen, had moved to Denver full time from D.C. about a year earlier, she had been seeing someone and things had gotten serious. She was moving in with him and like me, she was anxious to start a family, so they just started trying. She got pregnant almost immediately, it seemed. One day she told me they were trying and the next she was texting me a picture of a positive pregnancy test. She and her boyfriend planned to get married before the baby was due. It was just amazing how both of our lives had changed so quickly.

She left D.C. to get away from a breakup just as I was leaving Jake. We are both overweight, so I think we both were terrified of leaving men who didn't seem to care about our weight and entering a dating market that seemed overwrought by people obsessed with looks. But somehow, we both found new guys who loved us as we were. And she got pregnant! It gave me hope that my excess weight wouldn't be a factor in trying to get pregnant. She did, so why wouldn't I?

Eddie and I started trying the moment we agreed we wanted a family and we were coming up on eight months of trying. While eight months seemed like a long time on paper, it really didn't feel like it. It still felt new, like we'd only been trying for a couple months, probably because we'd had so many other distractions with the wedding and living together for the first time.

I was worried about coming up on the one-year mark of trying. I knew I would need to bring it up to my doctor at my next yearly checkup and that kind of scared me. I was worried she would take one look at me and say, "Well, of course, you can't get pregnant! Look at how big you are!" I hate going to the doctor. I've never been one to get sick very often and the doctor scares me. I've been (self-) diagnosed with White Coat Syndrome, which is when your pulse quickens and your blood pressure elevates the moment a person in a white coat tries to examine you. My naturally guilty conscious makes me think they are going to tell me I am "faking" whatever illness I am there to fix. So, the thought of going to the doctor because I couldn't get pregnant wasn't something I was too excited about. Knowing that my friend Helen could get pregnant naturally and almost immediately was something for me to hang on to.

"Wouldn't it be great if I got pregnant soon?" I said. "Our babies would get to grow up together and it would be awesome to go through all of that with my best friend!"

My mom beamed, "That would be really great."

"Preferably a girl!" Emma chimed in. "Not that boys aren't cool..."

Kate laughed, "Yeah, yeah, I have a lot of boys. We do need another girl in this family."

I smiled and laid down my final card and yelled, "Skip-Bo!" Emma and Kate groaned and started to shuffle the deck again.

Chapter 18

Emma

The day after we all descended on Mulberry, I awoke far too early considering it was three hours earlier in California. I slipped off the air mattress in my parents' basement as gracefully as possible, trying not to disturb Charlie. Once on my feet, I froze to listen to his breathing; it was still steady. I smiled at the man who dropped everything to fly to Indiana at a moment's notice. He hadn't even hesitated when I told him what had happened. "Your family needs us," he said, half asleep, and I loved him even more for embracing my family so completely. "We'll be there."

Upstairs, I found the boys spread across the living room, staring blankly at <u>The Secret Life of Pets</u> on TV. Christopher and Phillip were sitting sideways in my parents' La-Z-Boy recliners, munching on Eggo Waffles, while Alexander and Thomas were stretched out on the floor with bowls of dry cereal.

"Hi, Monkeys," I said, patting Alexander on the head as I weaved around them. I got four weak greetings and figured they were all still sleep deprived and shaken, so I moved on to the kitchen. There I found my mom emptying the dishwasher from the night before.

"Hi, Mom," I said, making my way to the coffee pot, which I knew would be full, thanks to my dad.

"Hi, Sweetie," she said, a little startled by my coming up behind her. "I didn't expect you for another few hours."

"I couldn't sleep," I said. "Where are Kate and Alice?"

"Still asleep, as far as I know," she said. I nodded and reached around her for a spoon to mix almond milk and sugar into my coffee.

"I'm sure Charlie will sleep until at least noon," I said, taking a seat at the small table under the window. "He's been so exhausted lately."

"Tough time at work?" she asked.

"Yeah, he's been working a lot of overtime," I said. "He's doing really great and everybody at the office loves him, it's just not exactly what he expected. He wishes he could be doing more creative work, but he's stuck doing a lot of the administrative stuff."

"That's too bad," she said. "It seems like neither of you are really getting to use your talents." She was right, but I didn't want to admit it. Moving had been more about Charlie and I getting to the same city and less about our jobs, but I had hoped that we'd both be feeling better about our careers at this point. "How's your new job?" my mom asked.

"Also, not great," I said, referring to my new position with *Inland Empire*, a regional magazine for the area east of Los Angeles. "I thought I was going to get to write about food and entertainment, things I'm actually interested in."

"What are you writing about?"

"Farming," I said flatly.

My mom laughed. "You could have written about that here!"

I couldn't help but laugh with her. I had moved about as far away from Mulberry as I possibly could within the contiguous U.S., and yet I hadn't been able to escape the farming culture that surrounded it. I shook my head and looked down into my coffee. "I don't know how long I'll last there," I said.

"Honey," my mom turned away from the dishwasher and walked over to the table. She put her hand on mine. "You can't keep changing jobs every six months."

"I know," I said. "I just can't figure out how to do what I want to do. What if I'm not good enough?"

"You are," she assured me. "You just need to find the right fit." She gave me a side hug and went back to the dishwasher. "I just think you should stick with this one for a little bit, until you're sure you've found it."

Later that day, Alice, Eddie, Charlie, and I took the boys to a movie so Kate and Steven could deal with the insurance company and start sorting out how they would rebuild their lives.

Alice and I took Alexander and Phillip in one car, and Charlie and Eddie took Christopher and Thomas in another.

"Are we going to live with Grandma and Grandpa forever?" Phillip's tiny voice asked on the way to the theater.

"No, Monkey," I said. "Just…for a little while." I looked at Alice, realizing I had no idea how to talk to the boys about what they had just been through. They were little and scared, and I had no answers.

"You'll stay with Grandma and Grandpa until your house is rebuilt," Alice offered.

"How long will that take?" Alexander asked. Alice looked at me. She didn't have the answers either. Kate was always the one with the answers. "I'm not sure," she said.

"Are we going to go back to school?" Phillip asked. "Will we get to see our friends again?"

"Of course," I said, willing to say anything to make my nephews feel better. I looked at Alice with wide eyes and shrugged. "Right?" I asked her.

"I'm sure you guys will still go to school," she said. "Your mom and dad will figure everything out."

"Hey, do you guys like Kidz Bop?" I asked, trying to change the subject. Alexander perked up a bit as I found a YouTube playlist and hooked my phone up to Alice's car stereo. Alexander loved music and always knew the lyrics to Top 40 songs better than I did. Thankfully, the distraction worked, and Alice and I made it the rest of the afternoon without having to answer more questions about what was next for the boys.

The next couple days were like a weird vacation. It felt like Christmas with all of us under one roof. We watched movies and played board games and spent the evenings sitting around the dinner table long after the meal was over, drinking wine and swapping stories and laughing until our eyes watered. And then we'd remember why we were there and the room would go silent again. In those moments, we'd smile softly at Kate and her family and say another prayer of thanks that they were all alive.

When it came time to head back to California, I had a hard time letting go of Kate as we said our goodbyes.

"Thanks for coming, Emmy," she said.

"I'm sorry we have to leave so soon."

"We all have to get back to reality," she said. "But this was a good vacation from my problems."

"*What About Bob*," I said. "Sorta." We laughed, then sighed as I finally let her go from our hug.

"Will you guys be okay?" I asked.

"Of course," she assured me, and I believed her.

At the airport, Charlie and I switched into "traveler" mode seamlessly. We navigated the security checkpoint like pros, instinctively helping each other juggle our belongings without a word. He handed me his bag of toiletries and I gave him my laptop, which he dropped into a bin. We piled our shoes and jackets into another bin and rolled our eyes when we got stuck behind a man who failed to remove his belt.

Once through security, I led Charlie straight to the Auntie Anne's stand for pretzels and a Diet Coke, and then to a newsstand to pick a magazine for the trip. We arrived at our gate with plenty of time to spare, so I opened the latest issue of *Travel & Leisure* to a story about one woman's journey along the Camino de Santiago in Spain. As I read, I stopped to share excerpts with Charlie every few paragraphs.

"Do you want to just read me the whole story?" he finally asked, after I had interrupted his music about 10 times.

"No, I'm sorry. I just…"

"What?" ·

"I don't know. I just want to do this," I said, waving the magazine in front of us.

"Hike the Camino de Santiago?" he asked, pulling his earbuds out of his ears entirely.

"No. Well, maybe," I said, looking at the pictures again. "But that's not what I mean. I want to write stories like this."

"So do it."

"You know it's not that simple. These types of magazines have to have job openings. And then they have to hire me out of the hundreds of people who also want that once-in-a-lifetime job."

"Maybe you should consider freelancing again," he said.

"I can't make enough money off freelancing," I said, feeling defeated by the industry I so desperately wanted to be part of. "At least not without more experience than I have now."

"What should we do?" he asked.

"Sell everything and buy an RV?" I smiled. We had toyed with the idea before, but we knew we didn't have enough money saved up to make that last.

"I wish," he said, taking the magazine from me and flipping through the pictures.

"I just feel like we're doing something wrong, babe. I mean, you're not happy at work either, are you?"

"No," he sighed. I could see the months of long nights and stressful meetings in his eyes. He looked tired and defeated. "But I hate admitting that. I dragged you out to California, and for what?"

"You didn't drag me anywhere," I said, wrapping my arm through his and leaning my head on his shoulder. "I wanted to go, and I love living with you. California isn't the problem."

"I guess not," he said. "But I feel guilty admitting that this job isn't what I hoped it would be. I haven't gotten to take a single photograph since I took this promotion. I'm a sellout."

"You're not a sellout," I said, taking the magazine back from him.

"I basically gave up photography to take a job that pays well," he countered. I could hear the frustration in his voice. Like me, he knew exactly what he wanted to do, but he couldn't figure out how to make it work.

"With what happened to Kate and Steven, I can't help but think about how everything can be taken away in an instant," I said. "If neither of us is doing what we want to do, and I'm spending all my time in jobs I hate and you're working too hard to enjoy anything else, what's the point?"

"What are you saying?"

"I think we need to reevaluate some things," I said, flipping through the magazine again. "I think we should go somewhere."

"We are somewhere," he said, reminding me that we had just spent four days away from work and Hoosier and our real lives back in California.

"Somewhere new. Somewhere neither of us has been to before," I said. He looked confused but intrigued. Charlie was always up for an adventure. "We need to go somewhere where you can take some pictures and I can write and we can find ourselves again. Do you feel like yourself right now?"

"No," he said, shaking his head.

"Then let's go."

October

Chapter 19

Kate

The cell phone lot at the Indianapolis International Airport is a quick study in Hoosier behavior. The main section is always full and always in motion. The parking spaces are very close together, so you almost always make eye contact with someone. Once that connection is made, it is generally understood that you'll nod and smile, and then politely look down and/or away and mind your own business.

There are exceptions to this rule. For example, it is not unusual to realize you know the person in the car to your right or left. When that happens, you get out, give hugs, and chat while leaning against your respective cars.

When I was waiting for Emma to arrive in mid-October, I decided to stage my own rebellion. I called it the "Stress Uprising." For 10 whole minutes, I was alone in my car and I was going to sing at the top of my lungs and dance in my seat, and I didn't give a flying crap-cracker who was staring at me.

For months and months, I had either been surrounded by people in Mulberry, surrounded by people in the car driving to and from Speedway, or surrounded by people at work. Any time I wasn't physically surrounded, I was on the phone with insurance people, bank people, construction people, concerned friends and family, concerned neighbors, and concerned school people. And every one of these people spoke to me with that tilted head scrutiny, watching to see if I was showing signs of cracking.

If any of them had been in an adjacent car as I belted out the "Hamilton" soundtrack at top volume with extra emphasis on the curse words, they would have felt justified in their concern.

Just as I was punching the air to declare that I, Hercules Mulligan, would "get the FUCK back up again," I got the text from Emma: "At door 3." I turned down my music, gave a crazed grin to my cell phone lot neighbors, accepted their looks of annoyance and disgust with dignity, and drove off to get my little sister.

I got out of my van, which was parked at a crazy angle in a half-hearted attempt to parallel park among the others in the loading zone. I had to wave Emma down because she didn't recognize the "new" van I had to get after the fire.

"The person next to me kept picking his nose!" Emma exclaimed with no preamble.

"Gross! What did he do with it?" I giggled.

"Do with it?" she looked at me quizzically.

"Yeah, did he eat it?" I said, eyes sparkling.

"You spend entirely too much time around boys," Emma said as she shook her head.

Emma loaded her suitcase into the trunk and a cat carrier into the backseat. I eyed the carrier suspiciously. No noise was coming from it. Emma and Charlie would be taking some trip (I could not remember where.) and before she met up with Charlie (I could not remember why they didn't leave together. Work?) Emma was bringing her cat to come live with us while they were away.

"Are you sure Hoosier hasn't gone to the litter box in the sky?"

"No! And don't say that. This is just a precaution. He's mostly fine. He just has days that I worry about him and I don't want a bunch of strangers at a kennel taking care of him if something happens. I need someone I can trust."

"I'm not sure the Angel of Death is your best choice," I pointed out.

"Who better to deal with it, if it comes to that?" she reasoned.

Emma then launched into a detailed list of instructions for Hoosier that made me think "mostly fine" was generous optimism. There were medications and things to watch for and procedures that were more elaborate than anything I'd ever done for my children.

"Please tell me you've written all of this down," I jumped in.

"Of course," she assured me.

"And I'm going to have you sign the Bryant Pet Hospice release. We will not be held liable should your animal decide to meet his maker before your return," I said, deadpanned.

Another unfortunate experience that helped fuel my death-shrouded reputation was that animals in my care often didn't survive the experience. It started with Alice's fish I cared for while she was on Spring Break in college. The stupid thing had lived for a head-scratching four years, but couldn't make it two more days until Alice got back. Then there was my neighbor's bird, the school hamster, and my best friend's turtle. When Christopher was little, there was a month-long slaughter of goldfish I kept replacing rather than break it to my son that his fish died. Our two cats had finally broken the cycle, but by then we had earned the Bryant Pet Hospice reputation.

"Do we have to go somewhere to get this release witnessed by a notary public?" Emma teased.

"You sign in blood. No notary needed," I smiled.

After the elementary crew piled into the car and managed to hug Emma over the back of her seat, we stopped by McDonalds to grab snacks and drinks and then headed to the junior high school to get Christopher. From there we swung by the house so Emma could see the progress being made.

"It looks just like your old house, really," she observed.

"Yeah, it basically is," I said, a little defeated.

"You didn't want more space? Maybe another bedroom or living space or something?" Emma asked. I could tell she was trying not to criticize, but she was confused.

"Insurance wasn't even enough for this. We've had to take out another loan, which caused a bunch of delay," I sighed. "It's all just a nightmare. We hope to be back in it in a month or so."

"No attic fans this time, I'm guessing?" she ventured.

"You know, we didn't even know there was an attic fan!" I shrieked. "Stupid thing had never worked, but it was alive enough to start the fire."

"My window will still look at the moon!" Phillip piped up in the back.

"Excellent, buddy!" Emma replied.

"And it will feel like our house still, but Mom said it might smell different," Thomas said.

"Only until you're in there for a few days," Christopher said. "Then it will just smell like you again."

"Mom!" Thomas protested.

"Christopher. Save the snark for people your own age. Flip on the movie," I instructed. "Let's get to Grandma's house."

When we finally pulled up to my parents' house, the boys vaulted from the van to go complain to my mother that they were all "starving." As I went around to pull Emma's suitcase from the trunk, she cut me off.

"Are you okay?" she asked with her serious-concern face firmly in place. I couldn't help but think about how this was the first time in months I wasn't annoyed by the question.

"I'm smiling, aren't I? Happy, smile. Sad, frown. Use the corresponding face with the corresponding emotion," I said as I showed all my teeth in a broad smile.

"French Kiss. And I don't believe you," she said. "Are you writing, at least? Going to any movies? Anything at all for you?"

I snort-laughed in a wholly unattractive way.

"I appreciate the concern, Emmy. I really do. But I literally don't even have time for this conversation. If I'm not in there to stop her, our mother will stuff my children with cookies or cupcakes or God knows what she baked today. And if I have to scrub puke out of one more carpet in this house, I'll scream."

"I thought your kids didn't puke on carpets anymore. They make it to a bathroom or you make it with a bucket or bag. I've seen you catch it in the cardboard tray of a drink holder at a baseball game," she said.

"All the rules have changed. They didn't survive the fire," I sighed.

I walked around Emma and forced the crease out of my forehead with my index finger. When I walked through the front door, I gently reminded my boys to only take one warm homemade cinnamon roll with icing an inch thick.

"I made plenty. They can have more than one," my mother interjected.

"One is enough for right now. They can't be buzzing on that much sugar when they are trying to do their homework," I explained in the most non-annoyed voice I could muster.

"I just thought it would be a nice treat," she offered with that horrible hurt undertone that said she was only trying to help and I was being unreasonable.

As I closed my eyes and took a deep breath that I hoped would prevent me from losing my shit in front of my sticky-faced children, Emma walked in the door. Thank you, sweet baby Jesus.

"Emma!" my mother dropped the plate of 10,000 calories and rushed to hug her baby.

While she was distracted, I ordered my children to surrender the rolls and get to homework. Then I opened the trash can, pulled out the top few items, shoved the half-eaten cinnamon monstrosities in, replaced the top trash, and swept the dishes into the dishwasher. When I turned around, Steven was standing in the doorway, watching me.

"What are you doing?" he asked.

"Preventing diabetes in our children," I told him as I rubbed at the crease in my forehead again.

"Why don't you just tell her to knock it off?" he reasoned.

"She's doing it to make them happy," I said. "She's worried we're all stressed and that's what she can do to help."

"But it's not helpful."

"What is?" I countered angrily. I did not want to have this discussion again. The covert trash operation was meant to avoid conflict, not just divert it from my mother to my husband.

"What do you mean?" he shot back with his own pent-up frustration.

"Well, if I tell my mother her way of helping is actually hurting, she'll be devastated," I said, trying to stay calm and regain some semblance of my control. "I might stand some chance of not wounding the woman who has generously housed us for the last six months if I can redirect her energies. But to what? What can she do that wouldn't be more intrusive or obnoxious?"

"She doesn't need to do anything," Steven said stubbornly.

"I know that!" I said, looking for another way to explain this without sounding unhinged. "But it isn't a matter of need. It's a maternal instinct. She sees her child, her son-in-law, her grandchildren in distress. She wants to help. She needs to help."

"Can't you convince her that letting us stay here is enough?" Steven asked. "We can handle the rest."

"Steven. It's easier this way. Seriously." I closed my eyes and willed myself to not sigh at my husband as if he was one of my children, trying my patience.

He huffed out of the kitchen and I picked up my phone.

Kate: Deliver us, Lord, from every evil and grant us peace in our days.

Alice: That isn't from a movie.

Kate: Nope.

Alice: Wait, is that what the priest says during the Our Father at church?

Kate: Good girl. You win a Catholic gold star.

Alice: What's up? Did Emma make it okay?

Kate: Yes, she's here. I just had a fight-like thing with Steven and I'm tired.

Alice: Fight-like thing?

Kate: You know. Married people thing. Not horrible, but tense and heavy. Not enough energy or venom to qualify as a straight-out fight. Anyway, Emma asked me if I've been writing or doing anything for me. I haven't even thought about screenwriting.

Alice: Totally justified. You've been slammed. But it's worth thinking about again soon. You need it.

Emma and my mother came back in. "Everything okay?" my mom asked.

As I turned to face them, I mentally instructed the corners of my mouth to rise. "Yep. Just house stuff. Emma, tell me about this trip you're taking," I said, shamelessly using my sister to change the subject.

Four days after Emma left, I was sitting on the bathroom floor at 1 a.m. pleading with Hoosier. He hadn't eaten a bite of food for three days and I couldn't tell if the water had been touched. I couldn't get his medicine in him and eight hours earlier his back legs seemed to have stopped working. "Don't do this, Hoosier. Emma loves you so much. Please?" The cat looked up at me with glassy eyes and meowed quietly. "You're right. I'm sorry. If you're in pain, you can go," I said as I pulled him into my lap, wrapping him gently in a towel. I leaned back against the bathtub and slowly pet his head, humming bits of a hymn that was rattling around in my head.

Steven peeked around the bathroom door. "What's going on?" he whispered.

"Hoosier's dying," I said flatly.

"You don't know that," he said. "I bet he'll rally if we can get some food into him. Why don't you come to bed and we'll take him to the vet in the morning? Maybe they can help?"

"He'll be dead in the morning," I told him with absolute certainty.

He considered me for a moment and then asked if I was going to stay up with the cat.

I nodded sadly. Steven walked away and I wondered if he was mad at me for spending the night in the bathroom. I felt so out of touch with him, I couldn't tell. Our stress levels were so high, we had taken to skirting around one another for fear that the other's burden would brush against our own and bring us both down.

He came back a minute later with a pillow and a blanket. I leaned forward and he put the pillow behind my back. Then he draped the blanket around my shoulders. He put one hand on Hoosier's head. "Bye, Hoosier," he said. "When I was a boy, I had a cat named Watson. Find him and he'll show you around. Tell him I miss him."

And with that Steven slipped out of the bathroom, and I let tears fall from my cheeks unchecked. I spent the rest of the night scratching Hoosier's head and telling him what a great cat he had been. I thanked him for being so wonderful to Emma for so many years and assured him that we would look after her when he was gone.

Sometime around 4 a.m. I realized that Hoosier wasn't breathing any longer. My alarm clock would be going off in an hour, and I was out of leeway with my boss. I knew that I had to be in the office on time if I had any hope of taking a day or two off at Christmas. So, I threw on my mother's boots and my coat and went into the garage. I found a shovel and made my way to a tree in the corner of the yard. In the frosty dark I dug a hole, reverently said a final goodbye, and filled it in.

By the time the boys got up for school, I was showered and dressed. My theater makeup skills came in handy to disguise my exhaustion and sorrow. I broke the news over breakfast, dried tears as we put on coats, comforted during the drive to Speedway, and forced myself to put my smile back on by the time I walked through the doors of my office building.

Safely in my cubicle, I let the smile fall, pushed aside the work that was waiting for me, and pulled out my "new-to-me" iPad. I took a deep breath and started reacquainting myself with the world of screenwriting.

Chapter 20

Alice

She's beautiful, Helen," I said, picking up her daughter and cradling her in my arms. My eyes filled with tears of joy as I looked at the tiny face that hadn't been in this world for 24 hours yet. Helen smiled at me from the hospital bed. She noticed my tears, went to speak, and then stopped herself. "What?" I asked.

"It's just," she started. "I hope holding Ella doesn't make you feel sad that, you know, you haven't been able to get pregnant yet."

"No!" I said, at an octave higher than my usual tone. "My struggles have nothing to do with your happiness. I couldn't be more excited to be here to help welcome this little one into the world." Baby Ella moved slightly in my arms as she continued to sleep. "Just look at her," I marveled. "She is so little and precious."

My heart did ache for a baby of my own, though. It was so powerful that "ache" didn't seem like a strong enough word to describe my desire. I was having conflicting feelings of happiness for my friend along with the bitter taste of jealousy. Over the years, I saw friends become overtaken by jealousy and I just didn't want to become that person. Someone else's successes had nothing to do with me. Helen didn't get pregnant to rub it in my face that I couldn't get pregnant. She got pregnant because she also longed for a baby. I believed deep down that it was my destiny to be a mother too. My path was different from everyone else's. I would get there.

I was mesmerized by Ella's ridiculously small features and felt hopeful once again for my own baby. I found that as the months of trying went by, I always remained hopeful. But since we had been trying for over a year and I was in my mid-30s, it was time to visit the dreaded doctor to see what was wrong with me...or Eddie. Ella began to fuss in my arms, so I handed her back to Helen and said my goodbyes as Helen anxiously tried to get Ella to nurse.

The following week, Eddie and I sat in a small doctor's office and waited for my doctor to return with our test results. My leg shook nervously. Eddie reached out for my hand and said, "No matter what she says, it's going to be okay. Once we know our hurdles, we can move forward, right?"

I gave him a weak smile and nodded. I felt on the verge of tears. Something was clearly wrong, right? I tried to focus on an object in the office to keep my emotions in check. My eyes landed on an abstract sculpture. It was black and oblong and either came from some African nation or Pier One. My doctor didn't seem like the kind of person who traveled to Africa for fun, so probably Pier One.

"Alice, Eddie," my doctor said as she entered the room. "I apologize for the wait." She extended her hand to both of us. Eddie and I both instinctively sat up straighter to brace ourselves for the news. "Well, from what I can tell," she started as I stared at the ugly statue, "nothing is prohibiting you from getting pregnant."

"What?" Eddie and I said at the same time.

"Well, Eddie has a good sperm count. They look healthy and strong. And Alice, you passed all the tests. You are ovulating regularly, monthly, you still have a number of viable eggs left, and your uterus is in good health and able to sustain life."

I stared at her and said, "But then why...?"

She shook her head slightly and said, "It's hard to tell, really. Perhaps you are experiencing too much stress in your daily life or you aren't having sex at the right times or perhaps your weight is causing an issue. Though your tests came back normal, some women do have a harder time conceiving when they are overweight."

"Oh," I said as she verbalized my one main fear.

"I suggest you try naturally for another couple months and then consider seeing a fertility specialist in the New Year. Don't have sex until the 12th day of your cycle, and then have it every other day until about the 24th day of your cycle. Work on destressing your life and trying to lose some weight. Even a few pounds can make a big difference. Go for walks and stay away from sugar. You know…the usual."

I continued to flit my eyes back and forth between my doctor and the most ridiculous statue in the whole world. I hated that statue. Who did she think she was? A cool doctor with fancy statues? She was cheery and confident on our behalf as if she was telling us great news. *There is nothing wrong! You can make a baby!* It wasn't comforting at all. I had hoped for a specific, hopefully minor, issue that we could fix and move on and get pregnant. But to say we were fine was infuriating. Obviously, something was wrong! Otherwise we'd be pregnant! And of course, my weight was an issue! It was the one constant in my life that I had never been able to control, so of course that was why we couldn't get pregnant. To me it seemed like a death sentence. As if someone said, "If you just stop breathing, you will get pregnant." It was that impossible for me. Eddie was holding my hand tighter than before. He knew what was coming. He had unfortunately witnessed my complete breakdown due to my weight issues before.

We thanked my doctor and headed to the car. I handed my car keys to Eddie because I knew there would be no way I could drive. The tears had already started to cloud my vision. As soon as I clicked my seatbelt into place, I reached behind the seat for the tissue box and the tears just started spilling out of me.

"Oh, Sweetpea, it's okay," Eddie soothed. "She was really positive."

I wiped at my eyes and shakily said, "She was positive because she is one of those small people who thinks weight loss is an option for me! I am 35 and I've been overweight

210

my whole life! I go from diet to diet, from exercise routine to exercise routine and nothing works! I've given up carbs and sugar and dairy, I've juiced and eaten organically and given up processed foods, I've boot camped and visualized and trained for 5Ks. Nothing works!" I felt my face crumple into the ugly cry. I threw my hands up to my face as my eyes squeezed tight together and my mouth stretched open in that silent scream position and then the sobs quickly followed. I gasped for breath and just wanted to curl into myself. Eddie patted my back as he pulled out of the parking lot. He knew I would just want to be home on our couch where I could cry into his chest while he rubbed my back.

Once home, we assumed our "Alice is having an emotional breakdown" positions after I gathered my water and tissues and Eddie had his coffee. I curled into him on the couch and inhaled his scent. He put his big arms around me and kissed the top of my head. I felt my body relax immediately. No one had ever had this effect on me before. Eddie made me feel so safe and secure and loved. I hugged him tightly and sniffed.

"I think it's important to focus on the good things the doctor told us," Eddie said into the top of my head.

I pulled back and looked him in the eye, "I know," I said. "I just feel so mad at myself. Kids have been an important dream in my life for the last five years. Why haven't I prepared my body properly? Why haven't I gotten serious about losing weight so I could be in the best possible position to have a baby? I've done everything else to prepare! I've got the great husband, the house, the job, the family love and support. Why didn't I take care of the most important thing: my body?"

211

Eddie used a tissue to wipe my tear-stained face. "Stop being so hard on my wife. You have been trying, you just haven't found the magic formula yet. You need something you can stick with for longer than six weeks."

I stared down at the tissue in my hand and felt tears boil up again. "You mean, I can't commit to anything?"

"I mean that you seem to have a very specific cycle. You get excited about something, go full bore, get bored, and then stop."

I looked up at him, my sadness becoming anger. "Well, great. I am destined to continue to fail."

"Whoa, Alice," Eddie said. "Why are getting so defensive? You're not hearing what I am saying."

"Well, what are you saying?" I snapped.

"I admire how you never stop trying to better yourself. You don't accept things that make you unhappy. You keep trying for what you want. I just think that when it comes to losing weight, you need to figure out what your cycle is, you know? I'm sure your diet failure starts way before you realize it. Some kind of trigger starts your downward cycle. You just need to pinpoint that and rise above it."

I took a deep breath. "You're right," I said. "I can take control of every other part of my life, I should be able to take control of this too." I smiled up at Eddie. "How did I end up with such a great husband?"

"Must have been that pact you made with the devil," he said.

"Oh right...damn. I did promise him our first born. Hopefully we will have twins so I can keep one!" Eddie and I laughed at my awful joke and then I continued, "You know, if we can never have kids, I think you and I can still have a good life." Eddie looked down at me with a question on his face. "I just mean that baby making is stressful and some couples don't make it through it. We will obviously have our ups and downs trying, but at the end of the day, we still have us. I say we try for kids until I am 40 and if it doesn't happen, then it doesn't happen."

"What about adopting or IVF?"

"I don't know if I want to go through all of that too," I said. "But I'm not sure. Right now, I just feel like we should try, be content in the knowledge that we gave it all we got, and then rethink our future. Become travelers or full-time artists or something ridiculous that you can't do with kids."

"So, both you and Emma would never have kids?" Eddie asked.

"Yeah, my mom would have a heart attack, but she will have known that we tried."

"Sounds like a good plan to me," Eddie said.

"I mean, I do think we will get pregnant. I just want to prepare my mind in case we can't." I gave Eddie another tight hug and took a few more deep breaths.

After a few minutes, Eddie broke the silence and said, "So do you not want to go tonight?"

I sat up. "Oh man, I forgot!" I slapped my hand into my forehead. "No, we have to go."

The restaurant was oddly calm for a Friday night. Eddie and I found his parents' table easily and joined them.

"Happy Anniversary!" Eddie's mom, Phyllis, said as she hugged us both.

Eddie's dad, Greg, joined in the hugs, "Has it been a year already? What are you doing hanging out with a couple of old people?"

Eddie and I settled into our seats and he said, "This is just the start of the anniversary weekend. We are heading to Glenwood Springs tomorrow for a relaxing soak in the hot springs."

"Oh, that sounds lovely," Phyllis said.

The waiter came to take our drink order and we all scanned our menus. We were at the same Vietnamese restaurant we were at when Eddie told his family that we were engaged. His sister and nephew were with us on that occasion. The whole family liked to talk, so it was a while before there was enough of a lull in the conversation for Eddie to make the announcement. He got their attention and said, "Everyone, I have some news. Alice and I are getting married. I proposed on Thursday night and she said yes!" The silence that followed the announcement scared me. I started to have thoughts of them hating me and braced myself for the "too fast too soon" talk, but thankfully, the message eventually seeped into their consciousness.

Phyllis had put her hand to her mouth and said, "Oh, thank God," as tears sprang to her eyes. Obviously relieved that her

42-year-old son was finally settling down. Greg slapped Eddie on the back and gave him a hearty handshake and Eddie's sister, Lisa, offered congratulations and immediately asked to see the ring.

"Oh, we are going to go pick it out tomorrow," I said.

"Eddie," Lisa said, "you better get her a good one! An expensive one. It should cost at least $5,000!"

Eddie choked on his soda and looked at me in horror. I put my hand on his arm and responded to Lisa, "I've already picked out the ring I want online. It's closer to $700. I love it and can't wait to have it on my ring finger." Lisa gave me a skeptical look and continued to bring up the issue until Eddie made a snarky comment about her never being married so how would she know about what was proper or not.

On the night of our one-year anniversary though, our group was smaller and we had nothing to announce. Our conversation progressed along nicely until out of nowhere, Phyllis said, "You can't go to the hot springs, Alice! What if you are pregnant?"

I set down my full fork and said, "Unfortunately, I am definitely not pregnant this month."

"Are you sure? You've been trying for so long!"

"Mom," Eddie started.

"I mean, the Bernard men are very fertile, so maybe..."

"We were at the doctor this morning," I said. "She confirmed that there is no baby in there."

"What else did the doctor say?" Phyllis was practically on

the edge of her seat. She was desperate for another grandchild.

Eddie took my hand and said, "She said that there is no obvious reason why we haven't gotten pregnant yet and to keep trying."

Greg nodded his head in approval and Phyllis looked perplexed. "But then why hasn't it happened yet?" she asked. "Did you put that fertility statue I gave you in the bedroom? It should be right next to the bed!"

I furrowed my brow, "What fertility statue?"

"The one I brought back from Africa! The two birds kissing, where did you put it?"

"It's in our kitchen," I said. "I didn't realize it was a fertility statue."

Phyllis looked horrified so Eddie jumped in, "We will put it in the bedroom tonight. Thanks, Mom."

But Phyllis continued, "Maybe you aren't elevating your hips properly after sex. Remember that move I showed you, Alice?"

I blushed remembering the time she got on the floor in her house to show me how to properly elevate my hips after sex to ensure that gravity worked with us. "Yes, I remember." I said. "I've been doing that, right, Eddie?"

"Yes," Eddie said, slightly embarrassed. "Mom, I promise we are doing all the right things. It will happen. It just takes time."

"I never had a problem getting pregnant. Lisa was an accident. Only Eddie was planned and even then, I got pregnant so fast. Remember, Greg?" Greg nodded and focused on his meal, but Phyllis continued. "Or Lisa, obviously. She also didn't mean to get pregnant!"

"Mom," Eddie said again, knowing she would just keep going.

"What about your family, Alice?" Phyllis continued. "Did your mom have a hard time conceiving you or your sisters? Clearly your older sister is very fertile, how many boys does she have?"

"Mom!" Eddie said again.

"Four," I said. "No issues of infertility in my family." I said calmly. "We just need to keep trying."

"Well, I don't think you should be going to any hot springs," she said. "Eddie, you'll fry up your little guys and who knows what it will do to your eggs, Alice."

"Mom!"

Kate: Happy Anniversary, Alice!

Alice: Thank you!

Emma: Oh...yeah...Happy Anniversary!

Kate: Real smooth, Kid. Doing anything fun for your first anniversary?

Alice: We are heading up to Glenwood Springs tomorrow to relax in the hot springs.

Emma: Oh man, that sounds great.

Kate: I take it you aren't pregnant this month?

Alice: Nope, not pregnant. Had our doctor's visit this morning. She basically told us everything looks good and to just keep trying for a couple months and then she will refer us to a fertility specialist in the new year.

Emma: That's good, right?

Alice: It is. She was very hopeful, but she did mention that my weight might be a factor. So, I don't know what to do about that. I mean, I know what I am supposed to do, it has just never worked for me, you know?

Kate: Well, maybe this will give you some extra motivation?

Emma: Or maybe don't listen to the doctor! Overweight people get pregnant all the time!

Alice: Yeah. I don't know. I think I'll just meditate on it for a little bit and try to figure out what is best. I look forward to seeing the fertility specialist.

Kate: Why does she want you to wait until the new year to see someone?

Alice: I'm not sure, but with the holidays coming up, I prefer to wait so it doesn't interfere with our trip to Indy for Thanksgiving and the crazy Christmas holiday. I'm just going to let it all go and refocus in January.

Emma: That sounds like a good plan.

Kate: Yes, yes. Quite good.

Alice: I already feel better about everything. Thanks, ladies. K, gotta go pack for the springs! Good night! Love you!

Kate: Night! Love you both too.

Emma: Ditto!

Chapter 21

Emma

There were cats all over Santorini. Every evening around 7 p.m., as we squeezed through the alleyways of the Greek island to meet our tour group for dinner, Charlie and I passed an old man feeding three kittens. His wrinkled skin was the deep kind of tan that only comes from a lifetime in the sun, and while his calloused hands hinted at a life of heavy labor, he was incredibly gentle with the cats, rubbing each one on the head as he put out a can of wet food.

"Animal shelters are not common around Greece," our tour guide Landon told us. "So, the locals take it upon themselves to care for the strays." These cats didn't belong to the old man, but feeding them was clearly his evening ritual. He seemed to enjoy it as much as they did.

I tried to ignore the pang of guilt I felt for Hoosier every time another cat ran across the stone walkways as we wandered the island. I felt terrible that I hadn't been there when he passed away, even though I knew Kate had taken care of him better than anyone else would have been able to. He had been there for me for 12 years, and I wasn't there for him. He had seen me through high school, college, grad school and more jobs than I could count. He moved from apartment to apartment like a champ, but he had had enough. I was comforted knowing he was laid to rest at my parents' house. Had we been home, we would have had to turn his body over to the vet, not having a yard of our own. This way, we'd be able to visit his grave when we went to Mulberry for Thanksgiving.

When we first got the news, Charlie and I were sipping sangria at our hostel's rooftop bar, waiting for the famous Oia sunset. I wasn't surprised, but I cried on Charlie's shoulder as the sun sank into the Aegean Sea, creating a masterpiece of purples, pinks and oranges in the sky. That night, instead of going to a club with our fellow travelers, we sat around a fire pit on the hostel's patio, raised a glass in honor of Hoosier and told stories.

"Remember that time Hoosier fell asleep on the back of the couch and he rolled off?" Charlie asked. I laughed and nodded.

"He was about as graceful as I am," I said, flipping through the pictures on my phone. Most of them looked exactly the same, but I hadn't been able to stop myself from taking them over the years. "Did I ever tell you about the time he got stuck under the bathroom vanity at my apartment in Boston?"

"No," Charlie laughed. "How'd he do that?"

"There was a hole in the baseboard, but it was tiny. I still don't know how he squeezed under there, but once he did, he couldn't get back out. I heard him meowing and it took me awhile to figure out where he was."

"So, what did you do?"

"I got a hammer and saved him."

"You ripped the vanity apart?"

"Just the baseboard," I smiled.

After that night, Charlie and I agreed to not let Hoosier's loss ruin the rest of our time in Greece. We had dropped a hefty chunk of our savings on this trip, and we were going to make the most of it. We had one more day in Santorini before our group, made up of 20- and 30-somethings from across the U.S., moved on to Athens. Charlie and I chose to travel with a company called Tied Down Travels rather than on our own because we wanted to meet like-minded people as much as we wanted to explore a new part of the world. We thought it would be inspiring to be around fellow young professionals who had a passion for travel and made it a priority. We chose to spend our last day on the island tagging along with Landon and his wife, Liv, with whom he had started the company.

To start the day off, our guides led us down steep, zigzagged steps to the base of the island where we found a cafe that sat along the turquoise waters. We sipped bitter coffee as fishermen tossed the morning's haul onto the docks beside us and local chefs eyed the merchandise. Taking advantage of our guides' undivided attention, Charlie and I launched a series of questions at Landon and Liv.

"How long have you been doing this?" Charlie asked.

"Well, we started leading trips when we were still working other jobs," Landon said. "We would use our vacation time once or twice a year, just like our clients, but we ditched the corporate world and went full-time with Tied Down Travels just over three years ago."

"Where did the name come from?" I asked.

"It's kind of a joke," Liv admitted. "When we had office jobs, we felt like there was always something tying us down, keeping us from traveling like we wanted to. So, when we started the company, knowing there were a million things that could get in the way, we decided to use our excuses as our motivation."

"That's exactly what we're struggling with right now," I said. "There's always something keeping us from doing what we want to do."

"What do you want to do?" Landon asked.

"Stay here forever," I said, laughing, but I could tell he wasn't going to let me off that easily, so I got more serious. "I'm a writer and Charlie is a photographer," I explained. "But we're not using our talents in our day-to-day."

"Why not?"

Charlie considered this for a moment. "When I got into advertising," he said, "I wanted to be on the creative side, but there weren't any openings for photographers, so I went corporate thinking it would be my 'in,' and now I'm stuck." I looked at him, brow furrowed. I had never heard him describe his career like that before. I knew he wasn't doing exactly what he had set out to do, but I had no idea he felt so trapped. I thought he had chosen his path purposefully.

Landon and Liv exchanged looks, then Liv shrugged and nodded at Landon. "We've actually been talking about expanding our staff," he said. I perked up.

"How so?" I asked, glancing at Charlie to see if his interest had been piqued too. It had.

"Well, we haven't worked out any details yet," Liv said, cautiously, "but we want to improve our social media presence. We know other companies similar to ours send writers and photographers on their group trips. So far, Landon and I haven't had the capacity to commit to a full-blown blog."

"Are you hoping to hire two people? A writer and a photographer?" I asked, trying not to get too excited. "Would they get to travel together?"

"Maybe," Landon said, glancing at Liv. "We need to think about it some more before we post any job openings."

"Of course," Charlie said, taking the last swig of his coffee. "Well when you do, let us know." I loved how direct he was. He was so much better at networking and promoting himself than I was. Had I been there on my own, I probably would have taken Landon's answer to mean, "it's never going to happen," but Charlie took it as an opportunity.

As we finished our drinks and gathered our bags, I stared up at the cliff we had come down to reach the cafe.

"It's going to be a long walk back up," I said.

"That's why we're not going to walk," Liv replied, nodding to the area behind me. I turned and saw eight donkeys poised and ready to bring passengers up the hill. My eyes widened, and I noticed Charlie looked a little unsure as well.

"We're taking donkeys?" he asked.

"You have to ride donkeys in Greece!" Landon exclaimed, patting Charlie on the back. "Come on."

Reluctantly, Charlie and I followed Landon and Liv to the donkey handler, who pointed each of us to the donkey he wanted us to ride. Mine was dark brown and stocky, and he wore an orange and cream striped mat on his back. I looked at him cautiously and whispered "hello" before climbing on his back. He immediately shifted and started stepping forward; I gripped the saddle with both hands.

"Woah!" I yelled. The handler barked an order in Greek and the donkey stopped.

"You okay, Emma?" Charlie asked from the white donkey behind me.

"I think so," I said. I pet the back of the donkey's head lightly. "Good donkey," I whispered. Then I turned back to Charlie. "How do you say 'good' in Greek?" Charlie shrugged.

Before I could ask Landon, who seemed to have a pretty good grip on the language, the handler called out another short command and we were off, with my donkey leading the group up the stone path.

"How's it going up there?" Landon asked over the *clomp clomp clomp*.

"Am I supposed to be guiding this guy?" I asked nervously.

"No," Liv laughed. "He knows where to go. Just enjoy the ride!"

Enjoy? I was fairly confident I was going to fall off at any moment. I bounced up and down as the donkey made his way up the winding steps, snorting and farting every few strides.

"Ugh, Emma! Your donkey smells!" Charlie said.

"It's not my fault!" Just then, the donkey took a wide turn up the next set of steps and nearly took out a pair of tourists who had paused to take in the view. "Sorry!" I yelled, bracing for impact and holding on as tight as I could. Thankfully, the couple moved out of the way just in time and we continued to climb.

When we finally made it to the top, I waited for the handler to steady the donkey before I slid off.

"What'd you think?" Landon asked.

"That was terrifying."

"Oh, come on, it wasn't that bad," Charlie said, playfully hitting my arm.

"Not for you! You had a strong, young donkey. Mine looked like he was going to keel over halfway up the hill. I'm lucky to be alive!"

Charlie shook his head and laughed. "You're so dramatic." He put his arm around me and the four of us made our way through the crowds to a restaurant near the hostel, where others from our group had already started on plates of spanakopita and jugs of wine.

The next day, the group left the beautiful beaches of Santorini for the bustle of Athens. We settled into our hotel room just as the sun was beginning to set and stepped out onto our private balcony that overlooked the Acropolis and the terracotta rooftops of the city. I marveled at how beautiful it was.

"I can't believe some people go their whole lives without seeing places like this," I said to Charlie. He wrapped his arms around me and took in the view for himself. "Wouldn't it be awesome to work for a company that fixes that?"

"Yeah, it would," Charlie said. "I would love to photograph places like this for a living. And if we could do it together? That would be perfect."

"Do you think we could pull it off?" I asked. "Our families would freak out."

"We'd still be based in the U.S., I think; we'd just be traveling a lot more," he said. "We'd probably see them as much as we do now."

"That's true," I said, considering it. "There's nothing really tying us to California, and I would leave my job in a second."

"For an opportunity like this? I would, too," Charlie said.

On the last night of our trip, Charlie and I sat at a rooftop bar with Landon and Liv, sharing a few final bottles of wine.

"I really need to visit more rooftop bars in my day-to-day," I said, swirling the wine in my glass.

"We could go to more in California," Charlie said, "but none with a view like this." He raised his glass in the direction of the gold-lit Parthenon in the distance. We paused to soak it in once again. Liv finally broke the silence.

"Landon and I have been talking more about the idea of hiring a writer and a photographer," she said. Charlie and I both sat up a little straighter and leaned forward. "We looked you guys up the other night. We found your last travel blog, Emma, and checked out Charlie's pictures as well. We think you two would be a really good fit."

"Really?" I asked. "You want to hire us?"

"Well, we need to think about logistics a little more," Landon said. "Ideally, we would send you two as trip leaders while Liv and I led other groups, so we'd be able to double the number of trips we offer. Then, we'd have you two write blog posts and take pictures to promote Tied Down Travels while you're away. We think we could realistically expand in about six months, but it could take a little longer until we could bring you two on board."

"That makes sense," Charlie said. "I think we're definitely open to exploring the options and learning more about what the job would entail."

"Great," Liv said. "When we get back to the States, we'll talk to our financial team and start putting together an expansion plan."

"There's nothing set in stone yet," Landon added. "We don't want you going home and quitting your jobs tomorrow, but start thinking about if this is really something you're both interested in, and we'll talk about it more soon."

"Sounds good," I said, raising my glass for a toast. "To possibilities."

Once we landed back in the States, I texted my sisters immediately.

Emma: I'm BAAAAACK! Did you guys miss me?

Kate: Hey! Welcome back! How was your trip?

Emma: It was amazing. Between the sights, wine and copious amount of pita bread, Charlie had a hard time getting me back on the plane.

Alice: I miss pita bread. And regular bread. And cookies.

Kate: You're sending Alice into gluten-envy, Em.

Emma: Sorry. The pita was actually rubbish.

Alice: Good.

Emma: Hey, thanks for continuing to use the "Sisters" thread while I was away. It was great turning my phone on and getting 347 texts all at once.

Alice: We didn't want you to feel left out!

Kate: We're considerate like that.

The apartment felt strange without Hoosier lurking around. He didn't take up a lot of room or make a lot of noise, but I could feel a difference without him there. I missed the way he nuzzled my hand when he wanted to be scratched behind the ears and the subtle sound of him scampering to investigate a noise outside. Other than that, however, our lives went back to normal almost immediately. We knew it could take a while before we heard from Landon and Liv again, so Charlie went back to the ad agency and I continued writing about California soil and the best farming equipment for every job.

"I hope it doesn't really take six months for us to hear from them," I said one night as we were finishing a meal of chicken kebabs, tzatziki sauce, and pita bread. Every night since we had returned from our trip, I tried a new Mediterranean recipe to keep the spirit of our latest adventure alive.

"Well, they have to make sure people will sign up for extra trips if they offer them," Charlie said.

"I know," I said. "I'm just ready."

"We're in no rush," Charlie said, bringing our dinner plates into the kitchen. "It's only been three weeks since they came up with the idea. It's best if they take their time and get everything sorted out before we hop on board. We have to make sure we can live off whatever they offer us before we leave our steady jobs."

"It's been three weeks?" I asked, thinking I might have misheard him from the living room. "Already?"

"Yeah," he said, returning to the couch. "We'll be in Mulberry for Thanksgiving next week. Time's flying."

Three weeks since we'd gotten back. That couldn't be right. I grabbed my phone and tapped the Google Calendar app. One. Two. Three. Four. Five. I froze.

Part 3

November

Chapter 22

Kate

Thanksgiving has never been my favorite. Sure, gluttony is swell and family is nice, but it's always seemed like a lot of effort for very little reward. The boys only eat turkey and rolls, no matter how much I try to get them to try a bite of green bean casserole or dressing. It's always turned into an exasperating reminder of how impossible my children could be. And this year, I just didn't need it.

We had assumed we would be in our new house by Thanksgiving. In fact, we had been assured we'd be in by then. But weather and inspectors and back-ordered everything had conspired against us. So, rather than celebrating and showing off our new house to our family, we were trying to make room for Alice, Eddie, Emma, and Charlie in my parents' already crowded house.

I stood in the kitchen with my mother on Thanksgiving

morning, ripping up pieces of rye bread for the spinach dip. "Why didn't you ask them to get hotel rooms?" I whined (yes, whined—I had been up half the night with Phillip because of fire nightmares).

"We would hardly get to see them if they were in a hotel," she explained.

"You hardly see them now when they all sleep in until noon," I argued.

"Plus, that wouldn't be fair. We let you stay here for months, but ask them to pay for a hotel for a few days? C'mon, Kate."

"Maybe we should go to a hotel," I suggested.

"Don't you dare. Your sisters would be so upset," she admonished.

"Well, we wouldn't want to upset my sisters," I said as I eviscerated the bread.

Alice walked into the kitchen and made a beeline for the coffee pot. "I need some caffeine. It's difficult to be up before noon, ya know," she shot me a look. I made a face at her to try to diffuse the situation, but I could tell she wasn't too happy with my early morning bitch-fest to our mother. Great.

"Mom," Alice said, "what's the full menu for tonight? Did I tell you I'm not eating meat these days? I've read so many studies about the bad effects it has on our bodies."

Not being surprised by Alice's new diet declaration made me snap at her. "Jesus, Alice. What DO you eat?"

"Plants," she said matter-of-factly as she stuck her tongue out at me and left the room.

233

Emma and Charlie came down about an hour later and commandeered the television to put on the parade. Phillip came into the kitchen to lodge a complaint while I cut sweet potatoes. "I hate the parade, Mom," he declared.

"You don't hate the parade, half-pint. Go watch it with your aunt. She'll tell you who all the people are."

"I don't care who they are!" he declared.

"Then go watch the basement TV," I said through gritted teeth. This kid didn't get enough sleep last night. He was going to be a wreck all day.

"Christopher is watching something," he said in a tone that matched the way I had spoken to my own mother.

"Tell Christopher he has 20 minutes, then he needs to do something else. You can have it then," I said.

"What can I do until then? I'm bored."

"Read, play a game, color a picture, do a puzzle, go find Thomas, or your Aunt Alice, or your father," I rattled off. The knife slipped and I took off a neat slice of my left thumb. I bit back a curse as white-hot pain exploded in my brain. I quickly scooped the now bloody sweet potato into the trash and rushed to grab a paper towel to put pressure on my thumb. I swallowed hard against the metallic taste in my mouth. Apparently, I was excellent at suppressing my distress or my son was just that oblivious, because my trauma didn't interrupt his onslaught of unreasonable complaints.

"But I wanna watch Teen Titans Go!" he whined.

"Kid, you're going to have to wait," I said very slowly and

deliberately. Phillip stuck his lower lip out and tears sprang to his eyes as he turned and marched out of the kitchen, betrayed by his mother who could not solve his problem. Great.

"Kate!" Emma hollered from the family room.

"What?" I snapped back.

"Just wanted to tell you the Broadway performances are starting," she said in a defensive tone.

"I'm busy!" I shot back.

"Geez, sorry," she muttered. Great.

The first aid kit fell from the cabinet and smashed my toe. My eyes darted around the kitchen to be sure I was alone. "Goddammit to hell," I swore quietly. "Fuck."

"Kiss your mother with that mouth?" Steven asked as he came into the kitchen.

"Is this kitchen some kind of sound amplifying freak of acoustics? Why can everyone hear me when they aren't in the room?" I exclaimed.

"Settle down, lady. I'm not gonna tell anyone you have a potty mouth," he said and smiled at me.

Christopher barged into the kitchen with his brothers at his heels. "Mom! Did you tell Phillip I can't watch my show?" he demanded.

"I said in 20 minutes!" Phillip defended himself.

"I can't find the Kindle, Mom," Thomas joined in.

"Phillip took my book! He said you told him he had to read and he couldn't find any other books!" Alexander added.

"Christopher, go finish your show and then socialize with your family. Thomas, the Kindle is on the charger in the front room. Phillip, give Alexander his book. That is way too old for you. Steven, take your youngest to the store and buy some triple antibiotic cream and two large sweet potatoes. Go!" The whole group turned tail and left the kitchen, leaving me with my throbbing thumb and a burning desire to go back to bed.

"Your boys crack me up," Alice started as she wandered into the kitchen a moment later. "Phillip said he was going to go buy sweet and sour potatoes with Steven."

"Yeah," I agreed half-heartedly as I pulled pots from a bottom drawer, causing an avalanche and a crash of noise that gave me an instant headache.

"What, you suddenly don't think they're adorable?" she asked.

"Let's see how adorable you think your kids are in a couple years when you've had no sleep," I grumbled. I looked up just in time to see Alice flush and dart from the kitchen. Great.

Chapter 23

Alice

I quickly made a beeline for the bathroom as I stepped over my nephews and hurried past Eddie. As soon as I reached the bathroom, the tears sprang from my eyes. I stifled a gasping inhale of breath and hoped no one knew I had run to the bathroom to cry. Kate probably knew. Nothing got past her. But seeing as she caused this mini breakdown, I didn't care. I promised myself I wouldn't become this woman, but it was apparently inevitable. I was a woman who was having a difficult time getting pregnant and any mention of my lack of children sent me into a tailspin of emotions. I hated it.

I frantically wiped away my tears and tried to stop the transition into a full on ugly cry. It was Thanksgiving and the last thing I wanted to do was to remind everyone that I was inexplicably unable to conceive. I dabbed at my face with a tissue in an effort to not have the "fresh cry" look. When I finally felt in control, I exited the bathroom.

I did a quick assessment and it didn't look like anyone knew I had been in the bathroom crying, thankfully. I eased back on the couch to watch the parade. As soon as I thought I was in the clear, my phone buzzed. I looked down and saw I had a text message from Eddie. "U OK?" I looked at him across the room and saw he had that worried look on his face. The look he got when he was both worried about me and ready to fight anyone who might be hurting me. I loved that look. Well, I didn't like that he got that look because it usually meant I was causing him worry, but I saw his immense love for me in that look. I gave him a shoulder shrug and stared down at my phone. A second text came through. "Let's go for a walk." I nodded and we both stood, grabbed our coats and snuck out the front door.

"What's going on, Sweetpea?" Eddie asked when we were a few yards from the house.

I sighed. "Ugh, you know. Same old, same old." I shuffled my feet along the pavement. "Do you ever get exhausted by my repetitive breakdowns? I can't get pregnant, I can't lose weight, etc. etc. etc."

"Breakdown? Did you have a breakdown?"

"Oh, yeah...a little one. In the bathroom," I confessed. "Kate basically told me that I don't understand her because I don't have kids. It was the way she said it that just cut right through me. I ran into the bathroom and had a little meltdown. I hoped no one noticed, but you obviously sensed something."

"I know you so well, babe," Eddie said with a smile. We only called each other "babe" when we wanted to add some light to a situation. We used to make fun of a couple on a reality TV show who called each other "babe" constantly. It then became our way to make the other laugh or smile. It worked, because I smiled at Eddie and wrapped my arm around his waist.

"I exhaust myself," I said. "Why can't I let snarky comments roll off my back?"

"Why did Kate say that? It wasn't very nice of her."

Like a good sister, my tune immediately switched over to defend Kate. "She didn't mean it. She seems really stressed today and I think it just kind of slipped out. It had nothing to do with me, per se."

Eddie raised an eyebrow and looked down at me. "Whether she meant it or not, she hurt your feelings. Shouldn't you talk to her about it?"

"No," I said quickly. "I'd rather just let it fade away. Get further from the comment and move on. It was nothing. I just projected my own insecurities onto something Kate said. She was talking about herself and her stress and I read into it."

"But wouldn't you feel better if you talked it out? Wouldn't it fade quicker?" Eddie's family liked to "talk" about their problems. But really, they'd just argue until someone was happy/got distracted.

"I don't like confrontation," I said. "I'd rather just vent to you and forget about it."

We walked in silence for a bit around the park behind my parents' house. Mulberry was quiet. It was always quiet. We were alone in the park as the wind blew and leaves rustled on the ground. The cold air was refreshing, but it was starting to infiltrate our warm coats. Finally, Eddie broke the silence and said, "You could never exhaust me, babe." I smiled up at him and veered him back toward the house.

I pushed open the front door to my parents' house and was greeted by the warmth and commotion of a full house. Everyone seemed to be up and moving. Eddie and I hung up our coats in the closet and stopped the first person to run by us. "Phillip, what's going on?"

He stopped and put his hands on his hips. "Dad and I just got back from the grocery store and Gramma can't find the cheese!"

"What?" Eddie and I said at the same time as Phillip ran up the stairs apparently in pursuit of the cheese.

We made our way into the kitchen to investigate for ourselves. My mom was in there rummaging through the fridge, clearly exasperated. We started to inquire about what was going on when Thomas came in the kitchen with tears in his eyes. "I did such a good job cutting the cheese and now someone stole it!"

Mom turned around and saw us. "There you are!" she said accusingly. "Did you take the cheese?"

"What cheese?" I asked. "What is going on here? We just went for a walk and came back to everyone searching the house like crazy people for...cheese?"

Mom gave a heavy sigh and explained. "Thomas and I cut up some cheese cubes for an appetizer and put it in a bowl and now the bowl of cheese is missing. I thought maybe you guys took it on your walk or something."

A shout came from Kate in the basement. "Nothing down here!"

A second shout came from the sunroom from my dad. "Sunroom is free of all dairy products!"

Eddie and I laughed. "You think we took a ceramic bowl of cubed cheese on our walk?" I said. "Mom, I'm lactose intolerant!"

"Right," she said and then gave Eddie an accusing side eye glance. "Well it didn't get up and walk away!"

"Maybe it was put in the wrong place by mistake," I said trying to help. I opened the fridge and noticed a bag of ice on the top shelf. "Why is there ice in the fridge?" I picked up the bag and opened the freezer to put it in the proper location. And there on the top shelf of the freezer sat a ceramic bowl full of cheese cubes. I took it out and handed it to my mom. "Here you go."

She looked at the bowl in amazement, then yelled, "Steven!" Apparently, Steven was the one who was supposed to put the ice in the freezer and the cheese in the fridge, but he clearly failed. The family gathered in the small kitchen to understand the mistake and make fun of Steven for causing the Great Cheese Scandal of Thanksgiving.

With the cheese located, my mom put out the appetizers and everyone went to grab some snacks. I waited at the edge of the dining room for my turn with my paper plate in hand. I had my back against the wall next to the entrance to the kitchen. I could hear Emma and Charlie talking in low voices and leaned toward the kitchen to hear better.

"What do you mean you don't know what you are going to do?" Charlie asked in a hushed tone.

"Well, clearly I can't tell anyone," Emma said. "And it's not what *I'm* going to do, it's what *we* are going to do! This is *our* problem, remember?" I couldn't understand what they were talking about and hoped they weren't having a fight. I didn't want to see my little sister upset. She continued, "There are so many things we need to think about. Are we keeping it? Getting rid of it? And I can't tell anyone until we decide. It would kill Alice to know I am pregnant with all that she has been going through."

I stepped into the door frame and stared, open mouthed, at them. Charlie saw me first and drew in a gasp. Emma slowly turned around to face me. Her face went ghostly white. "Al," she started to say but then grabbed the trashcan next to her and threw up. I turned on my heel and ran to the bathroom, slamming the door behind me.

Chapter 24

Emma

Charlie pulled my hair behind my head and put his hand on the small of my back, but I shrugged him off, grabbed a paper towel to wipe spit from my mouth and took off after Alice.

"Alice, wait," I said, trying not to yell. I didn't want to draw the attention of the entire family. By the time I reached the bathroom, she had locked herself inside and I could hear her gasp for air between sobs. "Alice, open the door." She blew her nose but gave no response. "Come on," I said. "I don't want mom and dad to hear us."

The door opened and I expected to be let in, but instead, Alice bolted past me and went right for the stairs.

"Where are you going?" I asked, confused. Did she want me to follow her? I covered about half of the distance between us when she made it clear she did not.

"I feel sick," she said loudly, so the entire family could hear. The conversation in the dining room about appetizers and football paused.

"Are you okay, Fiddle?" my dad asked.

"I'm going to go lay down," she said. I knew it would look strange if I followed her now. Well played.

Turning back toward the bathroom, I saw Charlie standing with our empty paper plates. He shrugged at me, looking worried. "She wouldn't talk to you?" he whispered.

"No. She just ran away. I don't know what to do."

"Can we go somewhere to talk?" He looked around. We were surrounded by people. The very people we didn't want to overhear us. Again.

"Mom?" I called out. "Do you have any root beer?"

"No," she came around the corner. "I thought you didn't like root beer."

"I don't," I said. "But Charlie does. We're going to walk down to the gas station to get some."

"Ok," she said suspiciously. She could usually tell when I was keeping something from her.

"Do you need anything else?" I asked with a fake smile.

"No," she said. "Is everything okay?"

"Yeah," I said. "We just want a little fresh air." I grabbed the coat I had left in Mulberry when we moved to California and handed Charlie one of my dad's jackets from the front hall closet. "We won't be long."

"I can't believe this," I said when we reached the end of my parents' street. "Did you see Alice's face?"

"It's not like we planned this," Charlie said. "She has to know that."

"I don't think it matters. She and Eddie have been trying to conceive for like a year, and now her little sister got pregnant by mistake? She probably hates me."

"Your sister could never hate you," he said, walking ahead of me. He was on edge.

"Can you slow down, please?" I stopped in the middle of the street. There wasn't much traffic in Mulberry on a busy day. On Thanksgiving, the town looked deserted.

"Sorry," he said, retracing his steps to be even with me again. "I think we need to focus on the bigger issue. Alice will get over it. But we cannot have a baby."

"I know," I said.

"So, you agree? That we shouldn't go through with this?" he asked.

"I don't know."

"What do you mean you don't know, Emma? What about everything we want to do? We can't travel the world with a baby in tow. Do you really want to give up on your dream job before you even start it?"

"I don't know." Tears were forming in my eyes.

"And do you know how much a kid costs?" he continued.

"We'd have to get a bigger place, which we can't afford, and pay for childcare, which we can't afford. I don't know if we will even be able to stay in California if you have a kid."

"We," I corrected him. "If we have a kid."

We reached the entrance of the gas station convenience store. He opened the door for me and rubbed his eyes with his other hand. "Yeah," he said. "We."

Inside, we didn't say another word to each other. I grabbed a two-liter of root beer while Charlie waited near the register. I placed the drink on the counter and a young woman came from a room in the back. Charlie looked at me out of the corner of his eye. *I see it*, I thought. She was pregnant, almost comically so. I wouldn't have been surprised if she was expecting twins or triplets.

"Is this it for you?" she asked, scanning the bottle and swaying from side to side. Her ankles were probably swollen.

"Yeah," I said, handing her the money. I couldn't help but stare at her belly. Alice would have looked at this woman and thought of the miracle of life and what a gift it was. I looked at her and saw exhaustion, discomfort, and bitterness. I have never felt the desire to be pregnant, and now that I was, I still didn't feel it. Every time I thought about it, I felt sick, and I was pretty sure it wasn't all morning sickness.

Back at the house, Alice hadn't come downstairs, and now Eddie was missing, too. I sent Charlie into the kitchen with the root beer and walked slowly up the stairs. I paused to work up the courage to knock on the closed door at the end of the hall, even though this had been my bedroom when I went home for breaks during college. I knocked on the door weakly and pressed my ear against the wood. There were whispers and some movement, then finally, Eddie came to the door.

"I need to talk to her," I told him, craning my neck to get a glance of Alice sitting on the side of the bed. She looked at me through bloodshot eyes. Charlie was only partially right. She probably didn't hate me, but I wasn't sure she would ever get over this.

"Now's not a good time," Eddie said.

"Come on, Al," I said, ignoring him. "You have to talk to me."

"Close the door, Eddie," she said, and he did.

I heard footsteps coming up the stairs. Thinking it was Charlie coming to see how things were going, I let my guard down and rested my head against the wall, feeling defeated.

"What's going on?" It was Kate. I stood up straight again, trying to look calm.

"Nothing," I said, but I had nowhere to go. Every other room around me had been claimed by Kate, Steven, and the boys. Ducking into one would admit to Kate that something was definitely wrong.

"Why are Alice and Eddie hiding?" she asked. "Is she still mad at me?"

"You?" I was confused. "What did you do?"

"Nothing!" she said defensively.

Just then, the bedroom door opened and Alice emerged again. Her face was red and puffy.

"Alice?" Kate asked, concerned. Alice walked right past both of us and locked herself into the upstairs bathroom. "Alice, what's wrong?" Kate pounded heavily on the door.

This, of course, alerted the rest of the family to the unfolding drama. Within minutes, our parents joined us in the narrow hallway and Steven and the boys were peering up the stairs at us. Charlie stood behind them, staring at the ground so as not to give away that he knew what all the fuss was really about.

"Alice, honey?" With his calming voice, our dad tried to coax his middle daughter out of the bathroom. "What's happened?"

"It's not fair," she said softly.

"What's not fair?" he asked cautiously. I tensed up and willed my sister to stop talking.

"I want a baby so badly." I felt the entire family lean in to listen. "And I can't have one." *Don't say it, Alice.* "And now Emma gets one she doesn't even want? It's not fair."

Slowly, nine heads turned to me. Even Phillip, who surely had no idea what was going on, was silent and still with his eyes locked on me.

"Emma?" My mom asked. I covered my eyes with both hands and slid down the wall. Charlie made his way past the boys and sat down beside me. I looked up at my family.

"I'm pregnant," I whispered. "And we don't know what to do."

"What do you mean you don't know what to do?" Kate

asked, instantly angry. For her, there was only one thing to do.

"I mean, we don't know what we're going to do," I said, more strongly. "We don't want to have a baby. Alice is right. It's not fair."

The bathroom door opened and Alice joined the rest of the family in the hallway. Eddie put his arm around her and she rested her head on his shoulder, sniffling every few seconds.

"Okay," my dad said, a little shell-shocked but still as calm as ever. "Well, little Fiddle, you don't need to have all the answers right now. We'll help you figure it out."

"Everything will be okay, sweetie," my mom said. "You and Charlie should say some prayers and reflect on what is best for you both. I know you'll figure it out."

"And we'll all be here for you, no matter what," my dad said. Looking at my sisters, however, I wasn't so sure they felt the same.

December

Chapter 25

Kate

I sat in the basement of my parents' house surrounded by bags, boxes, wrapping paper, tape, gift tags, and candy. I looked at my phone and realized it was no longer Christmas Eve. It was 12:30 on Christmas morning. I rolled my neck and tried to sit up straight. That lasted about 27 seconds and I sighed heavily.

Every year Steven and I made a huge effort for the entire month of December. We loved going to see Christmas lights and we went to every Speedway and Indianapolis holiday tradition we could fit in. This year was no different, even if we were still in Mulberry.

The only difference was that our usual killer schedule took on a new level of dedication from me and Steven. And since each carefully planned event required sacrificing our most precious commodity—time—we were bound and determined to make the best of each one.

We braved sleet and frigid temperatures for "Light the Night on Main" in Speedway. We bustled the kids into the Speedway Center for the Arts to eat Long's Donuts (the most spectacular donuts in the history of the world), to the Dallara Factory to see Santa Clause (who had arrived earlier in the evening in an IndyCar), and into Charlie Brown's to sip hot chocolate while shaking ice from our hats and out of our scarves.

We powered through "Christmas at the Zoo" to see the hundreds upon hundreds of lights with hundreds upon hundreds of Hoosiers because we could only fit it in on a weekend.

We walked around the Conservatory at Garfield Park an extra three or four times because the scavenger hunt was unusually easy and it had been a long drive to only spend 20 minutes there. I took my sweet time pointing out the cocoa tree to Phillip and explaining how those weird trunk pods were the beginnings of chocolate. I let Alexander sit and stare at the waterfall for much longer than anyone else wanted to.

And, in the greatest testament to our determination to make the most of every outing, Steven and I changed a tire on the side of I-65 in a freak pop-up snow storm, deposited two bags of vomit from Thomas on I-865 and I-465, fishtailed our way around downtown, and managed to make our reservation to take a horse-drawn carriage around the "World's Largest Christmas Tree" on Monument Circle.

To be honest, the whole thing seemed a lot like a made-for-TV Christmas movie. I even started five or ten screenplays with horrid names like "Finding Christmas on the Interstate" and "Have Yourself a Mobile Little Christmas." The sappiness was just too much for me to take seriously. Sentiment is not my strong suit, and I was using up all of it on family traditions with my real children. There was no more left for make-believe characters on the page.

It was a (mostly) fun month. And it drained me on a molecular level. I had been tired before, like when I had a newborn, a two-year-old, a four-year-old, and a six-year-old. But this. This was a tired for the record books.

"You almost done down here?" my mother asked as she came halfway down the stairs.

"I still have stockings to do," I admitted in a tone of utter defeat.

"Oh honey, that's going to take forever. Let me help."

I didn't argue. Steven was upstairs attempting to assemble an air hockey table, which we would have to disassemble and reassemble when we moved into our new house, but we decided the kids needed something amazing to wake up to on Christmas morning. So, it was going to live in the sun room until the day we packed up and moved back to Speedway.

I was starting to think we weren't ever going to move back. A week before, we received a frantic call from our contractor. He informed us the hardwood floors that had been installed in our entire house were being recalled for toxic chemical treatment. This would be another four- to six-week delay, which really meant another six- to eight-week delay.

The whole process was such a complete cluster. I wanted to

text my sisters right away, but we hadn't spoken since Thanksgiving. This was such an affront to our natural state that my very body was rebelling. I've never handled adversity or stress properly—I get stress hives. They usually blossomed on my ankles and legs. But when the stress was especially awful or prolonged, the hives would migrate to my arms and hands. A working mother of four cannot hide her hands.

Point in fact, when my mother settled down across from me to wrap tiny stocking presents, she immediately scowled at my hands. I ignored her and grabbed yet another roll of wrapping paper.

"I called your sisters today," my mom said.

"That's nice," I said as I scratched at my hand.

"I thought trying to do a video chat tomorrow morning might be a little hectic, so I told them we could just count tonight's call as our Christmas communication."

"Good," I said flatly.

"Kate. You're the oldest. You could stop all of this if you took the first step," she said.

"Mom, they could take the first step just as easily as I could. Our birth order has nothing to do with our ability to swallow our pride and pick up a phone."

"They are used to you leading the way, taking charge," she smiled at me. Why did my parents smile at me when I was pissed?!

"Well, I'm used to them not acting like irrational idiots," I muttered.

"Katherine!" That stopped the smiling.

"Can we not do this again right now, Mom? I'm just too tired."

"I can't stand this tension in our family. It would be horrible at any time, but at Christmas! Family is supposed to be a..."

"...safe haven," I finished. "Yes, Mom, I know."

"If you know, how can you be letting this happen? You need to fix it," she instructed.

Steven walked, or rather trudged, down the basement stairs at that moment. Saved by the husband.

"All done, honey?" I asked quickly, cutting my mother off mid-scolding.

"Yep. How much more do you have here?"

"Stockings. Grab some paper and get to wrapping, mister," I said. If it had been any other situation, I would have let Steven just sit and rest while I wrapped, but I needed him to make this whole enterprise go faster. I could not take much more tonight.

"Mom, why don't you head to bed. Steven and I have got this," I ventured hopefully.

"Okay, but please think about what I said. Merry Christmas."

"Merry Christmas, Mom." We watched my mother make her way upstairs and Steven gave me a look. "For Christmas, I'd like to be the middle or youngest sister," I said through a yawn.

"I don't know that you'd actually like to be either of them right now, honey. They both have some pretty heavy stuff going on."

"And we don't?" I shot back at him.

"I'm not saying we don't," he said. "It just seems to me like you could all use each other right now."

"You aren't really ganging up on me with my mother, are you?"

"No, of course not. But it's..." he leaned forward and put a bow on my head.

"Christmas," I finished for him, sadly.

Chapter 26

Alice

One of the great misleading lies of the movie industry is the three-minute wait for a pregnancy test to tell you whether you are pregnant or not. I'm talking about the non-digital kind. The package may advise you to wait three minutes for full results, but you can actually watch the pregnancy test go into action almost immediately. In the time it takes the urine to make its way up through the test, you can see your results. It's like watching a little race as the liquid moves its way through. It first hits the space where the "pregnant" line should be and then it hits the line everyone gets, pregnant or not. When I saw that first line appear followed by the second, I was in such shock that I had to sit on the edge of the bathtub for the remainder of the three minutes trying to process what was happening. That must be why the box advises a three-minute wait time. The time needed to wrap your mind around the reality. My heart was pounding so hard in my chest that I was afraid I might be having a heart attack. I took some deep breaths and as the words "I'm pregnant" slowly seeped into my head, the tears began to form in my eyes.

I left the bathroom, test in hand, and found Eddie sitting on the couch with his morning coffee. He had lit the Christmas tree and was petting Glenn, who was snuggling on his lap. Without looking up at me, Eddie asked, "So what's first? Cinnamon rolls? Presents?" Noticing I wasn't answering, he looked at me and said, "Oh, Sweetpea. I told you not to take the test on Christmas morning! I'm sorry."

I shook my head and tried to speak. A weak, "No," was all I could muster.

Eddie shook Glenn off his lap and came to assume his comforting position with his arms outstretched, he placed his hands on my upper arms. "We will keep trying."

"No," I said again. "Look." I held up the test for him to see and he looked at me quizzically. I realized he wasn't as accustomed to looking at these things as I was, so I explained. "Two lines," I said, gasping in for breath and feeling the tears start to move faster. "Two lines means pregnant!" It came out like a messy laugh/cry and a huge smile swept across my face.

Eddie dropped his hands from my arms. "What?" he asked. He looked at me, then at the test, then back at me. I could see his eyes becoming glassy with his own tears. "You're...we're pregnant?"

"Yes!" I exclaimed. "We are going to have a baby!" I cried and laughed, not knowing how to express the feeling of relief and happiness. "Merry Christmas!"

Eddie wiped at his eyes and took me in for a hug. His big arms wrapped around me and I buried my face into his chest. "This is the best Christmas gift I could have ever asked for."

It was so surreal to continue with our Christmas Day as if nothing had changed. But in reality, everything had changed! I couldn't get through the simplest task without suddenly remembering and pausing what I was doing to allow my mind to take it all in, and that feeling of excitement would hit me all over again. It was magic. Could it be true? Had it finally happened? I almost burnt the Christmas cinnamon rolls because I was busy imagining a little cluster of cells in my body that were going to become my son or daughter. I couldn't remember my gifts moments after I opened them because I was preoccupied with whether I should take another pregnancy test in a couple days to be sure it was true.

"Are you going to tell anyone?" Eddie asked after we had our traditional O'Riley Family Christmas lunch waffles.

"No," I said, taking my plate into the kitchen. "I don't think so. I kind of want to live with this for a couple days, you know? Let it really sink in...make sure it's real."

"Real?" Eddie asked as he started to fill the dishwasher with the dirty dishes.

I shrugged and said, "Well, at my age, I am at a higher risk for miscarriages...so I'd rather keep it between us for a little bit."

"You don't even want to tell your sisters?"

"You know we aren't talking at the moment," I said, putting

the margarine back into the fridge.

Eddie turned off the sink faucet, dried his hands on a towel and turned to lean against the sink and look at me. "First of all, I don't think I fully understand why you aren't talking. Second, you still sent each other Christmas gifts, so it can't be that bad. Third, your fight was about you not being able to have a baby. And finally, you need them. I've never known you to go this long without texting them. This isn't you. You don't hold onto grudges. I can see it affecting you. Wouldn't this be a great excuse to break the silence and reconcile?"

I leaned against the opposite counter from Eddie and held up four fingers so I could count off his points. "First of all," I said, mocking him, wiggling my pointer finger, "we aren't talking because I'm upset about…everything. I'm mad that Kate feels like she rules the world and is the only one who knows stress and she is like Super Mom and no one else can ever be a good mother, especially me and my inability to have kids."

"Former inability," Eddie said quickly.

We both gave big smiles remembering our little one grow-ing inside me. I continued, "I'm mad at Emma because she is just so irresponsible! It's not hard to remember to use birth control. She just flits about her life, jumping from job to job, travelling to Greece without a care in the world and oops! Gets pregnant. It just makes my blood boil. She doesn't know what she is going to do? Is she seriously considering an abortion? I know it is her right and all, but come on." I took a deep breath and put my pointer finger down then wiggled my middle finger and said, "Second, we still exchanged gifts because we aren't heathens! We know this silent time will pass and we obviously still love each other." I put my middle finger down and stared at my ring finger standing up with my pinkie and tried to remember his third reason. I shrugged and put the finger down and moved on to my pinkie and his fourth reason. "Finally, I do need them and we will reconcile, but I don't think I'm ready just yet. I do want to reach out to them to tell them the news, but not over text message. I want to live with this new reality for a couple days and then I'll reach out and tell everyone the news and I do think this will help us to reconcile. New Year's Day is in a week. That would be a good time to call them. A new year, a new beginning, you know? Until then, I will continue to be as stubborn as they are being because if you notice, neither of them have extended an olive branch."

Eddie smirked and said, "Kate literally gave you flavored olive oil for Christmas and Emma gave you a mosaic of a peace dove carrying an olive branch."

"And I gave them each homemade spa kits to help ease their stress and tension," I said matter-of-factly. "It's how we start to reconcile." I picked up Glenn who assumed we were congregating in the kitchen to feed him again. He meowed and I said, "It's a process. I will call them on New Year's Day, apologize and tell them the good news." Glenn jumped from my arms realizing he wasn't being fed and scampered off into the dining room to scavenge for scraps on the table. Eddie and I watched him sniff at the floor then up on the table.

"We don't have to name our child after a Richard Dreyfuss character, do we?" Eddie asked, referring to my lifelong obsession with naming all my pets after my favorite actor. There

261

was my fish from my childhood, named Matt Hooper for *Jaws*. My father actually named him and started the trend. The cat I got in middle school was named Dr. Leo Marvin for *What About Bob*. The two beta fish I got after college were named Curt for *American Graffiti* and Roy for *Close Encounters of the Third Kind*. And finally, there was Glenn, named after Mr. Glenn Holland in *Mr. Holland's Opus*.

I laughed and said, "Well, Moses Wine is a pretty solid name!"

Eddie shook his head and asked, "What is that from?"

"*The Big Fix*!"

"Never seen it."

"Ugh," I said in exasperation. "Now I know what we are watching next!"

Eddie laughed, rolled his eyes and went back to cleaning the kitchen. I went into the living room and sat on the couch, looking at the Christmas tree. I reflected on the year and a half Eddie and I had been trying to get pregnant and said softly, "I know you are in there, baby. I know you aren't much yet, but you will be and you will be the most wanted and loved human that ever lived. Take your time growing in there and in nine months your daddy and I will be so excited to meet you and hold you and hug you and love you." I put my hands on my stomach and leaned my head back on the couch. I was so happy it almost hurt. Glenn saw this as his opportunity to get warm and curled up on my lap.

After a few minutes, my phone buzzed. It was Helen.

Helen: Merry Christmas!!

Attached was a picture of Ella in her swing with a gold Christmas bow on her head.

Alice: Merry Christmas! What a cutie! Have you guys had a good morning?

Helen: It's been so nice. We've just been relaxing, enjoying our first Christmas as a family. Ella doesn't think much of it yet.

Alice: Well, she is only a couple months old. :0)

Helen: True. How is your day? Doing anything fun?

Alice: Yeah, we've had a good morning. Relaxing, gifts, brunch, etc. Going to Eddie's parents' house later for dinner.

Helen: What did Eddie give you?

Alice: The Hamilton book, some pretty earrings, art supplies, a scarf, a baby.

Helen: WHAT?!?!?

My phone rang and I picked up and said, "Hi, Helen."

She practically screamed in my ear, "What?! You're pregnant? Are you kidding me?"

I laughed out loud and exclaimed, "It's true! I took a test this morning! I'm pregnant!"

Eddie came into the living room and gave me a side glance. I shrugged and mouthed that I was talking to Helen.

Helen continued to scream excitement into my ear and I heard her tell Ella, "Ella! You're going to have a new friend!"

I laughed some more and warned, "You are the only person we've told, so keep it to yourself!"

"I will!" she said. She squealed with delight again and I just knew she was literally jumping up and down and it made me smile.

Chapter 27

Emma

T
he day after Christmas, I sat on the edge of my bed, staring at the blank wall. Charlie and I had never gotten around to hanging anything on the walls, mostly because we had been too lazy, but we also didn't really see the point. Before we got the offer from Tied Down Travels, we had been planning to buy a house, so the apartment—our second in two years—never felt permanent. Ever since I moved out of my parents' house, I have never lived anywhere for more than two years, so I didn't have a great track record of longevity. It was hard to put effort into a place I knew we wouldn't stay in. When the prospect of traveling full time came up, we halted all apartment-related purchases and what little drive we did have to make our place a home vanished. Now, I had no idea what we would do or where we would be in a year.

"What are you doing?" Charlie asked, entering the bedroom.

"They didn't text me," I said quietly.

"Your sisters?"

I shook my head. "No 'Merry Christmas;' no 'Thanks for the gifts.' I even put a Post-it note on Alice's peace dove to point out that it looked like her old art teacher. Nothing."

"I'm sorry, sweetheart," he said, sitting down next to me. "I really thought they would take the high road for the sake of Christmas. Your family gets so crazy about the holidays."

Fresh tears sprang to my eyes. I was a traditionalist when it came to the holidays. I wanted everyone to be together, I wanted everyone to be happy, and I wanted everyone to stick to the script. For years, I insisted my parents continue our Valentine's Day scavenger hunt for our boxes of chocolate long after Kate and Alice had lost interest in the game. I made a bunny cake for Easter every year because the one year I wasn't paying attention, my mom opted for pie instead, and I was irrationally upset for a 20-year-old woman. I took it upon myself to make sure the family stuck to the O'Riley family traditions that no one else really seemed to care about. Because I cared.

This year, the fact that neither of my sisters were talking to me only added to the pain that came with the absence of my dad's Christmas waffles and the afternoon viewing of a just-opened DVD. I had spent Christmas away from my family before, when we had been with Charlie's, but in years past I could always count on a video chat to get me over my homesickness.

I had never gone this long without talking to my sisters, and

I felt like I was slowly going crazy. I checked my phone every three minutes and I took to talking to myself whenever I had the urge to text one of them. Without them to talk to, I didn't know how to process anything or make a single decision for myself. My entire life, they had been my sounding boards, my voices of reason, my go-tos for everything from which pair of shoes I should buy to if I should be concerned about the bumps on my leg. Before Thanksgiving, I thought I was a grown, independent woman. I was wrong. I didn't know how to do anything without my sisters.

The next day, Charlie and I attended our neighbor's holiday open house, and I was happy to be distracted for a few hours. Jefferson lived in a million-dollar house two doors down from our apartment building, and we were told early on that he was referred to as "Mayor of Belmont Avenue." He knew everyone in the neighborhood and the entire Long Beach City Council. "If you ever have a problem with anything—a parking ticket, a lazy landlord—just give me a call," Jefferson said when we moved in. "I'll take care of it."

As a young retiree, Jefferson had taken it upon himself to keep an eye on the street, and nothing got past him. On street-cleaning day, he knew whose cars were parked in the way and in danger of getting citations, and he knocked on their doors to warn them. He was outside on his porch 98 percent of the time I walked by his house, and he almost always had visitors lounging in his Adirondack chairs and enjoying a few beers. In a land of people who kept to themselves, Jefferson was an anomaly; he was the definition of "neighborly."

Needless to say, everyone within a five-block radius was at the open house. With so many people buzzing around Jefferson's three-story mansion, it was easy for me to sneak sparkling cider in my glass so no one noticed I wasn't drinking alcohol. Charlie and I mingled with neighbors we often saw but rarely talked to. These Californians were much friendlier after a few beers.

When the party began to die down and Charlie and I said our goodbyes, we felt giggly and energized. We had been so secluded in the previous weeks, it was refreshing to interact with so many happy people. Back at our apartment, we put an album of Christmas songs on the retro record player I gave Charlie for Christmas, and we danced around the living room. It was the most carefree we had been in over a month.

A couple days later, however, the new year was approaching and I began to wonder how many holidays I was going to have to face without my sisters and how I was ever going to face this major life decision without them. I was back in my funk and Charlie caught me staring at the wall again.

"Emma," he said. "We need to figure this baby thing out." I didn't move. "I'm worried about you."

"I don't know what to do," I said for the millionth time.

"I know. And I don't think there is one 'right' answer," he said. "So, we need to figure out what's right for us." He was much more reasonable than me. I was emotional and constantly worried about everyone else's feelings. Charlie looked at facts and weighed options. We balanced each other out in that way.

"I don't want to give up everything we've dreamed of and worked toward," I said, cautiously. "But I don't know how I would live with myself if I went for the alternative." I couldn't even say the word. Years of Sunday School and weekly mass weighed on me. As a teenager, I had attended pro-life rallies on more than one occasion, but I never really thought about what it meant. I went because my friends did and it got me on a trip to D.C. without my parents; I never considered what I was actually marching for. As I grew older, my views about a woman's right to decide what to do with her own body had completely changed, but that didn't erase the Catholic guilt that was etched into my psyche.

"I would never ask you to do something you don't want to do," Charlie said. He looked more serious than I had ever seen him. "I will support whatever decision you make."

"But..."

"Even if," he interrupted me, then paused. "Even if you decide to keep the baby," he continued, "I will be here for you 100 percent." I started to cry again. I was a crier even before my hormones were out of whack, but it had gotten ridiculous.

"What about everything we want to do?" I asked through my tears.

"I'm not saying I won't be disappointed if we don't get to become full-time travelers," he said. "But I am not going anywhere without you." He lifted my chin with his hand so I had to look him in the eyes. "If you want to have the baby and move in with your parents in Mulberry, I'll pack my bags."

I smiled weakly. "We're not that desperate."

"Thank God," he let out an exaggerated sigh of relief and I laughed. We sat in silence for a few minutes as the gravity of Charlie's offer to give up everything to support whatever decision I made set in.

"I just don't think I could do it," I whispered.

"Okay," he said, as if that were it for him; he truly meant that he would support my decision.

"But I also don't want to be a mother."

"Okay," he said again. "What if we gave the baby up for adoption?"

"Yeah..." I said, considering the option. "But that still means I have to be pregnant. And if I'm pregnant, we won't be able to take the travel jobs in a few months, and then what if I can't give the baby up after I have it? You know how I grow attached to things."

"Then we would keep it," he said, then added, "I guess," less sure.

"But we don't want that either."

"You're talking in circles, Emma." He was trying not to get annoyed with me, but I could see I was trying his patience.

"I know."

"So, what do you want to do?"

"I want to talk to my sisters."

December/January

Chapter 28

Kate

I finally felt like I could breath. My parents had gone to spend the week of New Year's with my grandmother and we had the whole house to ourselves. I relished the freedom. It still wasn't our place, but it was the closest we had gotten in nine months. I wasn't constantly debating if I wanted to walk into a room and have another "discussion" with my mother about my sisters or if I could just go hide in another room.

Steven and I plopped down in front of the TV and didn't have to ask my parents what they wanted to watch. We didn't have to worry that we'd bother them if we turned it on or if a show was appropriate in mixed company. Steven happily watched clips of "Saturday Night Live" with reckless abandon.

I took great pleasure in surrounding myself with all my electronics at once. This drove my parents crazy. My hand-me-down laptop was precariously perched on the arm of my chair, my Craigslist iPad rested on my lap, and my phone was securely in my hand.

I hit "refresh" on a website for the two hundredth time in the last half hour. Still nothing. I went over to Facebook and refreshed the page. Nope. I went to Twitter and loaded the most current tweets. Damn it.

"What are you doing?" Steven asked me from the couch.

"What?" I smiled at him.

"You keep sighing dramatically."

"Finalists are supposed to be announced tonight for that screenwriting contest," I explained.

I had entered the ScreenTest screenwriting challenge on a whim back in October. Back when I thought we'd be moving back into our own home within a matter of weeks. Quite frankly, I had forgotten that I entered. It was an unusual contest because it didn't ask for an entire script. They only asked for the first fifteen pages of a script. I was so stressed and swamped, I figured 15 pages was about all I could muster then anyway. They would choose 10 finalists to win one-on-one instruction with a screenwriting teacher who would help develop a whole screenplay from those first 15 pages. I knew I could use a teacher. So, I labored over 15 pages while waiting in cars, over lunch breaks, even while folding laundry or sitting at sporting events, and I sent it in.

I'd been shocked and thrilled when I opened an email on Christmas Day to discover that my screenplay had made the quarterfinals cut. I'd been annoyed to discover they had actually made the announcement two days before on their web-site. Why wouldn't they email everyone the same day? And did they email the people who hadn't made the cut on Christmas Day too? Because that'd just be mean.

A few days later, I watched all day to find that I made the semifinals. That's when I started freaking out. I had a shot at making the finals. A real shot. There had been over 500 entries and I was in the top 50. What if I got it? I'd have to meet with someone who knew what they were doing and reveal that I had no clue what I was doing. But I couldn't afford an actual screenwriting class. Plus, I was in Indiana-not Los Angeles. Opportunities to learn the craft weren't exactly around every corner.

"BOYS! GAME TIME!" Steven hollered. Hollering at our children. God, I had missed hollering at our kids across a house.

Four voices, from four different parts of the house, hollered back—"Just a minute!"—at the exact same time Steven predicted the response in a high-pitched voice.

I started laughing and clicked the text messaging app on my phone. My fingers hovered over the thread marked "Sisters" and I suddenly remembered. Still not talking. I had assumed that the longer we went without talking, the less I would find my hands operating on auto-pilot and trying to text my sisters. Unfortunately, it was happening more often. Several times I had even started typing before I realized what I was doing.

"BOYS!" I yelled to distract myself from my subconscious need to communicate with my sisters.

"Can I just finish this level?" Alexander yelled back.

"I'm almost done with this world!" Thomas screamed.

"I'm trying to find my charger!" Christopher chimed in.

Phillip poked his head around the corner.

"Phillip! My son! You have won the 'Obey Thy Parents' award for tonight!" Steven held out a hand for a high five.

"Uh, can I watch Thomas finish the world first?" Phillip asked with a little blush.

Steven dropped his hand dramatically and feigned offense.

"Sure, sugar," I smiled at Phillip. "Just tell him he has five minutes maximum. Then I'm coming in there and pressing the power button no matter where he is in his world."

Phillip dashed from the room.

Christopher walked in with an armful of board games from my childhood.

"These are all the games I could find in the basement," he said. "Are we really just going to play these until midnight?"

"Traditional New Year's Eve when I was growing up, kid. If you want to stay up to see the ball drop, you must socialize with your parents. No hibernating with a device until then."

Christopher looked at all my devices with a meaningful look.

"Me too," I smiled, shutting everything off and hoisting myself out of my chair.

Eventually, we were all ensconced around the dining room

table with Ryan Seacrest on in the background. I spent a great deal of the night explaining games like "Ready, Set, Spaghetti!" and "Girl Talk" to my gaggle of boys who were downright slap-happy with exhaustion. They were all determined to stay awake to welcome in the new year.

The boys declared my childhood "super lame" when I tried to get them excited about the "Wheel of Fortune" board game and read them a few cards from an 80s version of Trivial Pursuit.

The night progressed with plenty of laughter and junk food and looking up "celebrities" on Google because we had no idea who Ryan Seacrest was talking with on TV. The boys grew increasingly excited and I could see the disappointment coming from a mile away. When we finally counted down and watched the ball drop, four pairs of eyes looked at me questioningly.

"That's it?" Phillip asked.

"That's it, peanut," I replied.

"Oh."

The boys gave a collective shrug and headed upstairs.

Steven and I fell into chairs and I pulled the contest's website up anxiously. My heart skipped a beat when I saw "Finalists Announcement!" blaze across the top of the screen.

I took a deep breath, clicked on the link, and closed my eyes.

"How can you tell if you made it with your eyes closed?" Steven asked.

"I'm scared to look. What if I make it? What if I don't?"

"Can I look then?" he asked.

"No!" I shouted and opened my eyes. There was my name! My name! "Oh my God. Steven. I got it!"

"Congratulations, honey!" he exclaimed. "I knew you would."

I quickly flipped over to my email and there was the message from the contest with all the details about what would happen next. My teacher would be contacting me via email within the week and we would set up a time to meet weekly by phone. There were also links to my teacher's biography and some suggested reading before our first meeting.

"I have homework!" I exclaimed happily. "Oh, this guy has actual screen credits. He has an IMDb profile and everything."

"I should hope so," Steven said.

"He wrote one of Emma's favorite shows!" I reported. My fingers had opened my sisters' text thread before I even finished the sentence. "Damn it!" I cursed myself.

"What's wrong," Steven asked, alarmed at my sudden about-face.

"I want to tell them! I'm so sick of this nonsense. I can't keep censoring myself. I have 10 million things to tell them and I want to celebrate with them."

"So, do it," he said. "What are you waiting for? Why are you pissed?"

"I'm probably just exhausted. We should get to sleep. It's a good three hours past our bedtime," I offered.

We looked around the room at the disaster left by our children and waved it off because we could. I was struck again with how much I missed making my own decisions about our environment. If we wanted to live in a mess this week, we could—guilt free!

We climbed into bed and fell asleep instantly.

"*Kate*" a voice echoed in my head. I bolted upright in bed as a chill shot down my spine.

"Honey? Are you okay?" Steven asked in a sleep-cracked voice.

"Someone called me. Warned me. About…something," I whispered, dazed.

"What? What are you talking about?" he asked.

"I heard my name. Clear as day. It felt like a warning."

"Was it your grandfather again?" Steven asked sincerely. I could have kissed him right then for not dismissing me as crazy.

"No. I didn't know the voice. That's what scares me," I said as I looked over at my phone and felt sick to my stomach. Something was coming.

"What can I do?" Steven asked through a yawn.

"Nothing. Go back to sleep. I'm sure it was just a bad dream," I said, never surer that I was wrong.

About two and a half hours later, I was staring across the dark room at my phone, trying to talk myself out of my panic and place the voice that had been bouncing around in my head. The phone sprang to life and the name "Eddie" popped up and I cried out in sheer terror.

"What's wrong?!" Steven yelled, instantly alert.

"Something's happened to Alice! The voice! It was my great-grandma! The one Alice was named after," I wailed.

"Answer it!" Steven demanded.

Tears were streaming down my face before I even got the phone to my ear.

Chapter 29

Alice

As consciousness began to flicker in my brain like a fluorescent light being turned on after a long hibernation, I tried to comprehend what was happening. Images moved in and out of my head, fuzzy, distant, and confusing. I tried to think about where I was and how I got there. My eyes were closed and I was laying down on my back, so I must have been in my bed, but I couldn't remember how I got there. Had I been drinking? Did I pass out? That didn't seem right. I could hear some beeping that I thought was my alarm clock. Was it time for work already? That didn't seem right either. I commanded myself to remember the last thing I had done. There was a celebration of some sort. Yes. New Year's Eve. Eddie and I had been at Helen's house celebrating New Year's Eve. I remembered the countdown, kissing Eddie and hugging my friends and clinking champagne glasses. Maybe I did have too much to drink, that seemed possible. But no, it wasn't right. Why wasn't it right? Then a wave of pure happiness rolled over me and I remembered my glass was filled with sparkling grape juice because I was pregnant! Of course, I hadn't blacked out from drinking. But then why…

All at once I remembered. Eddie and I said goodbye to Helen and her husband and I got behind the wheel of my trusty 2004 Santa Fe and we headed home. I was telling Eddie how excited I was to call my sisters the next day to reconcile and tell them the big news when those headlights came at us. I was driving through an intersection when a car T-boned the driver's side door. I heard Eddie scream, "Alice!" and then nothing. It all went black.

I started to take a mental inventory of my body. I felt like I was being held down by weights. Every part of my body was heavy. I tried to move but couldn't seem to move anything. I could still hear Eddie's voice ringing in my brain. It was his scream I heard before the car hit us and then it was him just saying my name over and over again. I tried to answer back but my mouth wouldn't cooperate with my commands. My mind said, "Eddie, Eddie," in response until I became overtaken by a fear I'd never felt before. My mind now screamed, "Eddie!" and I somehow managed to overcome the weight and blackness and my eyes finally shot open. I couldn't move my head, so my eyes began to frantically search as far as they could. I tried to speak, but my mouth seemed to be blocked by something. The beeping I heard earlier was beeping faster in my ear until a new noise entered my ear canal and I immediately started to calm down.

"Shhhhhh," I heard. "You're okay, Sweetpea." It was Eddie. "I'm here." I heard a chair scrape the floor as he stood up and came into my line of sight. My eyes filled with tears. He leaned into me and kissed my forehead and then placed his hand on my cheek. I tried to lean into it like I normally do, but my head wouldn't budge. Eddie then picked up a tissue and dabbed at my eyes and cheeks and then dabbed at his as well. Once the tears had been cleared for me, I could see Eddie had a big bandage on his forehead and a black eye. He didn't seem to have his glasses either. I tried to speak again, but remembered I couldn't, so I gave Eddie the best quizzical look I could. "We were in a car accident," he said. "Do you remember?" I gave an almost imperceptible nod and he continued. "Thankfully we are both okay. I will go see if I can find a doctor to take this tube out of your mouth, okay?" I gave another tiny nod and Eddie left.

I stared up at the ceiling of my hospital room and tried to comprehend what was happening. After a little while, a doctor came in and started shining lights in my eyes and asking me what seemed like a million questions along the lines of "Can you squeeze my finger?" and "Can you feel this?" Finally, I heard him say, "Okay, good. Let's get this tube out." I followed his instructions until finally I could take a deep breath on my own. Once the tube was out, the doctor said he would give us a few minutes and left the room, closing the door behind him.

Eddie went into the bathroom for a wash cloth and came back and dabbed at my dry, chapped lips. He held up a cup with a straw and told me to take a small sip of water. Once he felt he had completed the chores the doctor gave him, he sat on the edge of the bed like he did every morning before he left for work. I smiled up at him and wiggled my fingers that were at my side to alert him that I wanted to hold his hand. He obliged and slipped his hand into mine. I let out a sigh of relief. Happy to be alive and happy my favorite person in the world was alive and apparently doing better than me. After a while, I finally managed to squeak out a scratchy, "What happened?"

"A drunk driver," Eddie said matter-of-factly. "You were going through a green light at an intersection when we were T-boned by a drunk driver running a red light. The car seemed to hit your side of the car directly and we spun out. Thankfully, we stayed upright and didn't roll, or it could have been worse." He paused, seeming to remember the blow and his eyes filled with tears. "After we stopped moving, everything went so quiet. I hit my head on something. My glasses broke on my face and my forehead was bleeding profusely, but you," he gasped. "You weren't moving at all. I was so scared you left me!" Tears spilled out of his eyes and he held my hand tighter. "I just kept saying your name over and over and before long, I finally heard the sirens coming for us."

Eddie went on to describe the scene once the paramedics were on site. Eddie and the drunk driver were both conscious, so I became priority number one. They confirmed my heart was beating and I was breathing but I had been knocked unconscious. They carefully extracted me from the car and put me into an ambulance. They wanted Eddie to remain on the scene so they could stop his bleeding and get an account of what happened, but he refused to leave my side. Eventually they let him in the ambulance with me and they whisked us off to the nearest hospital. It wasn't until they ruled out brain and spinal injuries for me that he finally let them look at his head. He got 20 stitches on the right side of his head where he hit the window, shattering both the window and his glasses.

I managed to ask him if that was the extent of his injuries and he confirmed that aside from some whiplash and a concussion, the black eye and stitches were all that he suffered. "Me?" I asked him hoarsely.

"Broken left leg and arm, a couple broken ribs, lots of bruises and stitches..." Eddie said. "Looks like we've been through quite a ride." He smiled. I tried to lift my head to see my body, but I still couldn't move it. "They have your head strapped down right now," he said. "They just want to completely rule out any spinal injuries before they free you."

I relaxed my neck muscles and took a deep breath. I squeezed his hand and closed my eyes. I focused on my breathing until I remembered. I opened my eyes and before I could say anything, I began to cry again. Without hearing my question, Eddie knew what I was thinking. He started to shake his head slowly until he finally said, "I asked and the doctors told me we lost the baby."

My face scrunched in pain and I let out a deep wail. A noise I had never heard myself make before. Eddie reached for more tissues and leaned in to dab and cry with me. He put his cheek on my forehead and let his tears fall onto my face so I didn't know which were mine and which were his. When he came up for air, I asked, "How do they know? I'm not that far along..."

"You were bleeding pretty heavily down there when they

brought you into the ER," Eddie said. "I told the guys in the ambulance about the baby and they told the ER doctors, so they knew..." Eddie took a deep breath. "The doctor said that your body experienced a lot of trauma and it just couldn't hold on to the baby."

I closed my eyes again and felt the tears on my face dry into salty pathways on my cheeks. After a while, Eddie picked up the damp wash cloth and wiped my face clean again. He smiled at me and told me how thankful he was that I was still alive. I told him the same and then said a prayer of thanksgiving to God and a prayer of mourning for the baby that was almost ours.

The doctor returned to my bedside, conducted a few more motor skills tests and finally released my head from the brace that was holding it in place. He adjusted the bed so I was in more of a sitting position and I was finally able to see more of my injuries. I could lift my left arm a bit and see the cast, and I asked if I was able to get a bright pink cast like the kids get. The doctor said he would make it happen and then adjusted my leg in the sling it was dangling from to keep it elevated.

"Do you know what happened to the other guy?" Eddie asked.

"Well, he's alive," the doctor said. "Alice here sustained the worst injuries, I'm sorry to say. His airbag deployed and he had so much alcohol in his system that he still doesn't really seem to know what is going on." The doctor typed a bunch of things into the computer next to my bed, stood up, and then said, "Well, Alice, we are ready to move you out of the ICU. I know there are some people here who are anxious to see you, so let's get you moved and then you can have some visitors."

Eddie explained that as soon as he could, he called his parents and Helen and that they had been in the waiting room all night. He had been texting them updates periodically. He also said that he called Kate and she was spreading the word to my family. Before he knew whether I was going to wake up, he just couldn't make the call to my parents himself. So, like the rest of us, he relied on Kate to be the strong one to receive the news and pass it along.

"I'm going to go update everyone in the waiting room and then I'll give Kate a call as well." Eddie left the room and after about 15 minutes, he came back with his mom. She rushed over to me and smiled.

"I'm so glad to see you," she said. She took my hand into hers and sat on the bed. I smiled back and thanked her for coming.

"I left a message for Kate," Eddie said. Then his phone buzzed. "Oh, that's her." He answered the phone and went back into the hallway.

"Where's Greg?" I asked Phyllis, wondering where Eddie's dad was.

"We sent him to your house to get Eddie's backup pair of glasses. He was getting restless sitting in the waiting room, so he will be back in a bit." She patted my hand. "Helen is here. She said she will see you as soon as you get transferred to your room. Her husband is with the baby at home." I always appreciated Phyllis' ability to answer my questions before I knew I had them.

I stared off into the distance for a bit when I finally had to ask, "Did Eddie tell you about the baby?"

Phyllis' eyes filled with tears. "Yes," she said simply. She patted my hand again and rubbed my arm with her other hand. I began to cry again and she picked up Eddie's job of dabbing at my face with a tissue. Finally she said, "It's times like these we can only hope the good outweighs the bad. While we did lose one precious life, we still have two very important lives to be thankful for. I don't know if my Eddie would have been able to survive if he had lost you."

I nodded my head and said, "I don't think I would have been able to go on if I had lost him."

Eddie came back into the room. "Your family has booked early morning flights for tomorrow. Most should be here before noon."

I let out a shaky breath and nodded. "Good," I said. I knew I wouldn't fully feel okay until I had my parents and sisters with me.

Once they moved me to my recovery room, Helen and Greg joined us. Greg handed Eddie his glasses and gave me a pat on the arm and said something along the lines of, "You had us worried!" Helen cried when she saw me and cursed the drunk driver. After a while, my eyelids began droop and Eddie's parents suggested that it was time I slept. We said our goodbyes and Eddie pulled up a recliner next to my bed.

"Do you want to go get some sleep at home?" I asked.

"No way," he replied. "We will never be apart again, babe."

I smiled and let the sleep finally take over.

Chapter 30

Emma

W hen I flew to Australia back in college, the flight from LA to Sydney took more than 15 hours, but the two-hour flight from LA to Denver felt 100 times longer. Despite reassurances from Eddie that Alice was going to be okay, I wouldn't believe it until I saw her for myself. I spent the entire flight nervously bouncing my leg, much to the annoyance of my neighbor.

"Is this your first time flying?" the stranger asked me.

"No. I fly all the time," I said quickly. *And I generally like to be left alone,* I thought, opening an issue of *Farmer's Quarterly,* a competitor magazine my boss wanted me to read for research. I had no intention of reading it, at least not today. I couldn't focus on anything other than getting to Alice.

"You just seem really nervous," she said.

"I'm fine, thanks," I replied as I put my noise-cancelling headphones over my ears to really drive the point home. She scowled at my bouncing leg, shrugged to herself, and scooted further away from me before getting back into her book.

As soon as the plane landed and the "fasten seat belts" sign was turned off, I popped up and charged toward the front of the plane. I could hear my fellow passengers muttering their disapproval as I went, but I didn't have time to worry about being PC. Once the door opened, I practically sprinted up the jet bridge and through the terminal until I reached the people-mover that would take me to baggage claim.

As the car slowed and I prepared for another mad dash, my phone rang. It was Liv from Tied Down Travels. I paused, considered answering it, then let it go to voicemail. Charlie and I had gotten an email from Liv and Landon right before Christmas. They were anxious to start talking details, but Charlie and I still hadn't decided what we were going to do. We sent a vague reply about how we wanted to wait until after the holidays to discuss our options. Apparently, they considered January 2 "after." I shot a quick text to Charlie.

Emma: Made it to Denver. Liv called me. Didn't answer. Left a voicemail.

Charlie: What did she say?

Emma: Haven't listened to it yet.

I reached the passenger pick-up area and began scanning the cars for my ride. Kate and my parents had arrived a few hours before me and headed straight for the hospital, so Helen offered to pick me up.

289

Emma: Looking for Helen.

Charlie: Okay. Don't worry about Liv right now. Let me know when you see Alice.

Unsure of what kind of car Helen had, I awkwardly approached three different vehicles before realizing they were not waiting for me. I decided to stay put and let Helen find me. A few moments later, a blue Ford Escape pulled up to the curb and honked. I waved cautiously, still unsure if the honk had been directed at me and was relieved to see Helen wave back at me. I hustled to the back door so I could drop my bag, and I was surprised to find Ella in her car seat, cooing happily and clinging to a pink elephant stuffed animal.

"Oh, hello," I said awkwardly. "You must be Ella." I had always been bad at talking to kids. She smiled at me as I threw my bag on the floor, said hello to Helen, thanked her for coming to get me, and climbed in the front seat as quickly as possible so she could pull away from the chaos of passenger pickup before the traffic cop blew his whistle at us. As we left the airport and began the final leg of my journey to see Alice, I finally let myself take a deep breath. Just a few more minutes until I saw my sister.

Helen dropped me off at the front entrance of the hospital and told me how to get to Alice's room so I wouldn't have to waste time at the nurse's station. I walked as fast as I could without running and finally found room 216. Before anyone saw me, I paused at the door.

For the first time since I had gotten the call from Kate, I wondered if Alice wanted to see me. It had been 41 days since we had last spoken, and for a moment, I was nervous about seeing my sisters.

As I pushed through the door, my parents, Kate, and Eddie turned their attention to me. In turning around, Kate shifted in her spot next to the bed so Alice could see me entering cautiously.

"Emma!" Alice exclaimed, and all my fears instantly vanished. My eyes filled with tears as I rushed toward the bed and got my first glimpse of Alice. I bent down to hug her but paused halfway, worried I would hurt her. "It's okay," she said, wrapping her good arm around my neck. "Everything is okay." I knew she wasn't just talking about her injuries.

After I hugged the rest of my family, Eddie gave us the full account of the accident. The entire room was in tears, both thankful that Alice and Eddie were still with us and terrified at the thought of what could have happened.

"There's something else," Alice said, once Eddie had finished cataloging their injuries.

"There's more?" Kate asked, already overwhelmed.

"I was pregnant. We found out on Christmas," she said. I gasped and held my breath. She began to cry again. "But I lost the baby in the accident." I slowly exhaled and squeezed my eyes shut. It was too much to face.

"Oh, honey," my mom said, crossing the room to place her hand on Alice's forearm.

"Dammit," my father said quietly. He rarely used foul language and the weight of his curse filled the air. "I am so sorry, Fiddle." He joined my mother at Alice's side and kissed her forehead.

But Kate and I couldn't speak. We shook our heads in disbelief and joined our parents in surrounding Alice and Eddie. There was nothing to say. They had finally gotten the thing they wanted most, the thing they had prayed for and dreamt about for over a year, for much of their adult lives, actually, and within a week, it was taken away. There was nothing to do but cry with them.

After we had gone through an entire box of awful, hospital-grade Kleenex, I excused myself to call Charlie. Before I did, I listened to the voicemail from Liv.

"Hey Emma! It's Liv from Tied Down Travels. Landon and I just wanted to check in about when you and Charlie would like to discuss possibly coming to work with us. I know you guys wanted to know more about what the positions would entail and compensation and everything before you commit to signing on, so let's set up a time soon to video chat about the details. We're really excited and hope to hear from you soon!"

I felt sick. I had been hopeful that the opportunity to work with Tied Down Travels would come to fruition, but now that it was more within reach than ever before, I had a massive roadblock growing inside of me. After hearing what had happened to Alice, I was even more confused about what I should do. I called Charlie.

"Hey, how's Alice?"

"She's alive, but she looks awful. Broken arm and leg, bruises and stitches all over. She's pretty banged up."

"Oh man," he said. "Thank goodness she's okay."

"Eddie said he thought he lost her," I said, my voice catching at the thought of losing my sister. "But there's more."

"More?" he asked with the high-pitched voice he got when he was nervous.

"She was pregnant." He inhaled sharply. "But she lost the baby."

"Shit," he said. I could practically hear him shaking his head like the rest of us had, willing the reality to change because it was just so damn unfair. "That's awful."

We sat in silence for a few minutes before he asked the next pressing question. "How'd it go with your sisters?"

"It's all water under the bridge now," I said, breathing a sigh of relief that the stalemate had been broken, even if the reason why was so awful. "But no one has mentioned my current condition."

"No one has said anything?" he asked.

"I think it's too raw," I said. "Especially after Alice told us she lost her baby. It's too much."

"Yeah," he said quietly. I knew it made him nervous that I still hadn't made a decision. Not knowing what I was going to do and how it was going to affect him was driving him crazy, but he also didn't want to push me.

"I listened to the voicemail from Liv," I said, changing the subject. Sort of.

"What'd she say?"

"She and Landon are anxious to talk to us about some of the specifics of working with them. They want to set up a video call."

"Oh," he said. I could hear the pain in his voice as he felt his dream job slipping away. "What are you going to tell them?"

"I don't know. I need more time."

"We don't have much more time, Emma. If we decide to..." he trailed off. He knew from experience that even the word "abortion" caused me to shut down. "Our window of opportunity is closing, if that's the route we choose to take," he said instead.

"I just don't know how we could even consider that option after everything Alice has been through."

"I understand that, but it's not her body or her life. It's ours, and having a baby will change everything."

"I know," I said. I was tired of having the same conversation over and over again. It wasn't helping. If anything, I felt more confused each time. "I'm just going to tell Liv we need a little more time to sort some things out. I'll tell her it's because of Alice's accident."

"Why would Alice's accident cause us to need more time?" he asked.

"I don't know," I said, frustrated. "I'll just lie and say I have to take care of her and I can't take a travel job until she's better."

"I just hope they don't give up on us before we decide what to do," he said.

"Yeah," I said, feeling guilty once again for my inability to decide. "I have to get back to Alice."

Back in Alice's hospital room, I shifted awkwardly on the couch as I tried to get comfortable.

"They should get La-Z-Boys in here," I said as the vinyl squeaked below me.

"Yeah, that's what hospitals should spend extra money on," Kate said sarcastically, motioning for me to scoot over to make room for her. She slid back and forth on the plastic surface. "Actually, you're right. This sucks."

Alice laughed. "I'm sorry my hospital room is not to your liking."

"The picture of the dog with the watering can is nice," I offered.

"I had Eddie steal that from the room next door just for you, Em," Alice said, just as Eddie was coming back into the room with a fresh cup of coffee. "He had to fight off an old lady with a broken hip for it."

"Way to go, Eddie!" I joked.

"What are you talking about?" he asked, confused.

"If I had survived an old lady ass-kicking, I would want to brag about it," I said.

"*My Big Fat Greek Wedding*," Kate and Alice said in unison, and we all laughed. Eddie looked to my parents, who just shrugged. The three of us were finally back in our own little world; our parents weren't going to question it.

"Alright Fiddles," my dad said, standing up and stretching. "Mom and I are going to go back to Alice and Eddie's house for a nap, if that's okay."

"Of course," Alice said. "But the guest beds aren't made up."

"We can make a bed," my mom said, swatting away Alice's concern.

"I'll come with you, actually," Eddie offered. Then, turning to Alice, "I can set them up and then get a shower," he said, pushing Alice's hair back and giving her a kiss on the cheek.

With our parents and Eddie gone, it was finally just the three of us. After a moment of silence, we all jumped into apologies simultaneously.

"I'm so sorry, girls," Kate said. "I've been such a child. I should have reached out to you both weeks ago."

"I was being stubborn," Alice replied. "I took everything too personally and overreacted."

"I never meant to hurt either of you," I offered. "I need you guys now more than ever, and I hated not talking."

"It was stupid," Kate said. "I don't know how I would have lived with myself if we had lost Alice while we weren't talking."

"I can't tell you how many times I picked up my phone to text you guys," Alice said. "I felt like I was going crazy."

"Same!" I exclaimed.

"Living with our parents and my four children and not being able to talk to you guys was like the worst possible scenario," Kate said. "I had so much to whine about and so many funny boy stories to share."

"I can't believe you're still living there," I replied. "There's no way I could do that."

We spent the next hour covering everything that had happened since Thanksgiving. Everything except the one topic that loomed over us. Finally, after dancing around it as long as we could, Kate broke the ice.

"How have you been feeling, Emmy?"

The tears came instantly. No one could make me feel more vulnerable than my sisters. "I just don't know what to do," I said. "I want to do the right thing, but things were finally coming together for me and Charlie. We are this close to getting everything we want."

Sticking to our sister pact that no one cries alone, Kate and Alice wiped at their own eyes.

"I don't even know that I'm capable of being a mother," I went on. "Remember when the boys were little, Kate? Every time I watched them I called you about the smallest things because I didn't feel comfortable taking care of them myself and I was sure I was doing it wrong. I completely lack a maternal instinct. And when I was a little girl playing with my dolls, I always pretended I was the babysitter, not the mother. Even as a child I didn't think I could do it. And all the puke? I can't handle that."

"It's different when they're your own," she said.

I shook my head. "It just doesn't feel right. I don't have what it takes to raise a child. I've never wanted this."

They were silent, unsure of what to say or how to comfort me.

"Are you still considering having an abortion?" Alice asked meekly. I could tell it pained her to ask.

I looked down at the linoleum floor and traced the diamond pattern with my eyes. "I can't," I said quietly, finally admitting what I had known deep down all along. It wasn't until they let out huge sighs that I realized they had both been holding their breath.

"I guess adoption is an option, but I'm not sure how I'll do with that either," I said. "Remember when Alice gave my hamster away to one of her friends when I was in middle school because I wasn't taking care of it? I felt so guilty for giving it up and I wondered for years what happened to it. And I hated that thing!"

"I don't think this is the same thing," Kate offered with a small chuckle.

"Yeah," Alice finally spoke up. "You have to think about what's best for the baby."

"Can't you just take it?" I asked, looking down at the ground again. No one said anything. When I finally looked up, Alice was staring at me.

"Are you serious?" she whispered.

I wasn't sure.

March

Chapter 31

Kate

My motto for March was "A place for everything and everything in its place." As I supervised the distribution of boxes and furniture from the moving van to the house, I kept repeating that phrase over and over in my head. It was somehow comforting, especially in light of the fact that the moving van had to go to four separate places to collect things and drop them off in our newly completed (and insured and building-inspector-approved) home.

It had taken a full year, but we were finally home in Speedway. We were in our place. I knew I loved this town, but the total relief to be back was palpable. It was like I could finally take a deep breath and turn off the "high alert" that had been echoing in my brain since the night of the fire.

A parade of people welcomed us home with casseroles and cards and promises of 4-H geraniums that would arrive in

April. It was so wonderful to see happy faces. Not concerned faces. Not cautious, questioning faces. Not pitying faces. Just the smiling faces of our friends and neighbors.

It was a bit like Christmas, actually. There were boxes everywhere and every time we opened one, the contents were a surprise. So many people had donated things to our family, the boxes had been packed away and put in storage until we had a place to unpack them.

The boys thought this was a fantastic game.

"Mom! There's a Wii U in here!"

"Who gave us girls' clothes?"

"Everything in this box smells funny. Like bad funny. Like skunk butt and meatloaf."

"This whole box is books! Awesome!"

Beyond the "gift" opening, it also felt like Christmas because my whole family was gathering together to celebrate. Alice had gotten the "all clear" from her doctor and she, Eddie, Emma, and Charlie were all coming out to help us with the housewarming.

I was looking forward to seeing everyone, but just like the previous Christmas, I was dreading it, too. Whenever I thought of my sisters, I had a sick lead weight in my stomach. I had to talk to them about Emma's baby.

Back in the hospital, when Emma had suggested that Alice and Eddie could adopt the baby, my immediate reaction was "that's crazy" and I dismissed it. But one look at Alice's face and I knew this was far more complicated than my gut reaction. And, it wasn't really about me.

But the older sister and mother-of-four in me was screaming. There was no way they were ready for the emotional complication of such an arrangement. The problem was, we had literally just come together after a fight in which I had exhibited my most annoying older sister and mother-of-four characteristics. Namely, being a know-it-all and having an elitist "you can't possibly understand being a mother" attitude. I just couldn't throw cold water on the whole idea and our fresh reconciliation that day.

"Whoa, hold on here," I cautiously interjected. "This is a big...well...*gigantic* thing to think about. I don't think Alice is in any condition to make such a decision right now."

"But is it something we can think about?" Emma asked.

We were interrupted by a doctor asking us to leave the room so she could attend to Alice, and we tabled the discussion. Well, we didn't so much table it as much as I just dropped it. I was too afraid to open my mouth and alienate myself from them again. I knew Emma and Alice continued to consider it, but I only knew that from circumstantial evidence, not from either of them talking with me about it.

A couple days before everyone was coming to the housewarming, I knew I was going to have stop being cautious and speak up. I texted them.

Kate: We need to talk things out face-to-face. I know you two have been making plans and trying to make decisions, but I feel like I need to contribute to this discussion. As a mother and your sister. Fair warning.

Alice: Ominous, much?

Emma: Seriously.

Kate: I didn't want to corner you two unexpectedly. I was thinking we could slip away to get breakfast down on Main Street on Saturday morning. Besides, a healthy person is someone who expresses what they're feeling inside. Express, not repress.

Alice: In that case, you must be one of the healthiest people in the world.

Emma: French Kiss! You need new material, Kate. It's always French Kiss with you.

Alice: My ass is twitching. You people make my ass twitch.

Kate: Do you know that there are 452 official government cheeses in this country?

Emma: Of course you know him. All you bastards know each other.

The conversation continued purely in *French Kiss* quotes for another 20 texts because, frankly, it was much easier to quote a movie than acknowledge I had just made everyone apprehensive with my promise of a difficult future conversation.

Saturday morning was there before I knew it and I soon found myself sitting across from my sisters at Mister Lino's. I gripped my latte and looked from one to the other.

"Okay, here's the thing," I began. "I don't want to come off as condescending or superior. So, please know that whatever the ultimate choice might be, I will support wholeheartedly. I just want to make sure you are both considering all of the emotional baggage that will come with this decision, no matter which way it lands."

"Why are you so nervous, Kate? Spit it out. We obviously want to hear what you think, too," Alice said.

Emma nodded and angled her growing belly out of the way so she could dig into her breakfast sandwich better.

"Right. Well, I know you both understand that being a mother is a big commitment. And if you do this, it is going to be a commitment for both of you in different ways." I made eye contact with Alice and forced myself to keep it so she understood exactly how seriously I had thought about all of this. "Alice, being the mother of a baby is all-consuming. I know people always joke about a baby taking over their lives, but it's true. It is a deep and total rewrite of who you are and who you will be in the future. You won't even realize how total it is until the kid is old enough to be away from you for more than a couple hours. Every decision you make, every thought you have, will be affected. And you're going to have a whole other layer to this experience because you're going to constantly be considering Emma in the equation. You'll wonder if she wants to know more or less, if she wants to be involved more or less, if you are being the kind of mother she would want for her child.

"Which brings me to mom guilt. Mom guilt and doubt are ridiculous forces that often don't have much basis in reality. I feel guilty about things like telling Alexander I'll play a board game later instead of right now. I doubt that I'm doing the best thing for my kids when I let them watch a PG-13 superhero movie. I feel guilty when I don't tell them about basketball sign-ups or discourage them from taking up the saxophone. It is a near-constant inner battle. But with this baby, it's going to be an external battle, too. Because, Alice, when you are feeling guilt or doubt, you'll project it and magnify it according to what you think Emma might think of you. And as the child grows, you'll have the compounded doubt if he or she decides you're not the real mom or Emma would understand better. And you'll have to deal with the emotional confusion that this child will have about all of those things."

I took a deep breath and turned my focus to Emma. "Emma, I'm sure you are already understanding the connection you will always have with this child. When you can feel something move and grow inside of you, there is simply no denying that it is a part of you and always will be. You're going to have a totally different type of mom guilt that you won't be able to push down. I think many women who give up their children for adoption use the distance to cope. The connection and doubt are there, but they aren't faced with it on a daily or almost-daily basis. You will be. This baby will be in your life, but in a way that is going to have to be figured out every step along the way. There isn't a rule book or traditional way to handle this sort of thing and you are someone who operates on tradition and expectation. You and Alice will have to make it up as you go along and it will change constantly—with each new job or city, with each new stage of the kid's development, with each holiday or milestone. There's never going to be a 'normal.'"

I looked from one to the other. "Trust is going to have to be total here. Being a mother is hard enough without having someone second guess what you are doing. So, Emma will have to trust Alice in her choices. And if there is a disagreement, it must be discussed with care, kindness, total honesty, and away from the child. This also can't work if there isn't a guarantee that this is a permanent situation. So, Alice will have to trust that Emma won't change her mind and ask for the child back or to be placed with someone else. Once this is done, it has to be done-done."

I took a deep breath. "Finally, I just want to say that no family is perfect. No family is typical. No family just magically works. A family is a living thing that can thrive with the right attention and care. I know our family is strong enough to handle anything as long as we go into it with our eyes open and lots of love."

I looked from one of my sisters to the other and back again. They had both stopped eating and drinking and were staring at me, bewildered. "So that's it," I finished, lamely.

"I can see why you didn't want to try to text all that," Alice said, and we all burst out laughing.

Chapter 32

Alice

After breakfast, we all agreed to go our separate ways to reflect on Kate's words of wisdom. I thanked her for her insight and told her I was a little offended by her first statement about being ready to be a mom since it was the only thing I had been thinking about for over a year. As she continued, though, she did touch on topics that I hadn't thought of, and I was glad we were all able to have the time person-to-person to discuss what this really meant.

I always had conflicting feelings about adoption. The biological part of me wanted to pass on my genes. To see a little human that looked and thought like me and my husband. To roll the dice and see what features and attributes he or she got. To know that child would always have the security of knowing they were created from love and that they were always wanted.

The emotional part of me wanted a child to raise and love no matter where he or she came from. It believed that nurture does overcome nature. It believed that a baby raised by me would feel secure from day one and would grow up with the beliefs my husband and I instilled in him or her.

But adoption always had this great unknown attached to it. If you adopted from a foreign country, there were a lot of hoops to go through and the child was usually one or two years old by the time he or she got to come be a part of your family. Plus, it was an expensive ordeal. If you adopted through social services, the cost would be minimal, but there was always the risk that the child would have developmental or trust issues, and typically, it was the older kids who really needed good homes…sometimes with their siblings. An independent agency seemed a little more controlled, but you could wait years to get chosen by a birth mother and again, it could be quite expensive.

Needless to say, I was never sold on the whole adoption option. But now, I was presented with an entirely new fourth option. Adopting my niece or nephew seemed like such a safe way to go. The unknowns flew out the window. Plus, the baby would actually be related to me. It would have some of my genes, just not my husbands. If, God forbid, something happened to Kate and Steven and the boys needed a place to live, there would be no question. I would open my home to them immediately. Was this much different? Emma and Charlie needed a good home for their baby. I couldn't let my little niece or nephew go live with another family. I would open my home to this baby immediately as well. And now there was the added bonus that the baby would come to live with me from day one. It would think of me as it's mom and Eddie as it's father. It would be our baby.

When Emma and I returned to the hotel where we were staying, she paused before we entered our separate rooms. She rubbed her belly unconsciously as all pregnant women do and looked like she was going to say something, but didn't.

"What?" I asked. I leaned on my crutch and tried to scratch an itch under the sling on my left arm. She gave a small shrug and her bottom lip trembled a little. "You can tell me," I said.

"I just didn't think about those things Kate brought up," she said as a tear formed in her eye. "I mean, I *did,* but I didn't, you know?"

I pulled her in for a side hug using the right side of my body. "I know exactly what you mean," I said, tearing up as well. "There is nothing easy about this. Let's go talk to our men about what Kate brought up and then maybe we can all talk about it together a little later today."

"Okay," Emma sniffed and let herself into her room.

I entered my own room and was greeted by Eddie who was sitting up on the bed watching a morning news show. "Uh oh," he said when he saw me dab at my face with a tissue. "What did Kate say?" I could see his protective gear practically snap into place, ready to shield me from any and all pain.

I waved off his concern and shook my head, "No, no, it was a really good talk. She brought up things I don't think I was really thinking about. She did mention your concern about Emma and Charlie changing their minds in a year or two and wanting the baby back. She said that as hard as it might be, this deal must be full and final as soon as the baby is born. No take backs." I smiled thinking about the popular phrase we used as kids.

"Okay, that's good," Eddie said. "Come sit down." He got up and placed the twelve pillows we got from housekeeping into the necessary locations. Some for my back, some for my left arm, and some to elevate my left leg. I removed my arm sling and leg brace and carefully placed my appendages in the proper locations. My casts were thankfully removed about two weeks before we flew to Indy, but with the sling and brace, I still felt as inhibited as I did before. It was always a relief to take them off when I could relax. Once I was settled he asked, "What do you need? Water? Pain pills?"

"Water would be great," I said. I leaned my head back, thankful once again for my wonderful husband. My accident only solidified my belief that he was going to be a wonderful father. He was such a loving and caring husband, and I couldn't wait to watch him be a dad, no matter how we got there. Once I had my water, he hopped back onto the bed with me and turned off the TV.

"So, what else did Kate say?" he asked.

"I think the part that stuck out to me the most was when she said that not only will we be going through the same new parent emotions and self-doubt that everyone goes through, but we will likely also be thinking about Emma."

Eddie gave the quizzical brow look and asked, "How so?"

"Like maybe we will be constantly asking ourselves

whether or not Emma would approve. Or if the baby gets hurt, will we think Emma will come storming in accusing us of bad parenting and demand the child back or to be placed with a better family? Or will we feel like we need to constantly keep her updated with the baby's every move as if we are just baby-sitting?" I shifted my position on the bed and asked Eddie to place another pillow beneath my leg.

"How would we overcome that?" he asked.

"I think Kate was right when she said that this would need to be a full and final deal. We all have to agree that once the baby is born, it will become ours. We will need to think of it as 100 percent ours and Emma will need to make sure she doesn't feel like she needs to check in all the time or tell us what to do."

Eddie nodded. "So, when does this final decision happen? The baby is due in July. That's only four months away. We will need to start planning. Readying the baby's room and getting all the stuff."

"Yeah," I nodded. "I want to know right now that the baby will be ours, but it's not uncommon for women to change their minds at the last minute. They start to feel the baby move inside them and the connection starts and they can no longer imagine themselves giving it up. We just have to trust Emma will stick with her decision."

"Do you think she will?"

"I honestly don't know," I said, shaking my head. "There was something in her face just now..." I trailed off, trying to under-stand my gut instinct.

"Well, what does that mean?" Eddie said, starting to get upset. "I mean, we can't let her change her mind! If we are going to adopt her baby, then we need to know! She can't put you or us through that!"

I reached my good arm across my body and put my hand on Eddie's shoulder. "I know," I said. "It would be really unfair of Emma to back out at any time. Now or four months from now, but we have to allow her the chance to change her mind."

Eddie was shaking his head and I could see his anger rising. "That's bullshit, Alice. We can't live in limbo like that. We need to know. I can't..." his voice cracked. "I cannot watch you get your hopes up and prepare for this baby only to be told at the last minute that Emma wants to keep it. We can't go through the pain of losing another baby." Tears streamed down his face and mine quickly followed.

"You're right," I said wiping away the tears from both of our faces. "It would be extremely hard and unfair, but we have to allow them that choice. We need to make peace with that reality now whether or not it happens."

"I don't know if I can do that."

"Yes, you can," I said. "We will prepare as if the baby is coming and if at the last minute we learn we aren't getting Emma's baby, then we will figure out what we need to do next and we will be baby-ready. The doctor doesn't think the accident did any permanent damage to my baby-making ability, so maybe we will finally go to the fertility doctor and look at our options. We will just be the most prepared people in the world with a nursery before we know if a baby is coming."

"If we build it, baby will come?" Eddie asked with a smile.

"Exactly!" I took a deep breath and said, "I don't want the baby to come into this world surrounded by anger or jealousy. If Emma decides to keep it, then I want to be with her in California supporting her decision and helping her acclimate to being a new mom. I believe with all my heart that God will bless us with a family of our own. If this baby isn't the one to join our little family, then another will."

"Okay," Eddie said, clearly still hesitant and thinking that if that moment came, I probably wouldn't be as cool and calm as I was right then.

"Obviously, I reserve the right to be upset if that happens," I said with a smile. "But I know you will be there to comfort me."

Eddie put his arm around me and kissed me on my head. "We already have the perfect family between the two of us."

After I took a little nap, Kate, Emma, and Charlie joined us in our hotel room for the "all hands-on deck" talk. Once everyone was settled with Eddie and I on the bed, Emma in the lounge chair, Charlie in the office chair next to Emma holding her hand, and Kate on the edge of our bed, we got down to business.

I began. "Eddie and I have discussed adopting your baby from every angle we can think of," I said, speaking directly to Charlie and Emma. "At the end of the day, we would love to adopt the baby. We know we will be able to provide it with a loving home. Personally, I don't think I could bare it if you chose to give it up for adoption outside the family, but we know it is your decision.

"Kate brought up some good points" I continued. "If we do this, we need the security of knowing it is a final deal and you won't come asking for the baby back at any time." Emma and Charlie nodded. "In return for your promise, we promise to let you change your mind up to the moment the baby is born."

Kate shot me a worried look and Emma started to protest, but I put my hand up to stop them. "This is important to me," I said. "I need Emma and Charlie to understand that nothing is final until the paperwork is signed at the hospital releasing the baby to us. I wouldn't be able to live with myself unless I knew this is what you both wanted 100 percent. Your minds might change the moment you lay eyes on the baby so we need to keep the options open ended until then."

"But…" Kate started.

Eddie interrupted her objection, "Alice and I agree that when we get back to Denver, assuming Charlie and Emma are on board, we will start planning to become parents. We will get the nursery ready and start buying all the, ya know, baby things."

I picked up his thought and continued, "If, at the last minute, we aren't going to adopt this baby, then we will start working on our next plan. Maybe going to see a fertility doctor or whatnot. I strongly believe a baby will join us at some point." I smiled and looked at both my sisters. They were both nodding in agreement and Kate was wiping away a tear.

"You will both be great parents," Emma said. She paused

and looked at Charlie, who nodded, before going on. "Charlie and I have discussed this more, and we do want you guys to adopt her."

Kate, Eddie, and I jerked our heads toward Emma and Charlie who had big goofy grins on their faces.

"A girl?" I shrieked. Emma nodded. "Oh my God!" I hobbled from the bed over to her and she stood and we hugged. More tears came. These of happiness.

Emma pulled back and said, "Thank you for understanding our need for having a possible 'out' at the end. It really makes me feel better. I don't think we will need it, but it's calming to know it's there."

Kate came over and joined our hug. "Sounds like a well thought out plan to me."

Charlie came up behind Emma and said, "Alright, enough business, you two are going to be parents!"

"A girl!" Eddie said as he got up to shake Charlie's hand. The look they exchanged was one of understanding. Eddie could see that it wasn't easy for Charlie to admit how relieved he was that that baby was going to go to a good home, and Charlie could see that Eddie was going to be a great, caring, and understanding father.

We all laughed with excitement. I said, "Mom and Dad are going to flip when they find out they are going to have a granddaughter!"

Chapter 33

Emma

F or the first time in five months, I felt like I could breathe. Watching my sisters gush about pony tails and tiny dresses, I finally felt like I wasn't letting everyone down. Charlie was visibly relieved and I knew we were making the right decision.

Earlier, when I told Charlie what Kate said, we thought about what it would actually look like if Alice and Eddie adopted the baby.

"I know I'm going to have to find a way to deal with the mom guilt Kate mentioned, but more than anything, I keep thinking about something Alice said back in her hospital room in Denver," I said.

"What's that?" Charlie asked.

"She said I have to think about what's best for the baby."

"And what do you think that is?"

"I truly believe Alice and Eddie will be the best thing for her. They're ready for this. They want this. They will love her and give her the best life she could possibly have."

Charlie let out a sigh of relief. Since I returned from Denver in January, I went back and forth on whether I thought I could give the baby to Alice and Eddie, but I was finally feeling confident about my decision, and Charlie was beginning to let himself believe it.

"I don't know if we're just being selfish, but I don't think we are the best option for this baby," I continued, touching my stomach. "Of course we would love her and do our best to raise her, but I think we'd always have that feeling of regret for what might have been if we didn't have a kid. And that would seep into our daily lives, which wouldn't be fair for anyone. If we had no other options, I would say we should suck it up and deal with the situation we got ourselves into, but we do have another option. Alice and Eddie want a baby more than anything, and we can give them one."

"I hadn't really thought of it like that," Charlie said. "It's actually kind of cool that we can give them this gift. Do you think we'll be off the hook for the next 18 Christmases and birthdays?"

We laughed, for what felt like the first time in months. We had been so tense around each other since we found out I was pregnant, like we were both afraid of saying the wrong thing. With the hope of this arrangement ahead of us, it felt like we could be ourselves again.

"We need to figure out what our relationship with the baby will look like," I said. "I think it's something we need to talk to Alice and Eddie about, but I want to get your thoughts first."

"I have no idea..." he said, shaking his head and looking concerned again.

"I think it will be important for us to treat her the same as Kate's boys," I jumped in. I had already thought about it. "She'll be our niece, and we can't favor her over the boys or our niece and nephew on your side of the family."

"That seems fair," he said. He paused. "Will she know she was our baby?"

"I'm not sure," I said cautiously. "I think that's the biggest piece of the puzzle we need to figure out with Alice and Eddie. I don't think it's fair to keep it a secret from her, but I also don't know how to handle that. If we were to lie to her and she somehow figured it out down the road, she would hate all of us. But I don't know when you tell a kid she's adopted."

"Me either," he said. "Sounds messy."

"Like Kate said, there's no manual for how to handle this. I think we'll all have to figure it out as we go."

Charlie nodded.

"I think the important thing is that we, all of us, surround this baby with love the way we would any other child Alice and Eddie brought into their lives. We'll love her because she is part of our family, but ultimately, she will be theirs. We have to make sure they know we aren't going to judge their parenting or take her away from them. I think you and I know we can do that, but I don't think they are so sure."

"How do we convince them?" Charlie asked.

"We'll let them know that we won't be critiquing their parenting because we believe they'll do a better job than we would anyway," I said. "But ultimately I guess we'll just have to show them. The hardest part will be finding a balance between keeping up with them the way I would with any niece or nephew but allowing enough distance so they don't feel smothered and we don't feel guilty for going on with our lives while they raise her."

"Do you think we can do that?"

"I do. I just think we'll have to be very honest with them every step of the way. If we feel like they're shutting us out more than Kate and Steven, we'll tell them we want to be part of her life on the same level as them. If we feel like they're telling us too much, more than we need to know, we'll tell them."

"I think that's fair," he said, and we fell silent. After considering everything for a minute, he finally asked me, "How do you feel?"

"I feel like this is the right thing to do, for all of us."

"Me too," he said, pulling me in for a hug.

After our weekend in Indy, which involved several more family meetings about what this adoption would look like, long conversations about how everyone felt about the arrangement and celebrations that a girl would be joining the family, Charlie and I headed back to California with new hope.

Since New Year's, we had been talking to Landon and Liv about working with them and going over various details about what the jobs would entail, but we hadn't committed to anything or let ourselves get too excited. Thankfully, they bought the excuse that I needed more time to take care of Alice after her accident, and I convinced myself that growing this baby inside of me was a way of taking care of her, so it wasn't really a lie. They were both close with their own families, so they granted us more time without asking too many questions. Now, we felt confident we could accept their offer as long as they could wait a little longer, until after the baby was born. A week after returning to our normal 9-to-5 jobs, we felt even more certain we were ready to take the leap and sign on with Tied Down Travels.

In late March, we set up a video call to give them the news. We positioned the laptop so they couldn't see my belly; we thought it would be easier to avoid the whole thing rather than answer questions. We were so excited to put this opportunity in motion. After dreaming about it for so long, we were practically bouncing up and down.

"Charlie, Emma, I hope you have good news," Landon said. This was the first meeting we called, and they looked anxious to hear what we had to say.

"We know we've come off as overly cautious lately," Charlie began, "but we wanted to make sure we had everything figured out so we could give you a solid answer."

"We certainly appreciate that," Landon said. "We know this job would be a huge lifestyle change for you guys."

"We've thought a lot about it and discussed it at length with our families," I said. They looked hopeful and excited, like they were about to open gifts on Christmas morning. "And we want to do it." Charlie and I both gave cheesy thumbs up.

Landon and Liv erupted into shouts of joy. Honestly, it was hard to tell who was more excited.

"We are so happy to hear that," Liv said. "We were worried you guys were going to back out after our first couple phone calls. We weren't sure if you were still interested."

"We're sorry it took us so long," I offered. "Things have just been so crazy with my sister's accident and everything."

"Totally understandable," Landon said. "How's she doing?"

"Getting better every day," I said happily.

Turning back to the business deal, Charlie brought up specifics. "I'm not sure what you guys had in mind in terms of training, but we need to tie up some loose ends around here before we can pack up and hit the road."

"Absolutely," Landon said. "Do you guys have a start date in mind?"

"We were thinking after Labor Day," I said hopefully. Waiting until September would give me a couple months to recover, both emotionally and physically, after the baby was born. I was getting bigger every day and I knew I wouldn't be much help with packing up our apartment or selling most of our stuff in my current state. This would give me time to really get things in order before we took off.

"That's perfect," Liv said. I let out a sigh of relief. That was the final hurdle. It looked like this was actually going to work out.

"We thought we would take you guys on one of the group trips with us so you can really see what we do each day, from the administrative side," Landon said. "If you guys feel comfortable after that first trip, we'll send you off on your own. If not, we'll do another trip with all of us until you feel ready."

"That sounds great," Charlie said. I nodded with a big goofy grin.

"We have a trip to Barcelona that leaves September 14," Landon said. "What do you say you plan to meet us out in Boston on September 9, and we'll do some training before we leave?"

"Perfect," I said.

As we said "goodbye" to Landon and Liv, I shut the laptop and turned to Charlie. "This is really going to happen," I said.

He smiled and pulled me into him. "It is, babe. We're going to see the world. And there's no one I would rather see it with."

Epilogue

October

Kate

I climbed into the minivan and attached my phone to the auxiliary cable that worked about 67 percent of the time. I punched up a playlist I labelled "Vent" and cranked the volume to a level I would have scolded my children for using.

As I pulled out of the parking lot of my office, I started singing and stomping my left foot to the beat that shook the door panels. At this rate, I was going to go deaf due to stress-related jamming. Sitting at a stoplight, I quickly checked to see if a little red "1" had popped up on my email icon yet. It had not. So, I cranked up the volume a few more ticks.

By the time I pulled up to the place in the neighborhood where I met the younger boys after school, I had shouted my voice raw and turned the music back down so as not to alarm neighbors.

"What's wrong, Mom?" Alexander asked as he climbed into the van.

"Nothing, honey. How was your day?" I replied.

"You always tell me that 'nothing' is not an answer," he countered.

"You're right. I'm sorry. I'm a little anxious about hearing the results of that contest. They said the winner would be announced this week and this week is about over. Of course, in Los Angeles, it's only noon, so it could still be a while."

"Will you be sad if you don't win?" he asked with genuine concern.

"Well, it would be an amazing opportunity if I did win, but I'm not sure I'm ready for that sort of opportunity. So, I'll be sad and not sad at the same time, sweetheart."

"I know that feeling," he nodded.

In moments like these I could see the old soul in my second son and it always took my breath away. He had the most amazing ability to empathize. I couldn't help but send up a prayer that he be protected from the true horrors of the world. He'd feel them more deeply than most and I couldn't stand the thought of it.

"I'm starving!" Thomas yelled as he climbed into the van.

"I'm starving, too!" Phillip piped up in a comical Irish accent as he bounced over his brothers on his way to the far back seat.

"*Veggie Tales!*" Alexander said. The boys had picked up on the quote game my sisters and I played and adapted it to their own shared viewing habits.

"Well, it's Friday and mommy is stressed, so what's that mean?" I prompted.

"McDonalds!" the boys replied in unison. I laughed and pulled the van around to go get Christopher before heading to Mickey D's.

While we were waiting in the drive-thru line, I checked my email again. I had an email from the contest organizers. Oh, God. This was it. If I won, I'd be heading to LA for meetings with studios and managers.

I debated waiting to open it when I wasn't about to place an order from a van full of my children, but I'd waited long enough. I clicked on the message and knew at a glance that I wasn't the winner. The swift kick of disappointment hit me harder than I expected. I swallowed hard and put the phone down.

"Everything okay?" Thomas asked.

"Yep, I'm fine. What does everyone want?"

I ordered an embarrassing assortment of desserts and pulled around to the first window. The 60-something-year-old lady who knew way too much about my bad eating habits leaned out the window and smiled at me.

"Hey, sweetheart!" she grinned at me. "The van in front of you paid for your order!"

"What?" I was bewildered.

"Yeah! She said to enjoy your weekend!"

I looked at the minivan in front of me and saw the "Speedway Soccer" sticker and little heads turned in our direction in the back seats. Tears sprang to my eyes. It was a family we knew from various activities. We weren't particularly well acquainted; just connected through the common plight of the typical Speedway family. I stuck my hand out and waved a sincere "thank you" to them.

When I got everyone settled at home, I escaped to my bedroom, which still had a faint smell of paint and drywall.

Kate: I didn't make it. I lost the contest.

Emma: Oh, I'm sorry, Kate. That sucks.

Alice: What the hell do they know, anyway? Your script was amazing.

Kate: Thanks. I knew I wasn't going to win, but I also kinda thought maybe I could.

Emma: You told me you didn't really want to win.

Kate: I didn't. But I did. It's too soon. I don't know enough and the kids are too young for me to try to do anything like network and sell a script out in LA. But what if this was my shot?

Alice: If I've learned anything over the past year, it's that you never know when or where your chances come from.

Emma: Deep.

Alice: I am wise.

Kate: Ferris Bueller, you're my hero.

Alice: Life moves pretty fast. If you don't stop and look around once in a while, you could miss it.

At that moment, my four boys burst through the bedroom door and tackle-hugged me.

"What's this?" I asked.

"Alexander said you needed a hug," Phillip explained.

Thomas lost his balance and I overcompensated and we found ourselves in a giggling heap on the floor. Steven walked in and looked at us with a smile.

"You're home early!" I exclaimed.

The boys pulled Steven into the pile and I breathed in the presence of my family. I nuzzled into them when they were too busy laughing to notice.

"What is going on?" Steven asked.

"Great Grandpa said mom needed a hug," Alexander said. Everyone froze.

"What, honey?" I asked gently. Alexander smiled at me.

"You know," he said and bolted from the room.

Steven and I looked at each other. "I just got a great idea for my next script," I said.

Alice

Riley Ann Bernard came into the world exactly on time. She came on her due date when we were all gathered in California to welcome her and she came into my life at the exact moment she was supposed to. Eddie and I spent months painting and preparing her room in our home, and Helen threw us a great baby shower. We had everything we could possibly need. Everything but the baby, of course. Every moment we prepared, I got a little more excited. As it got closer to the due date, I started to envision myself cradling a baby in my arms and rocking her to sleep. By the time we flew to California, I was giddy with excitement. But below the excitement was a little voice reminding me to be cautious. It was saying, "She's not yours. She belongs to Emma. Emma has the final decision."

I spoke with Emma on the phone daily in the last month. She never once wavered from her decision to have Eddie and me raise the baby. I could tell she was getting more and more excited about her new job and she always referred to the baby growing inside her as her niece, not her daughter. While I remained hopeful and optimistic until the final day, I held onto the possibility that Emma might change her mind at the last minute.

Emma asked that only I be with her in the delivery room and it was a blessing to watch that little girl, *my* little girl, enter the world and take her first breath of air. The doctor placed her on Emma's chest and Emma cried tears of joy and kissed her on the head. The nurse then took her to get cleaned up and weighed, and when she returned with a clean little sleeping bundle, Emma shook her head as the nurse tried to hand her the baby. She said, "She is my sister's baby. My niece." The tears burst out of me at that moment in uncontrollable sobs and I realized I had been holding my breath. I then took her in my arms for the first time. She was beautiful. She was my daughter.

Eddie and I named her after my maiden name, as an homage to Emma really. We wanted there to still be that connection to her birth mother even if she wasn't going to have the same last name.

We spent about two weeks in California, and then we made our way back to Denver. The feeling we had when we brought Riley into our home for the first time was immeasurable. We showed her the house, her room, and the backyard, and we introduced her to Glenn, who sniffed her and moved on quickly to sniffing the car seat. It was surreal having a third person in our household. While I kept the knowledge that Emma gave birth to her in the back of my mind, it really felt like I gave birth to her. There was no question that this little girl was my daughter. Eddie's daughter. Our daughter.

When she was three months old, I was on the verge of going back to work full time. Riley and I had one final day at home alone and I cherished every moment of the day. She had this wonderfully playful personality and I couldn't wait to see how that was going to develop over the years. Kate called me in the morning to remind me to not freak out when we left Riley with Eddie's mom on Monday. My mom called me to see how we were dealing with the late-night feedings. And Emma called from somewhere else in the world to see how her niece was enjoying the little bear she sent from Spain.

When Eddie returned home from work, I was on the couch with Riley who was asleep in my arms. "Hello, Pumpkin," Eddie said as he kissed her head. Then he kissed me on the head and said, "Hello, Sweetpea." He plopped down next to us and put his arm around me and we both smiled at the deep breathing noises coming out of our daughter.

Looking at her, I couldn't help but think of the crazy journey we took getting to her...or the journey she took getting to us. All I knew was that at that moment on the couch, everything was perfect.

Emma

"Who needs more wine?" I made my way around the table, filling raised glasses and checking to ensure the bread and olive oil hadn't run dry. As I poured, Charlie snapped pictures of our first group of travelers—eight young professionals, five of whom had never left the U.S. before this—enjoying the evening in beautiful Florence. It was day three of our first solo-run excursion, and it was even better than we imagined.

Each night, the group gathered for dinner, usually a family-style meal served in a private back room of a local restaurant, and reminisced about the day. Charlie and I agreed it was our favorite part of leading the tour.

"I still can't get over the sheer size of David," one traveler said, taking a big bite of gnocchi and sighing as it melted in his mouth. We visited Galleria dell 'Accademia that morning, and it had been all anyone could talk about all day.

"My jaw literally dropped when we turned the corner," another said. "I have a whole new appreciation for Michelangelo. I didn't realize the scope of his influence."

I smiled at Charlie, who had put his camera down to indulge in his own glass of wine. It was amazing to watch how each person was transformed by the experiences we led them through. We always knew seeing the world could be life-changing, but now we were actively bringing that change into people's lives, and it felt right.

Back in our hotel room, I connected to the WIFI so I could text Kate and Alice.

Emma: Buongiorno Principessa!

Alice: Life is Beautiful! But it's 3 p.m. here.

Kate: 5 p.m. in Speedway. And there's two of us.

Emma: Whatever. You guys are lucky I even stepped away from the gelato long enough to say hello.

Kate: Is it wonderful?

Emma: Completely.

Alice: Woo! How's your first group?

Emma: They're great! Most of them have never traveled before so it's like leading a group of curious ducklings.

Kate: That sounds exhausting.

Emma: No, it's fun! Anyway, Charlie and I decided we want to send postcards to the kiddos at each of our destinations. Is Riley too young for postcards?

Alice: Yes. But I'm not! And I promise I'll save them for her. Ooh! I can make a little booklet out of them!

Emma: Perfect! Kate, you have to do that, too.

Kate: What?! I didn't sign up for craft time.

Emma: Too bad.

Just then, Charlie came into our room. "The group really seems to be bonding," he said.

"They seem like old friends," I agreed. During our training with Landon and Liv, they asked us to develop goals for the trips we were going to lead. One of the things we immediately agreed upon was that we wanted our tours to allow room for friendships to develop. When we moved to California, we saw firsthand how hard it was to make friends as adults, so we wanted to make sure our groups experienced a healthy balance of sightseeing, cultural experiences and opportunities to get to know one another. We made some of our best friends sitting in cafes and drinking pints at pubs around Europe, so we were intentional about leaving room for those moments.

"We're kind of killing it as tour guides," he said, sliding onto the bed next to me.

"Yeah, we are," I laughed, giving him a high five. "It's like we were born for this."

Before Riley was born, I was worried I'd feel weird starting the job and traveling around the world while Alice and Eddie were back in Denver. But everything changed the moment the nurse handed Riley to Alice. In that moment, I knew. She never belonged to us. She was born to be Alice and Eddie's daughter.

Acknowledgements

The Crawford sisters would like to extend their deepest gratitude to their beta readers who bravely subjected themselves to reading a novel of unknown quality so that they might offer feedback and encouragement to make it a novel of much better quality—Jen Cannon, Amanda Forbes, Erin Fry, Julia Gage, Jolie Kass, and Sue Scully-Rose. A special thanks also to Danielle Hinckley, our editor extraordinaire, who didn't judge us too harshly for our comma splices and em dash violations.

We thank our families for their support, love, and willingness to serve as inspiration for a story about the strength and importance of family. Mike, Peggy, Luke, William, Henry, Jack, Jonathan, and Richard, we love you.

Finally, we'd like to thank our cats. Because cats. They fill our hearts and our camera rolls. Thank you, Ace and Felix. Thank you, Dr. Leo Marvin. Thank you, Rafiki.

About the Authors

Megan (Crawford) Bickel lives and works in Speedway, Indiana, with her husband, three sons, two cats, and one immortal fish. She enjoys insisting that her children chew with their mouths closed and picking up the clear sticky straw wrappers from Capri Suns. At least we assume that is what she enjoys, as that seems to be all she does.

Elizabeth (Crawford) Dow lives in Bennington, Vermont, where she and her husband run the charming Beyond Gallery and Gift Shop. Her creativity and artistic spirit are matched only by her gift for organization and planning, which is an odd combination. However, that fusion is what enabled her to bring forth a cohesive novel written by three very different women.

Ellen (Crawford) Cooke and her husband don't seem to stay still long enough to qualify as "living" in any one place. She travels the globe with the dedication and ambition of a true adventurer. This makes complete sense to her sisters, as she has been a joyful adventure from the moment she came into the world.

Visit us at www.crawfordcontent.com for more information.

Made in the USA
San Bernardino, CA
18 March 2020